The Ultimate Millionaire
SUSAN MALLERY

Tame Me
CAROLINE CROSS

D1798624

MILLS & BOON
Pure reading pleasure

*First published in Great Britain 2008
by Harlequin Mills & Boon Limited,
Eton House, 18-24 Paradise Road, Richmond, Surrey TW9 1SR*

The publisher acknowledges the copyright holders of the
individual works as follows:

The Ultimate Millionaire © Susan Macias Redmond 2007
Tame Me © Jan H Heaton 2007

ISBN: 978 0 263 85888 4

51-0108

*Printed and bound in Spain
by Litografía Rosés S.A., Barcelona*

Tame Me

by Caroline Cross

"You shouldn't have to lose everything."

"And you're here to fix that?"

"Yes." Flashing on her reaction every other time he'd tried to offer his assistance, Gabriel thought it wise to add, "If you'll let me."

"I see. Well, here's your answer." Straightening, Mallory swivelled to face him, her eyes dark with something he couldn't identify – and anger so blatant a blind man couldn't have missed it. "Go to hell."

"What is your problem?" Gabriel demanded.

"You!" she shot back. "You arrogant, self-satisfied idiot!" Sucking in a breath, she yanked her arm free. "I don't want your pity or your charity. And I am not, nor will I ever be, some wrong you need to right!"

Available in January 2008
from Mills & Boon® Desire™

The Ultimate Millionaire
by Susan Mallery
&
Tame Me
by Caroline Cross

ᗞᗋᏕᏕᏕ

Merger of Fortunes
by Peggy Moreland
&
Back in Fortune's Bed
by Bronwyn Jameson

ᗞᗋᏕᏕᏕ

The CEO's Contract Bride
by Yvonne Lindsay
&
Melting the Icy Tycoon
by Jan Colley

MILLS & BOON
100 YEARS
of pure reading pleasure

100 Reasons to Celebrate

We invite you to join us in celebrating Mills & Boon's centenary. Gerald Mills and Charles Boon founded Mills & Boon Limited in 1908 and opened offices in London's Covent Garden. Since then, Mills & Boon has become a hallmark for romantic fiction, recognised around the world.

We're proud of our 100 years of publishing excellence, which wouldn't have been achieved without the loyalty and enthusiasm of our authors and readers.

Thank you!

Each month throughout the year there will be something new and exciting to mark the centenary, so watch for your favourite authors, captivating new stories, special limited edition collections...and more!

The Ultimate Millionaire
by Susan Mallery

He was playing her.

Fine. She could play, too. She could make him sorry he'd ever pulled her into his game. She grabbed a handful of his jacket, raised herself on tiptoe, wrapped one arm around his neck and pressed her mouth to his.

She was determined that this last a whole lot longer than that brief kiss they'd shared before. She wanted to teach him a lesson.

After a second of hesitation, Todd put his arms around her and kissed her back. He moved purposefully, like a man on a mission. There was so much heat and need and pleasure, she let him have his way and was rewarded when he kissed his way down her neck…

THE ULTIMATE MILLIONAIRE

by
Susan Mallery

SUSAN MALLERY

is the bestselling and award-winning author of over
fifty books. She makes her home in the Los Angeles
area with her handsome prince of a husband and
her two adorable-but-not-bright cats.

Dear Reader,

When I was twelve, a friend's mum gave me a book she thought I might like. It was called *Dark Star* and, I'm sorry to say, I don't remember the author. But I do remember everything about that story. The dark and dangerous hero, the innocent English secretary who fell in love with her boss. It was my very first romance and it changed my life forever.

From that moment on, I read romances and Mills & Boon were my favourite. I always had one with me, even occasionally reading a chapter or two behind a text book in class!

Now I have the great privilege of writing romances. I still get a thrill from the dark, sexy heroes and I love creating funny, strong heroines who are more than willing to take on the men of their dreams.

Mills & Boon, congratulations on 100 years of wonderful books, and thank you for allowing me to be a small part of this great legacy.

Susan Mallery

One

"Would you do it if I beg?"

Marina Nelson was careful to keep from smiling at Julie's dramatic plea. Of course she was going to agree to help her sister, but not right away. After twenty-four years of being the baby of the family, it was nice to finally have a little power.

"You know I'm busy," she said slowly. "It's the start of a new quarter and I have a full class schedule."

Julie sighed. "Yes, and your work is very important. But so is this. I wouldn't ask if it wasn't. I really need someone to take charge while I'm on this business trip. We have similar taste and you're organized and I thought…" Julie tucked her blond hair behind her ears and looked sad. "Am I asking too much? I am. I know it's crazy. I'm the one getting married, not you. So I should do the planning. But this trip to China is a once-in-a-lifetime opportunity. Six weeks of Ryan and I working together before we settle in to being married *and* parents."

Marina glanced down at her sister's stomach. Julie was only about three months along and not showing at all. One of the advantages of being tall, she thought humorously—it takes longer to see the bump.

"I can see how a trip to China would be far more thrilling than the messy details of choosing a menu and picking out flowers," she said, still not allowing herself to smile. "Not to mention deciding on a dress. What if you hate what I pick?"

They were close enough in size for the actual gown itself not to be a problem. Any minor tailoring could be done right before the wedding, after Julie got back.

"I won't," Julie promised earnestly. "I swear, I'll love it. Besides, you'll send me pictures, right? We talked about that. You'll upload them into e-mail and I'll write back with my opinion." Her blue eyes widened. "Marina, please say yes."

Marina sighed heavily. "No. I can't. But thanks for asking."

Julie's mouth dropped open, then she reached behind her for one of the small, floral sofa cushions and swatted Marina with it.

"You're horrible! How could you let me go on and on like that? I was practically begging."

Marina laughed, then grabbed the cushion. "There's

no 'practically,' Julie. You begged. You whined. I have to tell you, I was a little embarrassed for you."

Julie sighed. "So you'll do it?"

"Of course. You're my sister. Just give me a list and I'll take care of everything."

"You have no idea how you're helping. Between getting married and our trip and closing on the new house, my life is a nightmare."

They sat in Ryan's study—an uncomfortably modern condo in West Los Angeles. It had a great view and electronic everything, but it lacked color and soul, except for a few throw pillows Julie had contributed. Rather than try to make it homey, Julie and Ryan had decided to buy another house that they both liked. Marina knew that Willow, their middle sister, was going to oversee the minor renovating Julie and Ryan's new place needed, which left the wedding to Marina.

"I think of this project as practice," Marina said with a grin. "I can figure out what I want and don't want should I ever take the plunge."

"Oh, please. You'll get married," Julie said confidently. "The right guy's out there somewhere. You'll find him."

Marina wasn't currently looking, but it would be great when it happened. Assuming she could trust herself to fall in love without losing her soul in the process.

"Until then, just call me the wedding planner," Marina said. "Now, where's that list of yours?"

Julie reached into her purse, then straightened without removing anything. "There's just one other thing."

"Which is…"

Julie drew in a breath. "Okay, so this is Ryan's wedding, too, and he's a little nervous that it's going to be too girly. He wants a vote in what's happening."

Marina didn't get the problem. "Fine. You two can argue all you want, then e-mail me the compromise. I don't care."

"Um, yes, well, that's not exactly the plan. Ryan wants a representative to be with you for all the important decisions. The food, the cake, the band, the decorations, the flowers."

"A representative? Like his mother?"

Marina had never met the woman. No doubt she was perfectly lovely, but another opinion could seriously slow the process.

Julie tried to smile and failed miserably. "Actually, no. More like Todd."

"Todd? As in Todd Aston the Third, all around rich guy and jerk?" Marina couldn't believe it. "Anyone but him," she muttered.

"He's Ryan's cousin and they're as close as brothers. You know that. Todd is the best man and he offered to help. Do you hate me now?"

"No, but I should." Marina sighed. "Todd? Yuck."

Nearly six months ago, the three sisters had been introduced to their maternal grandmother for the first time in their lives. Grandma Ruth had been estranged from her only daughter, the girls' mother, ever since Naomi had run off and gotten married.

Now Ruth was back and she wanted a relationship with her daughter and granddaughters. In addition, she had a burning need to connect her family with her second husband's family through marriage.

In a moment of dinner conversation that Marina was confident would go down in family history, she'd offered each of her granddaughters a million dollars if one of them would please marry Todd Aston the Third, her nephew—or maybe great-nephew, no one was sure—through marriage.

Julie had fallen in love with Ryan and Willow had found Kane Dennison, which left only Marina for toady Todd. Talk about bad luck.

For reasons she was still trying to figure out—maybe it had been a momentary brain injury—Marina had agreed to one date with the obnoxious Todd.

It's not that the guy wasn't good-looking—at least, that's what Marina had heard. She'd never actually seen the man. He was also wealthy and successful in his own right, rather than just inheriting from Mommy and Daddy. Ryan liked him and Marina thought Ryan was okay—especially after he'd shown the good taste to fall for her sister. But Todd?

His idea of a significant relationship was to date the same woman twice in the same week. He went out with models. How could she ever have a serious conversation with a man who dated women who were paid to starve for a living? It violated the female code.

Plus, initially he'd tried to break up Julie and Ryan. Marina thought that was pretty low.

"I'm not asking you to have his baby," Julie said. "Just work with him on the wedding. Besides, it won't be too bad. He's a guy. He'll get bored at the first meeting with the florist and disappear. You'll have to deal with him once. Twice at the most."

"I don't want to deal with him at all," Marina said mournfully. "He's everything I don't like in a man." Talk about emotionally useless. Or so she imagined.

A sound came from the doorway. It sounded like someone clearing his throat. When Marina looked up she found a pretty good-looking guy leaning against the door frame.

He looked more amused than annoyed, but based on Julie's gasp and sudden blush, Marina was willing to go out on a limb and figure this was the infamous Todd Aston.

"Ladies," he said with a nod. "Ryan let me in and said you were meeting in here. I've shown up for wedding duty. I'm also accepting a humanitarian award at the end of the month. Perhaps the two of you would like a shot at writing my bio for the event. It would certainly be entertaining."

"Oh, man," Julie muttered. "I'm sorry. That all came out more harshly than I meant it to."

Marina studied him. He was the walking, breathing definition of tall, dark and hunky. Great face with soulful eyes and the kind of mouth that made a woman dream about being taken against her will. Broad shoulders, a muscled chest and jeans skimming over narrow hips and yummy thighs. All in all, a great package. Too bad Todd's personality was stuck inside it.

He smiled at her. "You must be Marina."

"I am. Nice to meet you, Todd."

"Nice?" He raised one eyebrow. "That's not what I heard. You've already decided I'm an ass. Or is it an idiot?"

She shifted on the sofa, feeling just a tiny bit uncomfortable. "You go out with models. Their airbrushed perfection in magazines make regular women feel bad about themselves."

"Because of that, models shouldn't be allowed to date?"

Logic? He wanted to use logic in a discussion about the objectification of thin, young women in modern society?

"Of course they should be allowed to date," she said smoothly. "I'm simply not interested in someone who's interested in them."

"Right," he said folding his arms over his chest. "Because you assume that if they're beautiful they must be dumb. Therefore I like dumb women."

"I didn't say that, but thanks for clarifying."

His mouth twitched as if he were holding in a smile. "I don't date dumb women."

"You should probably make up your mind about that," she told him.

"I'll get right on it."

"If you two are finished…" Julie pointed to the chair opposite the sofa. "Okay, then. So, we should get started with all this. The wedding."

Todd strolled across the room and took the seat offered, then pulled a PalmPilot out of his shirt pocket. "I'm ready."

Marina looked at him. "You're actually going to participate?"

"Right down to the organic seed we'll be throwing

at the happy couple when they head off on their honeymoon." He leaned forward and lowered his voice. "We don't use rice. The birds eat it and it's bad for them."

She opened her mouth, then closed it. "Someone's been spending a little too much time on the Internet."

"Internet, bridal magazines, whatever. When it comes to wedding planning, I'm your guy." A challenge brightened his dark eyes. "I'm in this all the way. Are you?"

If he thought he could scare her off, then he was in for a wild ride. "I'm in. And just for the record, I define stubborn."

"Me, too."

Ha! No way. He might think he was all that, but Marina was more than willing to take him on and win.

Julie sighed. "I thought you two might not get along, but I never considered this might become a competition. Listen. We're talking about a wedding. My wedding to Ryan. We need help, not a Las Vegas-style show. Bigger is not better. Don't be too creative. Let's just make it low-key and elegant, okay?"

Marina felt Todd's gaze shift to her. She stared right back at him and refused to be the first one to blink. "Julie, have I ever let you down?"

"No," Julie said slowly, as if she didn't want to admit it.

"So trust me."

Julie gave them each a copy of her list. Todd scanned his, then turned his attention back to Marina Nelson.

She was blond like her sisters, only her hair was

darker—more honey-gold. She was about an inch taller than Julie, with the same curvy build. They were obviously sisters and could almost have passed for twins. The main difference—aside from hair color—was the "I'm willing to take you on, big guy" attitude in the set of her chin. Julie was far more agreeable.

Todd had a rule when it came to women—why work hard? There were plenty of attractive females more than happy to come on to *him*. Some of it was due to his success as a businessman, some of it was about his looks. Most of it was about the family fortune.

Whatever the reason, he rarely had to go searching for company. His romantic life was an ongoing series of short-term relationships with minimal commitment and effort on his part. That was how he liked things.

Marina was going to be anything but easy and he wasn't even trying to get her into bed. But Ryan had asked for his help, so he would put up with the overly verbal Nelson sister for the sake of his cousin.

He was even willing to admit—only to himself—that he was looking forward to taking her on. It had been a long time since a woman had done anything but let him get his way. Working with her would be good for his character, even if he did plan to win in the end.

"Basically we have the invitations done and that's it," Julie said as she studied her own copy of the list. "Grandma Ruth offered her house for the wedding and Ryan and I agreed it's an amazing place. But there are decisions to be made. It's a winter wedding. Do we want to risk the outside thing? It could be seventy-five or it could be raining."

"She mentioned something about a ballroom," Marina said. "On the third floor. Want us to check that out?"

"I've seen it." Todd kept his attention on Julie. "It would easily hold three or four hundred. A few less if you're interested in a sit-down dinner."

"We are," Julie said, making a note.

"But the guest list isn't nearly that big," Marina told him. "It's about a hundred."

"Ryan said it was closer to two hundred."

Marina turned to her sister. "That many?"

"It keeps growing."

"That's a lot of tables."

"I know. So I need you to check out the ballroom and see how it would be. Is there still room for dancing with all the tables in place? Where would the band go? I'm torn. Being outside would be great, but I'm not sure I can trust the weather, and I won't need to be stressed about one more thing."

"We'll decide that first," Marina said, taking notes. "That will affect all the other decisions. What's next?"

"Flowers, favors—nothing stupid, please—food, entertainment, a photographer and my dress. Oh, and you and Willow have to pick out bridesmaids' dresses."

Ryan was so going to owe him, Todd thought humorously. "Tuxes," he said.

Julie stared at him. "Oh God. You're right. The guys need tuxes."

"I'll take care of the dress myself," Marina said, smiling at him. "The dress is purely a girl thing."

"Do you plan to get a say in the tuxes?" he asked.

"Sure."

He waited while she began sputtering.

"Wait a minute," Marina said. "A bride's dress has to be something special. She's only going to get married once."

"I could say the same thing about Ryan. He'll want to look good and you don't trust me to make that happen. Why should I trust you?" Of course he had no real interest in the wedding gown, but fair was fair.

Julie waved her hand. "I don't care who goes to the bridal shop. Just find me an amazing dress. Nothing fitted at the waist, of course."

That's right, Todd thought. Julie was pregnant.

He knew Ryan was excited about being a father. While Todd never intended to marry, he liked the idea of having kids. The lack of wife would complicate things, but didn't make the situation impossible.

"I can't believe you want a say in the dress," Marina muttered.

He leaned toward her. "Think of all those models I've dated. Some of their fashion sense must have rubbed off on me."

"Did you talk about fashion much?"

"We didn't talk at all."

He heard her grind her teeth together and nearly laughed.

"Willow works for that nursery," Marina said as she ignored him. "I'll ask her for recommendations on the florist front."

"Good idea," Julie said.

"I know a photographer," Todd told her.

Marina widened her eyes. "Does he take pictures of people with or without clothes?"

"Both. You'll enjoy looking at her work."

"I don't care about naked," Julie said. "Does she do weddings?"

"They're her favorite."

"Good. Put her on the list. Marina, nothing too artistic. Just regular pictures."

"Gotcha."

They went over a few more things, then Julie left to find the dress pictures she'd torn out of magazines.

Todd turned his attention to Marina. "I think this is going to be fun."

"Oh, me, too."

"You don't like me much."

"I don't know you."

"You don't want to."

"Actually I haven't decided that. Amazingly enough, you haven't been on my mind at all."

One point for her side, he thought. "You didn't say nice things about me before. I heard you."

She tilted her head as she stared at him. "You have a reputation which, personally, I think you enjoy. But people form impressions based on that notoriety."

"You think I'm shallow."

"I don't think you've ever had to work very hard at anything but your company."

"Still, you agreed to go out with me. One date. You promised. Aunt Ruth told me."

Her gaze narrowed. "It seemed like a good idea at the time."

She might be uncomfortable with the idea of dating him, but he was the one who had to live with the reality of his aunt offering her granddaughters each a million dollars if one of them would marry him. It made him feel like a loser. What the hell was so wrong with him that a woman had to be paid that much money to make a commitment?

Not that he wanted to get married, but it was the principle of the thing.

Fortunately Julie and Willow were both out of the picture, which left only Marina. He would have refused even a single date with her, but Aunt Ruth had looked so happy at the thought and although he would rather face medieval torture than admit it to anyone, he was a sucker when it came to his aunt Ruth.

"It's only one date," he said. "What's the worst that could happen?"

"It will be three hours that will seem like a lifetime?" But there was a flash of humor in her eyes as she spoke.

"The wedding," he said. "We both have to be there, we're both in the wedding party, which means it wouldn't be much fun for anyone else we brought."

She nodded slowly. "We will have just spent all that time arranging the event, so we'll have plenty to talk about."

"We can have lots of champagne."

She grinned. "Always a plan. All right, Todd Aston the Third, I'll be your date for my sister's wedding."

Two

Grandma Ruth's three-story Bel Air mansion was just as awe-inspiring the second time Marina pulled in to the stone covered circular driveway. It was massive and out of place—this was Los Angeles, not eighteenth century England. But the rich lived different lives, Marina thought as she climbed out of her aging import. Lives with live-in staff. Her idea of help at home was a package of premoistened glass cleaning towelettes.

She glanced at the double door leading into the house and decided to wait until Todd showed up before going inside. Okay, sure, she shouldn't be intimidated by her grandmother's maid, but she was. So what? She had other positive attributes she could focus on.

Less than a minute later, a gleaming silver Mercedes

pulled into the driveway. The car was a sporty two-seater model, the kind that cost as much as the national debt of a small third world country.

The guy who climbed out of it was just as impressive. Tall, well tailored and sexy enough to encourage smart women to make some really stupid choices. She would have to make sure she didn't fall into the category. Fortunately he wasn't her type.

"Marina," Todd said with a grin. "I thought you would have already scouted the house and made the decision."

"We're a team, Todd. I totally respect that." Or she would as long as it suited her.

Speaking of suits, his was dark gray, with a subtle pattern in the weave of the fabric. His pale blue shirt contrasted with the deep burgundy tie. While she preferred a more casual look, he wore his power extremely well. She, on the other hand, looked like a college student with a limited budget. Although her skinny jeans had zipped up with no problem, which made this a very good day.

She collected her digital camera and a small notebook, then followed him to the front door. "I have about an hour," she said as she checked her watch. "Then I have to be back at UCLA for a class."

"What are you taking?"

"I'm not. I'm interpreting." She glanced at him. "I'm a sign language interpreter for deaf students. I specialize in chemistry and physics, mostly the upper division classes."

He raised his eyebrows. "Impressive."

"It's not that hard for me. I've taken all the classes

myself, so I understand the material. I have three advanced science degrees. Eventually I'm going to have to pick a Ph.D. program, but I'm not ready yet. I already knew how to sign, so I decided to do this for a couple of years."

His eyes widened. "*Three* advanced science degrees?"

She loved people underestimating her. "Uh-huh. It's less impressive when you know I started college at fifteen."

"Oh, sure. It's practically ordinary. You're pretty smart."

She smiled. "Smarter than you, big guy."

He laughed. "I'll remember that."

He knocked on the front door and when the maid answered, he greeted her by name.

"We're here to see the ballroom, Katie," he told the woman in uniform. "Then check out the backyard."

The maid nodded. "Yes, sir. Your grandmother told me you'd be stopping by. Would you like me to show you upstairs?"

"We can find it. Thanks."

Marina smiled at the other woman, then followed Todd across a huge foyer and up a wide, curving staircase.

"So how big is *your* staff?" she asked as they reached the second floor and walked along a long, carpeted hallway. There were dozens of paintings on the wall and pieces of furniture that were probably impressive antiques, if she knew anything about them.

"Five live-ins, six dailies."

"What?" she asked. She'd only seen his house from a distance—and it had been bigger than this one—but still. "What do they do?"

He turned to her, touched his finger to the tip of her

nose and smiled. "Gotcha. I have a housekeeper who hires people to keep the house clean and take care of the grounds. She comes in three days a week. I'd rather not have any staff, but the house is old and big and I'm not willing to deal with it, so she does."

Okay, one housekeeper *was* better than five live-ins.

They took a second staircase that flowed into a landing that was bigger than Marina's apartment. A wall of ornate doors opened into a ballroom the size of a football field.

She stepped into the center of the room and turned in a slow circle. There were gilded mirrors on the walls and dozens of sparkling chandeliers hanging from the ceiling. The parquet floor gleamed and reflected the sunlight from the windows.

The walls had been painted a neutral pale beige, so any color theme would work.

"We're talking about tables of either eight or ten," Todd said as he pulled out his PalmPilot and pushed a few buttons. "We can fit as many as thirty tables in here and still have room for people to get around."

Marina did the math. "Can we fit twenty-eight tables and still have room for dancing and the band?"

Todd looked at her. "Orchestra. Not band. Julie said elegant. Bands aren't elegant."

Maybe not, but she'd never been to a wedding with an orchestra. "You think the L.A. Philharmonic is available?"

He grinned. "I'd have to check their schedule, but I was thinking of something a little smaller. I have a group in mind that I've heard play at other venues."

Venues? So while the rest of America went to the

mall, the über rich had venues? "What sort of venues would these be?"

"Mostly fund-raisers. A couple of weddings. I'll find out where they're playing in the next couple of weeks and we'll go hear them. They're great. Trust me."

Trust him? Not yet.

She put down her notebook and began taking pictures of the vast space. "I really like this room," she said as she turned slowly to get every angle. "I'll e-mail these photos to Julie as soon as I'm done with class."

"There's more," he said and led her to a series of French doors. He unlocked the first one and opened it, then motioned for her to lead the way.

She stepped out onto a wide balcony that overlooked the property. Although if one couldn't see where the fence line was, did that make it an estate?

The grounds were stunning. She could see the terrace and the pool and the gardens beyond.

"This would give us extra space," he said as he joined her. "A place for people to get some air. We could put lights in the garden for the view."

"I like it," she said more to herself than him. "Anyone can get married in a backyard, but this is incredible. A once-in-a-lifetime opportunity."

She turned back to the ballroom where she could imagine the tables and guests and flowers. Talk about making some memories.

"So you prefer the ballroom?" he asked.

"I do, but it's Julie's choice. Let's go downstairs and take some pictures of the garden so she and Ryan can decide. Once we know which way they want to go, we're free to start making other arrangements."

They made their way back downstairs, then stepped out onto the manicured terrace. It looked more like the grounds of a five-star hotel than someone's home, she thought as she took pictures, not sure how she felt about her grandmother living here.

Something of her confusion must have showed because Todd asked, "What's wrong?"

She pocketed the digital camera and tucked her notebook under her arm. "I keep thinking how strange this is—that a grandmother I never knew about was alive and well about fifteen miles from where I grew up. That this is her world and I can remember times when we didn't have enough money to have meat with dinner."

She shook her head. "I'm not complaining. My mom was great and my sisters and I always had plenty of everything we needed. Money was tight, but that's how it was with most of our neighbors. I'm okay with that. But now, to find out there's a whole other way of looking at things, it's strange." She looked at him. "I'm not explaining myself well and this is more information than you wanted."

"Of course this is different. For what it's worth, Ruth regrets all the years she was apart from you and your family. Her husband, my uncle, was a hard man. He didn't believe in forgiveness. Ruth simply didn't have the strength to stand up to him."

"That's what she said."

"It's true."

Great. So it seemed she came from a long line of women who surrendered heart and mind to their men. All the more reason not to get involved.

He looked at her. "You should try to understand what Ruth went through."

Todd Aston the Third being sensitive? "Okay, now I'm freaked out on two different levels. The contrast between what I'm used to and this, and your emotional perception."

"I'm a man of great mystery."

That made her laugh. "Of course you are. Wealth, power and mystery. You should put that on your business cards."

He led the way around the side of the house toward their cars. "I'm way ahead of you, Marina. I have it tattooed on my back."

She grinned. "I thought you'd have a stick up your butt," she said before she could stop herself.

"They know how to fix that now. Isn't modern medicine a miracle?"

She sighed. "You know what I mean. I thought you'd be…different."

"Unpleasant?"

"Imperious."

"I can be, if that would make you happy."

"No, thanks." She opened her notebook. "Okay, venue research complete. Which leaves us with food, the cake, flowers, a photographer and all kinds of other messy details."

"The dress," he reminded her. "We'll have to look

at something off the rack. There's no time for a custom gown."

She glanced at him, surprised he would know that. "Let me guess. More bridal magazine research? Although somehow I can't see you sitting down with a latte and a bridal magazine."

"I can't have a latte then. Black coffee to combat all the girliness. It's about balance."

Until this moment, she hadn't thought of Todd as a person. At first he'd been just a name, then he'd been the guy who tried to break up her sister and Ryan. Then an annoyance who would get in her way about the wedding. But now…

"Why do you hide who you are behind your reputation?" she asked. "The money thing. The model thing."

He unlocked his car. "I've dated maybe three models in my life, Marina. You need to let go."

"You're right. I will."

"Good." He sat in his car and grinned. "Of course, two of them didn't speak English."

They didn't… Then how… She glared at him. "You had better be kidding. Not speak English?"

He nodded. "I was simply doing my part to improve American relationships with our neighbors." He smiled angelically. "I know a great caterer. I'll set something up and get back to you with the details."

With that he was gone.

Three days later Todd stood in front of the catering office and watched Marina walk toward him. She wore jeans, a UCLA sweatshirt and her hair pulled back in a ponytail. Not someone who dressed to impress.

There was also an air of determination about her that made him anticipate plenty of flying sparks. Planning a wedding might not be his idea of a good time, but so far Marina had been a pleasant surprise. Smart and sexy. He'd been looking forward to seeing her again.

When she stopped in front of him, she put her hands on her hips and glared at him.

"I looked you up on the Internet," she said. "The models in question spoke perfectly good English, albeit with an accent."

"Albeit?" he asked as he raised his eyebrows. "Are we in a Jane Austen novel?"

"What do you know about Jane Austen?"

"Every good useless male who only dates models knows all about chick flicks and Jane Austen. It's required. I not only saw *Bridget Jones's Diary* twice, I've seen the special features. Ask me anything."

She burst out laughing. The sound was light and sexy and made him want to touch her. All of her. Unexpected heat swept through him, startling him with its intensity.

He immediately took a step back, both physically and mentally. He and Marina were on a mission. He was here to protect Ryan's interests and not die of boredom in the process. If tweaking Marina's assumptions about him got him through the day, then he was up to the task. But actually enjoying her company—not a good idea. Getting involved with his aunt-by-marriage's youngest granddaughter wouldn't be very intelligent.

"This place comes highly recommended," he said as they made their way to the front door. "It's supposed to be good food with more choices than beef or chicken. If this is the one we pick, we'll be able to customize the menu. Or in our case, argue over food options."

"You think we're going to argue?" she asked.

"I'm counting on it."

"I'm a pretty agreeable person, but I'm sure you're difficult," she said as he held open the door. "I'll be flexible on food, but not the dessert thing."

"What dessert thing?"

She smiled at him. "That we have dessert. It's one of the great thrills of a wedding. You get dessert *and* cake. How often does that happen in life?"

"Far be it from me to get between a woman and her sugar fix."

"Pretty and smart," she murmured. "How impressive."

"I know." He turned his attention to the receptionist and introduced them.

"I'm Zoe," the woman said with a smile. "We're ready for you. If you'd come this way?"

They were led in to a small room set up like a dining area. The table for six had two place settings at one end.

Zoe seated them, then pointed out the menu printed on a single sheet by the plates.

"We'll go in order," she said. "We'll start with soups, then the salads and so on. Please make notes or write down any questions."

She left and then returned immediately with three small bowls for each of them.

"Lovely presentation," Marina said as she picked the sprig of garnish out of one of the bowls. "Why do they have to put some garden weed on top of a dish? What is it? How do we know where it's been?"

"The not knowing adds to the thrill of the moment."

She looked at him, her blue eyes wide. "Are you thrilled?"

She was close enough that he could see a couple of pale freckles on her nose and hint of a dimple in her cheek. Once again he thought about touching her...and didn't.

"Beyond words."

"Liar," she murmured, then took a taste of the first soup. "Split pea with something else. Not bad."

He tasted it and shook his head. "No, thanks."

They both passed on the creamy mystery soup, while he liked the chicken vegetable and Marina complained it was too healthy.

"We're at a wedding. Do we really have to get our five servings of fruits and vegetables in the first course?"

He poked around the bowl. "Not a lot of fruit that I can see."

"You know what I mean." She set down her spoon. "What about tortilla soup? Or a quesadilla? Doesn't that sound good?"

"You want Mexican food at your sister's wedding?"

Marina's shoulders slumped. "Not really, but I could go for some right now. I should have eaten before coming here. I'm really hungry."

"So you like food."

She narrowed her gaze. "Yes, some women eat. I

eat. Shocking, but true. I also run every day, so I can pretty much eat what I like and enjoy it. Do you have a problem with that?"

"Running with that chip on your shoulder must help with your workout. The extra weight would increase intensity."

She opened her mouth, then closed it. "You're saying I'm a little sensitive about the food thing?"

"Would I say that?"

"You're thinking I'm overreacting because you date models and I don't feel I measure up to their ideal."

"You're doing all the talking."

"I'm not intimidated. Mostly not. Sometimes, maybe a little. But I'd like to point out that these are my skinny jeans. They've fit all week and they look fabulous on me."

"Yes, they do." He'd admired the curve of her hips and her long legs when she'd first walked up. He was willing to take another look, if that would make her happy.

"I don't seek approval from anyone but myself."

"Why would you?"

She smiled. "You're humoring me."

"It seems safest. You have some attitude on you."

"I know. I don't get it. I'm actually a fairly calm person. I'm not sure what it is about you that pushes all my buttons."

"It's because I'm so smooth and handsome," he said as Zoe came in with several salad plates, along with a basket of rolls. "You're uncomfortable."

Marina waited until they were alone to respond. When Zoe had picked up the soup bowls and left, she said, "I'm not uncomfortable. You have an ego the size of Antarctica. You're not that special."

"Of course I am. You researched me. Who was the last guy you researched?"

"The men I know are totally normal. Researching is not required. You make me crazy."

"Then my work here is complete."

She shook her head. "Eat your salad."

He took a bite of the first salad. There were a lot of strange looking lettuces and shavings of things he didn't recognize. Salad was highly overrated, he thought grimly.

"Think about the guys you usually date," he said, enjoying the fact that he could get to her. "Scruffy, poor grad students. When compared to me, they don't have a chance."

She glared at him. "Oh, right. Why would dating the next brilliant man who will change the course of history by improving the world be considered interesting?"

He picked up a roll and leaned toward her. "They're nerds. They're not interesting yet and they're not good in bed. Admit it."

Fury darkened her eyes. She opened her mouth, probably to yell at him. He stuck the roll between her lips.

"Not bad," he said, pointing at the second salad. "I like the blue cheese. What do you think?"

She pulled the roll away and glared at him. "I think you're a pompous, egotistical ass."

He tasted the third salad and grimaced. "So you like me."

"I don't."

"Of course you do. But I was asking about the salads. What do you think?"

She pointed at the one he'd tasted third. "That one works."

He shook his head. "Not a good idea. There's too much garlic in the dressing."

"Since when do you know anything about cooking?"

"I don't." Could he help it that she set him up with one good line after the other? Sometimes a guy couldn't help cutting a break. "But I do know about weddings." He glanced around, then leaned toward her and lowered his voice. "Kissing. Lots and lots of kissing at weddings. You don't want the guests to have garlic breath."

Awareness crackled in the room. He thought Marina might get nervous or change the subject, but her gaze never left his. The humor was gone, replaced by a tension that quickly flared into need.

What would it be like to kiss her? What would her mouth feel like against his? How soft? How hungry? How sexy?

Was she the kind of woman who took charge, or did she like to be convinced? The possibilities were endless and suddenly he wanted to explore them all.

"I think you're overstating the problem," she said. "I don't think the garlic is that big a deal, but if it is, we could simply change the dressing on the salad."

"There's only one way to find out," he said and leaned in farther, then brushed his mouth against hers.

There was heat and need. They competed for his attention. Marina didn't move, but he heard her breath quicken. But before he could take things to the next level, Zoe returned.

"What did you… Oh. Sorry. Should I come back?"

Todd straightened. "No. We know what we need to do."

Three

Marina felt as if she'd been hit by a truck. Well, that wasn't right, she thought as she blinked to bring the room back into focus. Nothing bad had happened and she certainly wasn't squished. But she was out of breath and feeling a little two-dimensional all the same.

Talk about wow. The heat, the tingles, the need to jump Todd's bones and make him have his way with her. All from a teeny, tiny, innocent kiss. What would happen if he kissed her like he meant it?

A dangerous question, she told herself. Todd was nothing like she'd imagined. He was funny and charming. Too charming. She had to remember that any contact with a woman was just a game with him. That he had the emotional depth of a cookie sheet. She should enjoy the superficial attraction for the momentary pleasure and let the rest of it go. He didn't do relationships and she didn't do anything else.

Although technically she didn't do relationships, either. It was the whole fear thing. She didn't want to get lost in a man.

They sampled several entrées, which were okay and the desserts, which were great.

"Are you going to finish that?" she asked, eyeing his barely tasted dish of chocolate mousse.

Todd pushed the bowl toward her. "You're welcome to it."

She dipped her spoon into the creamy, foamy delight and then savored the burst of rich chocolate on her tongue. He watched her, his expression unreadable.

She wanted to think he found her passion for chocolate fascinating, but no doubt he was comparing her normal appetite to his dates' lack of appetite and finding her just a little odd.

"Finished?" he asked when she'd scraped the last of the pudding from the bowl.

She nodded and they walked out to the reception area. After collecting prices and a brochure from Zoe, they promised to be in touch within a couple of weeks, then left.

"What did you think?" Todd asked as they walked to their cars.

"It was good," she said, "but not dazzling. I want to be dazzled. I think the food should be spectacular, not just good."

He glanced at the price list. "Considering what

they're charging, I agree. So we still need a caterer. Do you have any suggestions?"

"I don't cater much, but I can ask around."

"I'll do the same. I'll also check with Ruth."

Ah, yes. Her grandmother. "She does the charity circuit," she said. "At least she's mentioned it. So she should be a great source of information." Marina frowned. "I wonder why she hasn't offered us advice."

"She promised not to meddle," Todd told her. "Don't get too excited—it's not going to last. She's a meddler by nature." There was a tone of affection in his voice.

"So you've forgiven her for coming to me and my sisters and offering each of us a million dollars if one of us were to marry you?"

He winced. "I'm working on it."

"Why?"

He shrugged. "She always had time for me and Ryan. Our parents took off for months at a time and left us behind. Aunt Ruth stepped into the void. When we were with her, it was like family."

Marina didn't know what to say to that. On the one hand, it explained Todd's fondness for his aunt. On the other, this was the same woman who turned her back on her own daughter.

"You're thinking about your mom," he said, surprising her.

"Yes. My mom was seventeen when she fell in love with my dad. That's pretty young. I can understand her parents being upset with her choice, but there are a lot of options between saying it's okay and kicking her out forever. How come they didn't try any of them?" She drew in a deep breath and let it go. "You're going to tell me it was because of Ruth's husband, Fraser. I've heard it all before. He was a difficult man who ruled his house and didn't give anyone second chances."

He was also the only father Marina's mother had ever known. Her biological father, Ruth's first husband, had died before Ruth had even realized she was pregnant.

"My mom was Ruth's only daughter," Marina said. "She should have tried harder. She should have made sure her daughter was all right."

Todd surprised her for maybe the third time in less than two hours when he put his hand on her shoulder and squeezed gently.

"You're right," he said quietly. "She stood by her husband instead of her daughter. Because of that, she spent the next thirty years regretting her decision, but being too afraid to do anything about it. That's got to be a hard way to live, for all of you. She'll never get back what she lost and neither will you."

She blinked at him. "That was really compassionate and understanding."

He scowled at her. "I am capable of rational and emotional thought."

"I know. I just didn't think you'd bother."

"That's flattering."

Now it was his turn to touch him. She grabbed his hand. "I'm sorry. That came out wrong. It's just the way you're presented in the local press and how people talk about you."

Maybe he wasn't a cookie sheet, she thought. Maybe he was actually a jelly roll pan.

The image made her smile, which made his scowl deepen. "You're really starting to tick me off," he muttered.

"I thought you said you had a well-developed sense of humor."

"I do. You're not being funny. Whatever you think about me, you're wrong."

She was beginning to think that might be a possibility.

He pulled out his trusty PalmPilot and pushed some buttons. "We still need a caterer, a photographer, flowers, a cake, a dress, tuxes. It's a long list."

"We'll get through it. I'll e-mail Julie the information on this place. At least we know we're having the wedding and reception in the ballroom. That's something."

"Lucky us."

She stared into his dark eyes and smiled. "Thanks for being so understanding about everything with my grandmother. It helps to talk about it."

"Yeah, yeah. I'll call you and we can set up our next taste testing."

Then he stunned her by bending down and kissing her. Only this kiss wasn't about garlic or proving anything. At least she didn't think it was. Instead it was quick, hot and bone-melting.

His hands rested on her shoulders, holding her in place. His mouth claimed hers with an expertise that made her more than willing to take this wherever he wanted to go. She lost herself in the pleasure of touch and lips and need.

He wasn't what she expected. *This* wasn't what she

expected. She found herself responding to him in ways she hadn't expected.

He tilted his head and brushed her lower lip with his tongue. She parted for him. He swept inside, teased into arousal, then pulled back and straightened.

"See you soon," he said.

What? He was leaving? He was going to kiss and run?

"But you... Why'd you..."

He smiled. "We were interrupted. I like to finish what I start."

To Marina_Nelson@mynetwork.LA.com
From Julie_Nelson@SGC.usa

I can't thank you enough. I really, really owe you for all your hard work. Thanks for taste-testing the first caterer and sorry it didn't work out. But you're right. I want fabulous food at the wedding and so does Ryan.

Interesting about the whole garlic/kissing thing. I hadn't thought that too much garlic could ever be a problem, but at a wedding? You're so right. So, did Todd demonstrate the perils of garlic kissing? ☺ Just kidding. I know he's not your type. Not earnest enough and yet lacking in character. But not totally awful. At least he's cute. Remember that when he starts to make you crazy.

We're having the best time. I can't wait to get more pictures and e-mails from you. Again, you're a total goddess for doing this!

Love and hugs, Julie

Marina opened the cardboard box and reached for the

tape dispenser. After sealing the bottom of the carton, she flipped it over and then looked at the bookshelves in the hallway.

"Does Julie really need to keep all these?" she asked, even though she already knew the answer.

Willow stuck her head out of the bedroom where she'd gone to tackle clothes. "Of course. They're books. She'll keep them forever."

"Does Ryan know what he's getting into? The whole pack rat thing?"

Willow grinned. "She's not a pack rat and yes, he knows exactly what he's getting into."

"Well, I didn't have a clue," Marina grumbled. "Between helping you pack Julie's place, you handling the renovations at their new place and me planning Julie's wedding, she is going to owe us big time. We're going to have to break our legs or something and force both of them to serve us."

"She'll be there every second of our recovery," Willow promised. She held out her left hand and pointed. "Would you hand that to me?"

Marina didn't turn to see the object in question. Instead she stared at her sister's ring finger—or more specifically, at the stunning diamond ring glinting there.

"You're engaged!" Marina yelled. "I'm so happy for you."

Willow laughed, then they were hugging and jumping up and down together.

"It's so beautiful," Marina said, grabbing her sister's hand and studying the impressive cushion-cut stone surrounded by baguettes. "When did this happen? You didn't say anything. How could you not blab the second you saw me?"

"It was hard," Willow admitted. "But I wanted a great reaction and you gave me one." She stared down at the ring. "As to the when, it was just last night. Kane and I had talked about getting married before, when he came to his senses and realized he loved me. But between then and now there hasn't been a word. I was willing to give him time to get used to the idea of just being in a serious relationship."

They moved into the living room and fell onto the sofa. Marina smiled at Willow's happy expression.

"Who would have thought that the strong silent type would turn out to be such a great guy," she said, thrilled that Kane had been the one in a million Willow deserved.

Her sister sighed. "I know. It's a miracle. He's incredible. Last night we were having dinner together. It was really romantic and there was music and suddenly he was on one knee and holding out the ring and saying he wanted to marry me and be with me forever." Tears filled her eyes. "I never thought my life could be so wonderful."

Marina hugged her again. "I'm happy for you. Beyond happy. Delighted. Giddy. There are other words I can't think of right now."

"I'm happy, too," Willow said.

Marina leaned against the cushion. "Two of my sisters getting married. I'll be the old maid aunt, a favorite of the children, but you adults will worry that I'm slowly slipping into madness."

Willow rolled her eyes. "Please. You're too smart for that. But I would say to be careful. Love is in the air and all that."

Marina shook her head. "I'm immune. Which is fine with me. I'm not looking to get married anytime soon."

"What about falling in love?"

"Maybe next year."

In truth, she liked the idea of falling for a guy. But along with the desire to be in love was a healthy dose of fear. Giving away her heart looked a little to much like giving away her sense of self. First Aunt Ruth, then her mother. Marina wasn't willing to be like either of them.

"So, another wedding," she said. "Have you two picked a date?"

"We're thinking spring. Well, after Julie's wedding, but before the baby's born."

"I can help with the planning. I'll be an expert."

"I would love that," Willow told her. "I wouldn't know where to start."

"Just ask me anything. Or Todd. He's actually pretty good at the whole wedding planning thing. Just don't tell him I said that."

Willow shifted so they were facing each other. "Really? He's not awful?"

"No," Marina said, still surprised by that bit of news. "He's actually nice. Funny, charming...I like him. I didn't expect that at all. I thought he'd be a jerk. I really didn't want to work with him on the wedding, but even though we don't agree on everything, I like having him help. It's a big responsibility and I like having someone to share in the process. Plus, he's fairly good-looking. Even if my day is going badly, it's fun to have a little eye candy to look forward to."

"I don't think he's the kind of guy who likes being called eye candy."

"Probably not, but we won't mention it."

Willow studied her. "So this is good?" she asked. "With Julie and Ryan getting married, Todd is kind of in the family now. We'll all be friends?"

"I think so. We'll mock his choice of women when he brings dates, but that will be entertaining."

"Something to look forward to," Willow said. "Todd's not the kind of guy to hang out by himself."

Marina nodded in agreement, but found herself wondering about the other women in Todd's life. No doubt he was seeing someone right now. Who was she? Some socialite or heiress? A high-powered businesswoman? Marina would guess that whoever she was, her wardrobe consisted of more than jeans and UCLA sweatshirts.

Not that she, Marina, was trying to impress him. They were working together on the wedding. Nothing more. Except he'd kissed her. She still couldn't seem to forget the flash of heat and need and desire that had nearly overwhelmed her. And that had been from a kind of nothing kiss. What would happen if he kissed her like he meant it?

"He's actually my date for the wedding," Marina

said. "We both promised Grandma Ruth we'd go on one date and the wedding seemed the easiest."

"Once again I encourage you to marry him so I can have a million-dollar nest egg," Willow said with a grin.

"Kane has money."

"Yes, but that's *his* money. A fortune of my own would be kind of fun."

Marina shook her head. "Sorry. I don't have any big plans to marry Todd. Not even for a million dollars."

"What about five million? I'll bet Grandma Ruth would be delighted to cough up a little more cash."

"Not interested."

Willow sighed. "I thought our sisterly love was supposed to be unconditional. I hate that it has limits."

"Life can be tragic."

Willow glanced back at her ring. "There are some bright spots. I have Kane."

"Yes, you do."

Willow looked at her. "You're next. Things happen in threes. First Julie, then me, so it's your turn."

"I don't think it works like that."

Not that she would say no to her own happily ever after, but there were complications. Falling for a guy meant trusting him completely. While she could see that happening, it also meant trusting herself, which she was a lot less sure about.

Four

Marina sat on the front stairs of her apartment waiting for Todd. As her watch ticked over to the exact minute he was due, his sleek, silver, expensive convertible rounded the corner and pulled up in front of her building.

She stood and sighed. "Pretty car," she said when he stepped out and walked toward her. "Very pretty car." Of course he looked good, too. The man knew how to wear a suit. But she didn't feel the need to share that.

He held out the keys. "Want to drive?"

She blinked. "Excuse me?"

"Drive. The. Car. You're supposed to be the smart one here. It shouldn't be such a complex concept. I've seen you drive. You know how."

She looked from him to the Mercedes and back. "But

it's your car. You're a guy. Guys don't share their cars. Certainly not really expensive ones like this."

"It's just a car, Marina. I buy what I like, but it's not my life." He shook the keys. "Now answer the question. Do you want to drive?"

She snatched the keys from him before he could change his mind. "Absolutely."

But as she made her way to the driver's side, she glanced at him. Sure, Todd had money and if something happened to this car, he could easily get another, but it was the principle of the matter. This wasn't normal behavior. Was he really so secure with himself that he could let her do this without a second thought?

She settled into the leather seat and surveyed the interior. There were the basics she was used to, along with a GPS display, dual zone air-conditioning and a sound system that looked complicated enough to be on the space shuttle.

"It's nice today," he said. "Want to put the top down?"

"Oh, yeah."

She scanned the controls and found the one that took care of the top, then put the key in the ignition and turned to watch the show.

It was a marvel of German engineering, she thought as the top automatically folded down and a built-in cover slipped over it. All without her doing anything.

Then she faced front, adjusted the mirrors, started the engine and prepared to be impressed.

"How fast can I go?" she asked.

"How much are you willing to pay for a ticket?"

"Good point. So where to?"

He pulled a piece of paper out of his shirt pocket. "Today we're taking care of table linens, place settings, tables and chairs, party favors and the tuxes." He glanced at his watch. "We have an appointment at the linen place, so let's go there first."

He gave her the address and she pulled out into the street. The car responded to her every instruction, the engine purred smoothly and she could feel the power hovering just a press of her foot away. The day was warm, the wind wiped her hair around and she felt pretty darned happy.

"I could get used to this," she said as she came to a stop at the light.

"So you're tempted by the dark side?"

She grinned. "More than tempted." Obviously a car like this wasn't possible on her budget, but maybe a used convertible wasn't out of the question. It could still be fun.

She drove to the rental place and resisted the urge to take an extra trip around the block, just for the driving pleasure. Instead she parked and climbed out.

"Thanks," she said, handing over the keys. "That was great."

"Anytime."

"As if you mean that. Still, I'm deeply impressed you let me drive it at all. You're very secure."

"I'm a macho kind of guy."

She laughed. "Not to mention modest. You're extremely modest."

They walked into the rental showroom.

"I called ahead," Todd told her. "They'll have tables set up for us. We can get some idea of what colors work well together and how formal or informal we want things to be."

She pulled her camera out of her purse. "I'm prepared to take pictures."

They walked into the showroom and saw nearly a dozen tables set for dinner. Each table was done in a different color, with coordinating china and a centerpiece.

They introduced themselves to the clerk there, who invited them to walk around and get ideas.

Marina immediately moved toward a round table with a pale pink tablecloth and elegant light yellow napkins.

The plates were cream, trimmed in silver; the centerpiece was a combination of pink and yellow flowers that trailed across the center of the table. Even seated, the guests would be able to see each other and the colors were warm and cheerful.

"I like this one," she said, only to realize she was talking to herself. Todd was across the room in front of a table done in deep reds and purples.

She winced as she got closer. The china was black, the napkins dark and the flowers looked like something out of a nightmare rather than appropriate for a wedding.

"It's elegant," he said when she paused next to him.

"It's scary. I don't think we're going to have many children attending, but what if the ones who did come were terrified?"

He glanced over his shoulder at the one she'd liked. "What if we didn't set the table for an Easter brunch?

Julie said low-key elegant. Bunnies and colored eggs don't fall into that category."

Marina looked at the table she'd loved. "Okay, maybe it's a little pale, but this is awful. I don't like the really tall centerpiece. You can't see the people across from you."

"Which could be a good thing if you didn't like them."

She smiled. "We can't guarantee that will be the case. What about that?"

She pointed to a table done in deep rose, with accents of green. The cream china provided a neutral backdrop for patterned salad and dessert plates. The centerpiece was more botanical than floral and it sat low enough to see over.

Todd studied the settings. "It's not fussy. That's good. The colors are a little girly, but the green's okay. I like the centerpiece."

"It's certainly different," Marina murmured as she got out her camera and started taking pictures. "Rose and green would be pretty colors, with cream sort of blending in."

She snapped pictures of the other tables, but concentrated on the one she and Todd agreed on. Then they went to the clerk at the front of the showroom and asked about a price list.

Todd held out the sheet so they could both see it. The charges were broken down by type of rental, as well as number of units needed. The more rented, the less the cost per item.

"We didn't talk about the glasses," she said.

"Honestly, I can't see Ryan caring. If it holds wine and champagne, he'll be good with it."

"You're not going to argue on general principle?"

"Only to keep things interesting."

They were standing close together. Close enough for their arms to brush. Marina was aware of how much taller Todd was than her and how the heat from his body made her just a tiny bit squishy inside.

She did *not* want to be attracted to Todd, she reminded herself. It was that stupid kiss. If that hadn't happened, she never would have thought of him as more than just Ryan's friend and someone she had to learn to deal with for the next few weeks. He wouldn't have been…a man.

She forced her mind to focus on the project at hand. "Look, they can recommend a florist," she said. "That's good. We need more recommendations. The chair rental isn't too bad. We're going to need chair covers, though."

He swore softly. "They're four bucks each. With two hundred chairs, that's eight hundred dollars to throw a piece of cloth over the chair? Can't they be naked?"

She patted his arm. "No. They look better covered."

"Ryan and I are in the wrong business. If you rent out those covers twice every weekend, even with the cost of the initial purchase and cleaning, you're still raking in the money."

"So invest in the bridal business."

He looked around and shook his head. "It's too emotional. Give me a good high-tech start-up any day."

"But you could expand. Diversify."

"Maybe." He sounded doubtful.

She looked up at him. "So how did you get started?

Do you wake up one morning and think 'Hey, let's be venture capitalists'?"

"Not exactly. Ryan and I had a buddy back in college. He had a great idea for software, but he didn't have the money to manufacture or market it. We decided to finance his business."

"So you used your allowance money for the week?"

He shook his head. "Trust fund money."

"Oh, of course," she said knowingly. "That's where I go when I'm short on cash. It's so handy having that spare billion or two to fall back on."

"You enjoy mocking me, don't you?"

"It's pretty fun."

He folded the price sheet and handed it to her. "The company took off. By the time we graduated, Ryan and I had made our first million."

Impressive, she thought, but she wasn't going to say that to him. "Does the silver spoon ever choke you?" she asked.

He ignored her. "We both paid back out trust funds with interest and never had to tap into it again. Our company has been profitable ever since."

So except for his start-up cash, he'd earned his fortune the old-fashioned way. She would never have guessed. "Make any mistakes?"

"A few. Fortunately they didn't cost too much. Not every new company is going to make it and all the experts in the world can still be wrong. But we have good instincts."

And money, she thought. "No wonder you're considered a hot bachelor. How is it you've survived all this time without being trapped by some determined young woman?"

He smiled, but his eyes were cold and distant. "I've been burned enough times to not trust anyone."

"That can't be fun," she said, wondering if they had the same problem for different reasons. "How can you get close if you don't trust?"

"I don't need to get close to get what I want."

Which made sense, she thought, but was also sad. "That's got to get lonely."

"You don't have a guy in your life. Are you lonely?"

"No." Not exactly. Sometimes she wanted more, but the price of that always scared her away.

"So we're not so different," he said.

"Except for the millions and the fact that you date models, we're practically twins separated at birth."

"You're never going to let the model thing go, are you?"

"Um...not really."

The tux shop was well lit and elegant. Not exactly like those places at the mall. Marina felt distinctly underdressed, especially when the salesperson, a gorgeous brunette in her mid-twenties, stepped out from behind the counter in an outfit that looked as if it cost as much as Marina's rent.

"May I help you?" she asked, her gaze locking on Todd.

"We're here to look at tuxes," he said. "For a wedding."

The woman—Roxanne, according to her nametag—sighed. "Yours?"

"No. I'm the best man. The groom is out of the country. I'm supposed to make the right decision without him."

"I see." Roxanne turned her piercing green gaze on Marina. "And you are?"

"The sister of the bride. I get a vote."

"Wonderful."

Roxanne's attention swung back to Todd. Marina had a feeling it was never going to stray again.

"We have an amazing collection of designer tuxedos," Roxanne said, her voice low and sultry. "They're available for rent or purchase. Does the groom have your build?"

Todd glanced down at himself, then at Marina. "We're about the same size, don't you think?"

Marina nodded. "Pretty much. We want something simple, but elegant. Unfortunately the colors haven't been picked yet, so we're not ready to place the order."

Roxanne continued to gaze at Todd. "That's fine. You can try on whatever you like to see what makes you happy, then come back later."

Marina had a feeling Todd could visit every day and Roxanne wouldn't mind.

The three of them walked over to the display rack of tuxedos. Roxanne eyed Todd's body in a way that made Marina feel that she had stumbled into something intimate, then pulled out several selections.

"There are color choices, of course," Roxanne said. "Traditional black, various shades of gray, a few in other colors such as dark blue."

Todd grimaced. "Black or gray works for me. We're just looking for a regular tux. Bow tie and cummerbund."

"I like vests better," Marina said. Todd looked at her, Roxanne didn't.

"Vests?" He sounded doubtful. "I never wear a vest."

"How often do you put on a tux? Cummerbunds remind me of a high school prom. A vest can be elegant."

He shrugged. "Okay, but then I want a regular tie. A vest with a bow tie makes me feel like a grandfather."

Roxanne ran her hand down his arm. "You're certainly not that, are you?"

Marina held in a gagging noise. "At least try on both," she suggested. "If you hate it when it's on, then you can whine to Ryan."

"I don't whine."

"Oh, please. I've heard you."

Roxanne moved between them. "Let me get your size," she said, whipping a tape measure out of the jacket pocket of her very tailored and body-hugging suit. "Just hold your hands at your sides and relax."

Marina leaned against the counter as Roxanne did a very *thorough* job of the measuring. There was so much touching and cooing that even Todd started to look uncomfortable.

"All right," Roxanne said when she finally finished. "Let's get you into a dressing room and see how things go."

As she went into the back to get the samples, Marina grinned. "I hope she's quiet, because I embarrass easily. If the two of you start moaning, I'm out of here. Oh, give me the car keys so I can abandon you."

Todd gripped her arm. "You're not going anywhere. That woman scares me."

She laughed. "Oh, please. Is the big, bad millionaire frightened by the little girl in the tux shop? Poor Todd."

He narrowed his gaze. "You think this is funny."

"It kind of is."

It would be different if she were in a relationship with him. Then Roxanne's act would be a little disconcerting. But as it was, she could just have lots and lots of fun at his expense.

There was a tiny twinge of something buried inside her stomach, but she wasn't going to worry about whatever stray feeling she might have. It wasn't jealousy. It couldn't be. This was Todd. Someone she could never in a million years care about.

He pulled her into the dressing area with him. "Who's laughing now?" he asked as he jerked open a slatted door leading to a big dressing area, complete with a wooden chair. "Have a seat."

She folded her arms over her chest. "Excuse me? I can't sit here and watch you undress." Her cheeks got hot just from her thinking about it. She lowered her voice. "I barely know you."

"I'm wearing briefs," he said. "What's the problem? Pretend we're at the beach. I'm not going to be left alone with that woman."

He was serious. She wasn't sure if she was shocked or about to break out in hysterical laughter. "You expect me to protect you?"

"Damned straight."

She felt her lips begin to twitch, but she managed to hold in her grin. "All right. If it's that important to you. I'll sit here and watch you try on clothes. But I have to tell you, I'm a little disappointed. I thought you'd be better with women than this. It's another hope dashed. Any more disappointments like this and I'll need therapy."

He glared at her. "I know her type. She's not going to take no for an answer."

"And the big, bad millionaire doesn't want to hurt her feelings," Marina said, mocking him with a baby voice.

His eyes narrowed, but before he could respond, Roxanne appeared with several tuxedos. She came to a stop when she saw Marina in the dressing area.

"You're helping?" she asked in a voice that indicated such a thing could not be possible.

"Absolutely," Todd told her. "Marina has perfect taste."

"He's pretty helpless without me," Marina said with a smile. "Practically unstable."

Todd's gaze lasered in on her face and she had a feeling she might have to pay for that later, but who cared? This was a side of him she could never have imagined and she planned to enjoy every minute of it.

Not only seeing him as someone with flaws and weakness, she thought as Roxanne hung the tuxes on a hook and flounced out of the room, but as someone who was a lot more interesting than she'd first realized.

It wasn't until he pulled off his tie and began to unbutton his shirt that she realized the small detail she'd overlooked. The dressing room was oversized, but still relatively close quarters considering she and Todd hadn't known each other very long and he was about to take his clothes off in front of her.

He'd said to pretend they were at the beach. In theory, briefs wouldn't show any more than swim trunks, but they *weren't* at the beach and a really good-looking guy was undressing. Where was she supposed to look? Or not look?

He shrugged out of the shirt. His broad chest was well muscled and defined. She liked the faint dusting of hair that trailed down to his waistband. But when he reached for that waistband, she found herself suddenly staring at the floor.

"Ryan had better appreciate this," Todd muttered.

"You'll figure out a way to make him pay," she said, noting his socks were dark and looked new.

There was a rustle of movement, then he pulled on the pants from the first tux. Safety at last.

She decided to distract herself from the process by being busy. After handing him his shirt, she slipped the jacket off the hanger and studied the weave of the fabric, then fingered the lapel.

Roxanne appeared in the doorway. "Vest or cummerbund?" she asked, holding out one of each.

"Vest," Marina said, taking it from her and handing it to Todd. "You said you'd try."

He grunted, then slipped it on. Marina admired the way the cut emphasized the breadth of his shoulders and the narrowness of his hips. A faint tingle quivered to life somewhere behind her belly button.

He took a tie from Roxanne and eased it under his collar. After securing the knot, he put on the jacket.

"There's a three-way mirror out here," Roxanne said.

He followed her into the large center area of the dressing rooms. He stepped onto the platform in front of the mirror and stared at his reflection.

"What do you think?" he asked.

"Magnificent," Roxanne purred as she stepped up behind him and began smoothing down the shoulders and pulling at the hem of the jacket.

Marina agreed with the sentiment, even as the other woman's need to touch every inch of Todd got on her nerves. This was a business, not a petting zoo.

Determined to be mature and let Todd handle the situation, she ignored Roxanne and her roving hands.

"I like the vest," she said.

Todd nodded. "Me, too. I see what you're going for. It's less traditional than the cummerbund, but it looks great. We can't order anything until Julie and Ryan pick colors, but we can give them a few ideas."

"We have a Web site," Roxanne said, leaning toward his ear and pressing her breasts into his back. "I'll write down the item number so your friend can go online and see which tux you're talking about. If he looks half as good as you in this, it's going to be some wedding."

Marina held in a groan as Todd sidestepped Roxanne. "Great. Why don't you go get that information now?"

She reluctantly stepped back. When she'd left the dressing room, he turned to Marina.

"You're supposed to be protecting me."

"You're big enough to protect yourself."

"We're supposed to be a team. I'd rush to *your* rescue."

She couldn't figure out what he wanted from her. Did he want her to act like she was jealous? Was this his ego talking? Did he need every woman on the planet panting for him so that he could sleep at night? Or was it something else? Was he seriously uncomfortable?

While she wanted to believe the best of him, his reputation made it impossible. So he was playing her.

Fine. She could play, too. She could make him sorry he'd ever pulled her into his game.

She walked to the edge of the platform and grabbed a handful of his jacket, then tugged until he stepped down onto the carpeted floor. Then she raised herself up on tiptoe, wrapped one arm around his neck and pressed her mouth to his.

She was determined this should be a whole lot more than that brief kiss they'd shared before. She wanted to teach him a lesson. So she kept her lips slightly parted and pressed against him as if she meant it.

After a brief second of shocked stillness, Todd put both his arms around her, hauled her closer and kissed her back. He brushed her lips with his, then took advantage of her invitation and swept inside.

He moved purposefully, a man on a mission. He tasted faintly of coffee and mint—and he knew how to kiss.

The second his tongue touched hers, passion exploded. The feeling was so intense, she half expected the building to shake. There was so much heat and need and pleasure in the way he explored her mouth, teasing, flicking, retreating, returning.

Wanting blindsided her. She couldn't think, so she

reacted instead. She tilted her head and kissed him back. When he moved his hands up and down her back, she explored his shoulders, then his arms. He was all honed muscle and warmth. One of his hands got tangled in her long hair. He tugged slightly, pulling her head back. She let him have his way and was rewarded when he kissed his way down her neck.

The soft, hungry, openmouthed kisses made her want to whimper. Her entire body clenched as her breasts swelled in anticipation. She wanted to be on her back, on any flat surface. She wanted him between her legs, taking her hard and fast and damn the consequences.

That thought—one she'd never had before in her life—stunned her. She pulled back just as she heard the sound of a very irritated person clearing her throat. She turned and saw Roxanne standing in the entrance to the dressing room.

"You two should get a room," the saleswoman said, her voice icy.

"Interesting thought," Todd drawled.

Roxanne turned and left.

Marina stood there, not sure what to think let alone what she should say. Talk about unexpected passion. And awkward.

Several comments floated to the surface of her brain, but they all sounded stupid. Even if they didn't, she wasn't sure she could speak. Her throat was dry and tight and she had a bad feeling her voice would sound breathless.

"Marina," Todd began.

She held up a hand to stop him, then swallowed and forced herself to look at him.

Big mistake, she thought when she saw the hunger in his dark eyes. Her gaze zeroed in on his mouth…a mouth that could obviously drive a woman wild wherever it kissed her.

"I was teaching you a lesson," she said, her voice shaking a little. "At least I was supposed to."

"You're not what I expected, either."

Was that good or bad?

"You're not my type," she continued. "I want to plan my sister's wedding. Nothing else."

She met his gaze. Some of the hunger had faded, but there was just enough there to make her want to throw herself at him and do it all again.

"I agree," he said.

It took her a second to realize he was responding to what she said, not what she'd thought.

"So this never happened," she told him. "Nothing happened."

"Something happened. But we can ignore it—if you prefer."

Which was as close to a good answer as she was going to get, she thought. She left him alone to change back into his street clothes and walked out to wait by the car.

It wasn't the fact that she'd enjoyed the kiss that bothered her. It was that she'd been willing to give herself to him without knowing him. Without deep feelings. Her level of passion scared her.

Todd was a lot more interesting than she'd ever

imagined. Liking him was a surprise. Wanting him, equally startling but there it was. But the two together? No way. They made the situation more than dangerous—they made it deadly.

She couldn't afford to fall for someone like him. If she did, she would be destroyed. She'd seen it happen. She knew what it cost.

To Marina_Nelson@mynetwork.LA.com
From Julie_Nelson@SGC.usa
What do you mean you kissed Todd! You can't just e-mail "oh by the way, I kissed Todd today" and then hit send. It's wrong on so many levels. You kissed him? On the mouth?

Why? That's so not like you. It's not about the million dollars is it? Please say it isn't. That's not like you, either. Todd? Seriously? How was it? Wait. I'm not sure I want to know.

He's nothing like your type. You always fall for sweet, nerdy guys who are going to save the world. Not powerhouse alpha males with attitude. He dated models. You remember that, right? Are you okay?

On a completely different topic, we love the sage/rose combination for our colors. Go with that, but nothing too matchy-matchy, please.

To Julie_Nelson@SGC.usa
From Marina_Nelson@mynetwork.LA.com
I'm fine. Totally fine. The kiss just kind of happened. It's a long story and I thought he was playing me, so I kissed him. It doesn't mean any-

thing. I wouldn't have mentioned it except I thought maybe he'd say something to Ryan and then Ryan would say something to you and then you'd be mad because I didn't tell you myself. That's all. Although now that I think about it, Todd isn't the type to brag.

As to the kiss, it was just a kiss, you know? Nice. I know he's not my type. You have nothing to worry about.

I'm glad you picked colors. That will help with the planning. I love the rose/green combo, too. And I swear, nothing that matches in a cute way. We'll go for shades and variations on a theme. It's going to be fabulous.

To Marina_Nelson@mynetwork.LA.com
From Julie_Nelson@SGC.usa

OHMYGOD!! You already know what type Todd is? What else do you know that you're not telling me? What else is happening there? You'd better not fall for him, Julie. I mean it. I'm thousands of miles away and I'd miss everything.

To Julie_Nelson@SGC.usa
From Marina_Nelson@mynetwork.LA.com

LOL. Don't sweat it. I'm not falling for Todd in any way. You have nothing to worry about.

Five

Todd drove slowly through the traffic around UCLA, then pulled over to the curb. He scanned the crowd of students, then saw Marina talking to a young woman.

Not talking, he reminded himself. Signing.

The two women faced each other, their hands moving in a graceful dance he couldn't decipher. Marina nodded, then glanced over her shoulder. She saw him and waved, then pointed at the car and signed something to her friend. The friend nodded, they hugged, then Marina started toward him.

He watched her walk. In her jeans and long-sleeved T-shirt, she fit in with the other students around her. He let his gaze linger on her swaying hips, then moved his attention to the way her long golden hair fluttered. She looked like a commercial for some sexy product. Buy whatever it was and get a girl like this.

She opened the passenger side door and slid inside. "Hey," she said. "Going to let me drive again?"

"No. Too much power will go to your head."

"So typical," she muttered as she fastened her seat belt. "Why do men feel they have to hold out on women? Don't give the poor females too much responsibility or power. They won't be able to handle it."

"Women control the majority of wealth in this country."

"A fact that makes me smile every time I hear it. I know you don't want me driving because my skill level threatens your masculinity."

"Not for long. I'm in therapy."

She laughed and he joined in. Their last meeting had been at the tux shop, where she'd kissed the hell out of him and had left him wanting more. He hadn't yet decided what, if anything, he was going to do about that wanting. For now it was enough to simply enjoy Marina's company.

As he pulled back into the traffic, he tried to remember the last time he'd wanted to just be with a woman. To hang out and talk and tease without counting the minutes until he could get her into bed.

It wasn't that he didn't want to sleep with Marina— he did. But he also liked her.

When was the last time that had happened? Liking. He'd almost forgotten how that felt. Not that he trusted her. He trusted no woman. But he'd been looking forward to being with her today ever since the last time he'd seen her.

"How did you get interested in sign language?" he asked.

She glanced at him. "I'm embarrassed to admit I first learned because one of my girlfriends had a hunky older brother who was deaf. I was about fourteen at the time. He was older and brooding and I knew that inside he was really deep and fascinating and that he would fall madly in love with me if only we could communicate. I took a beginning sign language class and really enjoyed it, so I kept going."

"What happened with the guy?"

"He turned out to be a total jerk who just happened to be deaf. Still, I'm grateful he put me on this path. I became a certified interpreter. It was a great part-time job for me through college."

She glanced at her watch. "I'm sorry I have to split up our day."

"No problem."

"It's an important class. So I appreciate you being flexible."

"Far be it from me to stand in the way of someone's education."

"Spoken like a true member of the elite."

They were heading over to a different caterer to sample food, then meeting up later at his place to interview a florist.

"Now that Ryan and Julie have picked their colors, we can make some firm decisions," he said. "I let the florist know what the colors were and she'll bring appropriate samples."

"Good. I think the rose-green combo gives us lots of room and areas of compromise. The boy stuff can be green, the girl stuff pink."

"Then everyone's happy."

"Exactly." She smiled at him.

He braked for the stoplight and smiled back. While they were looking at each other he said, "That was some kiss the other day."

Instantly her eyes widened and color stained her cheeks. She jerked her gaze away from him and stared out the windshield. "Yes, well, you said you needed protecting."

He'd wondered what she'd thought about their kiss. Had it been as powerfully erotic for her as it had been for him? Now he knew the answer to that was yes. He also knew she was a little embarrassed and wondered why.

"Not that I thought you really needed protecting," she said, still not looking at him. "You can handle women like that in your sleep."

"I'm more interesting when I'm awake." He drove through the intersection. "I wasn't expecting the passion."

"Just because I'm smart and into science doesn't meant I'm not like other people."

"You're not like other people, but that's a good thing. I'm not complaining, Marina. I like who you are."

"Oh. Good. Not that your opinion matters."

"Of course not."

She glanced at him. "It *was* a pretty hot kiss."

"I agree. I might need to be rescued later."

"I don't think so. You can save yourself without help from me."

"That's kind of cold."

"Live with it."

He chuckled and she smiled. Then she started talking about what Julie had said about the place settings. But most of his attention was on another, more interesting topic. Namely the idea of getting Marina into his bed.

He wanted her. That wasn't the question. He knew they would be great together. He'd learned that the first real kiss told a hell of a lot about chemistry and compatibility and desire. He and Marina had it all times ten. But sleeping together wasn't exactly intelligent.

For one thing, they would be connected to each other for the rest of their lives. Between his aunt by marriage being her grandmother and her sister marrying his cousin, they were in each other's worlds. Having sex would only make a complicated situation more awkward.

For another thing, she wasn't his usual type. She didn't play when it came to men and he didn't believe in getting serious when it came to woman. Better to keep things simple.

But it had been a great kiss. Thinking about it had kept him up much of the last couple of nights and that hadn't happened to him…ever.

Marina stared down at the small plate of pasta in front of her. While she appreciated the artful presentation, she was starting to get a little paranoid.

She leaned closer to Todd and whispered, "Is it just

me, or has every dish been covered with some kind of cream sauce?"

"It's not you," he whispered back. "The salad dressing, that creamy soup, the chicken, the crab cakes."

"Now this pasta," she murmured. "If we picked this place, we'd have to have white as our accent color."

She raked her fork through the perfectly cooked fettuccini. She couldn't complain about the food itself. The shrimp were delicate, the diced vegetables crisp, the sauce a decadent blend of cream and cheese and whatever spices went into it, but still.

"We can leave," he told her.

"Do you hate the food?" she asked.

"No. It's good. It's just…"

"Too much?"

He nodded. "Exactly."

A few minutes later, the dessert samples arrived. Marina managed to hold it together while the hostess explained what each dish was, then began to giggle when the women returned to the kitchen.

Todd raised his eyebrows. "Which will it be? The molten chocolate cake in cream sauce? The berries with cream sauce? The bread pudding with a chocolate cream sauce or the selection of sorbets with a ginger-cream topping?"

She took a bite of the bread pudding. "It's delicious," she said. "Really fabulous."

"I like the food," he said, sounding doubtful.

"I do, too. It's just so rich. My stomach already feels funny. Maybe the owner was a cow in a previous life and all this cream sauce is a way to get back to her roots."

Todd stared at her. "That's odd, even for you."

"I'm searching for an explanation. Okay, I'll e-mail Julie and tell her the food is amazing, but it's cream sauce central. Then they can decide."

They stood. She put her hand on top of her stomach. "Can we stop at a mini market on our way back? I'm dying for a soda to wash away the cream sauce flavor."

"Right there with you."

After her class, Marina drove to Todd's place to meet with the florist. Although she'd been to the gatehouse in back a few months before, she'd never seen the main house up close until today.

As she drove through the open wrought-iron gates, she stared up at the giant four-story mansion. There were dozens of windows and actual gables.

"And I thought Grandma Ruth's place was impressive," she muttered.

The grounds were manicured and endless. When she parked in front of the house, her car looked like a toy that had been left out by a careless child.

Sure, she'd known that the rich were different and that Todd was rich, but until this moment, she'd never realized exactly how rich. She had a bad feeling they were talking billions.

She headed up to the wide double doors, then paused as she glanced down at her jeans. Should she have dressed for the occasion?

Just then the front door opened and Todd stood there. "Take it all in?" he asked.

"Not yet. Do you give tours on alternate Wednesdays?"

"Only for a select few. Come on."

He'd changed out of his suit and was also dressed in jeans and a long sleeved shirt, which should have made her more comfortable. But he looked too good—all hard muscles and sleek sexy male. So between his butt and the elegance of the house, she didn't know where to look first.

She walked onto a marble entry floor and resisted the impulse to step out of her shoes. The foyer was large and oval, with a baby grand piano by the staircase. Right. Because every decent foyer *should* have room for a piano. There were incredible pieces of furniture that were probably antiques and paintings that looked both real and important.

Todd closed the door behind her. "What are you thinking?"

"I'm wondering how many bedrooms."

"More than ten."

"Okay. Good. So do you rent out to large families or simply invite small countries to move in?"

"It depends on my cash flow for the month."

He was joking, but there was something about his expression. Something almost…wary.

"Am I reacting wrong?" she asked. "Should I pretend I'm not impressed and a little intimidated?"

"It's just a house."

She laughed. "It's a really big house and you live here by yourself. That's a little strange."

"I grew up here. It's big and expensive to keep up, but it's been in my family for three generations and now it's my responsibility."

She looked around at the massive chandelier and the fresh flowers. "It's like a really great hotel. Show me the fluffy robe and the room service menu and I'll move in."

"We don't have room service."

She sighed. "Then forget it. Room service is a deal breaker for me." She looked at him. "How do they usually react? The other women?"

"They start by calculating how big a settlement they'll get when the marriage ends."

"Ouch. Not everyone you've dated has been in it for the money. A few of them must have actually liked you."

He chuckled. "You're not very good for my ego. Many of the women I date actually like me. The money is just a big plus." He put an arm around her shoulders and led the way through an arched doorway. "I don't usually show them the house."

"I wouldn't. Not until you're fairly serious. The ones who are in it for money won't be able to pretend anymore and the ones who are will be scared to death."

"*You're* not scared."

They were close enough that she could feel the heat of his body, which made her remember how it had been to be in his arms. How he'd pulled her close and kissed her back and made her tingle all over.

"We're not dating," she reminded him. As far as she was concerned, they never would. Todd was too danger-ous for her peace of mind. She wouldn't have thought she could be scared by a guy, but in some ways he would never know about, he terrified her.

If only he didn't turn her on. Reluctantly she stepped free of his embrace.

They stopped in a large family room. There were two sectionals, a couple of armoires, side tables, a writing desk and nothing about the room felt crowded.

"Nice," she said, appreciating the warm colors and overall comfort of the space. "You have a decorator."

"Of course. I'm a typical guy. If it were up to me, the entire world would be beige."

Somewhere in the distance, she heard the sound of chimes.

"The doorbell," he said. "Probably the florist. Have a seat and I'll let her in."

She crossed to one of the sectionals and sat down. To her right was a drinks cart made of incredibly beautiful inlaid wood. Instead of liquor, there were an assortment of soft drinks, along with ice, flavored water and a few snacks.

"Somewhere a housekeeper or cook is lurking," she murmured to herself as she put ice in a glass and popped the can of her favorite soda. There was no way Todd had put this together himself.

What must it be like to grow up in a place like this? She couldn't begin to imagine. While the house was something out of a movie, she had a feeling it might not have felt very comfortable for a kid. Todd was an only child. This was the kind of house that screamed out for bunches of kids. Had he ever been lonely?

Todd returned with a tiny woman of indeterminate age. He was laden down with armfuls of books and portfolios. She had two baskets with dozens of flowers in them.

"Marina, this is Beatrice. Beatrice, Marina is the bride's sister."

"How lovely that the two of you are planning the wedding together," the other woman said with a smile. She glanced around at the furniture and turned to Todd. "Perhaps some kind of dining room would be better suited?"

"Sure. Right this way."

"Can I get you something to drink first?" Marina asked.

Beatrice glanced at the cart. "Water, please, dear. Bottled if you have it."

Marina filled a second glass with ice, grabbed a bottle of water and trailed after them. As they moved from the family room to the dining room, she braced herself to be both impressed and intimidated.

Good thing, too, because the dining room could easily seat thirty, although the table was currently set with only a dozen chairs. Still, by the way it sat in the center of the room and the number of thick legs clustered together, she would guess there were about eight or ten leaves that fit into it.

Two hutches flanked leaded glass windows, while a long buffet sat in the center of the opposite wall. There were four chandeliers and a fireplace.

Todd set the books on the table, while Beatrice began to lay out dozens of flowers.

"I understand the bride and groom have chosen their

colors," she said as she clustered various blooms together. "That's always helpful. Rose and green will be lovely. However, I have some ideas for something a little different. A twist on the ordinary. For example, here we have dusty-rose colored tulips with green gladiolus. Not traditional, but they look beautiful."

Marina wasn't into plants or flowers, but as she knew what tulips looked like, she could figure out the gladiolus by default. The green petals were amazingly lush and the color was perfect next to the deep pink of the tulips.

"They're gorgeous," she murmured, then looked at Todd. "What do you think?"

"Nice."

She smiled. "Too much girly stuff?"

"I'm not into flowers. This seems fine."

Beatrice pulled out a spiny looking display. "Here we have bromeliad, ginger and anthurium. Again, not traditional, but the colors are perfect and these arrangement could make a charming table."

She handed Marina a ball of flowers in a yellowish shade of green. "Chrysanthemum balls. Very elegant. This sort of thing can be hung from the back of chairs." She thrust a handful of green berries at Todd. "Hypericum berries. A perfect green."

She brought out more and more flowers until Marina couldn't hold anymore. Todd was equally laden down.

Then Beatrice turned to the books. "I have pictures from various weddings. We'll look at them now."

She flipped through dozens of photos, explaining the different flower possibilities.

"You said there would be a separate room for the ceremony?" she asked.

Marina nodded. "There's a perfect room off the main ballroom. We'll set it up with rows of seating, so that space will need flowers, as well."

Beatrice began to talk about what they could do, but suddenly Marina found it difficult to listen. She felt hot and flushed, although at the same time, she felt a chill. Her stomach had taken a turn for the uncomfortable, as well. It seemed to flip over on itself in a way that made her want to gag.

Cautiously she put down the flowers. She'd never been allergic to anything before, but maybe the overdose of pollen was getting to her.

Todd looked at her. "Are you all right?"

Her stomach gave another lurch and she had a bad feeling she was about to throw up.

"Not really," she said, interrupting Beatrice midexplanation. "Is there a bathroom nearby?"

"Sure." He put down his armful of flowers. "I'll be right back," he told the florist and led Marina out of the room.

Down a very elegant hall she was in no shape to appreciate, was a spacious guest bath.

"It's my stomach," she said. "I don't know what's wrong."

"Don't worry about it. I'll handle Beatrice."

Despite the suddenly twisting sensation in her stomach, she managed a smile. "I don't think anyone can handle Beatrice, but you go ahead and try."

"Come out when you feel better."

"Sure. I'll probably just be a minute."

She closed the bathroom door behind her and two seconds later lunged for the toilet.

Marina had no idea how much time had passed. She'd already thrown up twice and had a bad feeling she wasn't done. She felt shaky and weak, hot and cold, and a distinct longing to never feel this horrible ever again.

She sat on the marble floor, her eyes closed and wondered if she had the strength to drive herself home. The task seemed impossible on a couple of different levels. First, she doubted she could make the trip without vomiting again. Second, she couldn't seem to focus on anything but how miserable she felt.

There was a knock on the bathroom door.

"Marina?"

She recognized Todd's voice. Why had this had to happen here of all places? With him around?

"Yeah?"

"How's your stomach?"

"Awful. I can't figure out what's wrong."

"I can. Food poisoning. All those cream sauces."

She remembered what they'd eaten and groaned. "You, too?"

"You bet. I got rid of Beatrice. Come on. I'll take you upstairs to one of the guest rooms. The bathrooms are more comfortable and you can crawl into a bed between events."

She hesitated for a second, then staggered to her feet. Stretching out on a bed sounded really good right now.

She opened the bathroom door and saw Todd looked about as bad as she felt. He was pale, slightly green and there were shadows under his eyes.

"Aren't we an attractive couple," she murmured as he took her hand and pulled her toward the stairs.

"We'll take a picture. We have to hurry. I don't know how long I have."

Despite how sick she felt, she started to laugh. "You sure know how to show a girl a good time."

"Tell me about it. At least it's Friday. You don't have classes on the weekend, do you?"

"No."

"Good. Then you can crash here as long as you'd like. There's a phone in your room if you need to call anyone. There are robes in the closet. I put a couple of my T-shirts on the bed, so you could sleep in something more comfortable than your clothes."

They reached the second-floor landing. She glanced at him. He'd thought of all that while feeling as horrible as she did? Talk about a great guy. "Thanks. You're going way beyond what's expected."

He put a hand to his stomach. "It's going to be an ugly few hours. Basically we have to get all the bad food out of our system."

She didn't want to think about that. "We should—"

Todd cut her off with a shake of his head. "Third door on your right. T-shirts on the bed. Water on the nightstand."

He turned and hurried in the opposite direction, ducking into a door at the far end of the hall.

Marina watched him go, then felt a faint rising in her own midsection. She didn't have much time herself.

She ran into the guest room and found everything as he'd described. There were two clean T-shirts on the bed, three bottles of water on the nightstand and a robe in the closet. But before she could deal with any of that, she ran toward the bathroom and wondered if she could possibly survive the day.

Six

Marina woke up sometime around six Saturday morning. She'd spent quality time in the bathroom until about midnight, then had crawled into bed and slept like the dead. After brushing her teeth with a conveniently placed new toothbrush, she slipped into the fluffy robe and headed out into the vast expanse of Todd's house to find the kitchen.

Passing through the dining room, still littered with flowers, she made her way toward the rear of the house and walked into a kitchen that could easily satisfy the pickiest chef known to man.

She also found Todd there. He wore sweats, a T-shirt and hadn't shaved. There was a slight shifting in her stomach, but this one had nothing to do with the food she'd eaten and everything to do with how delicious the man in front of her looked.

"Morning," she said, doing her best to act normal around the sudden fluttering in her chest. What was wrong with her? This was Todd. A guy she borderline despised. Except she couldn't. Not really. He'd been just as sick as she had been yesterday, but he'd taken the time to get her settled before spending his evening in his own bathroom.

He looked up and smiled. "Hey. How you feeling?"

"Better. My stomach is so empty I can practically hear coyotes howling. You?"

"I wrapped things up about one in the morning, then crashed. I'm going to make an executive decision here and say no to the cream sauce caterer."

She laughed. "I won't fight you on that. I don't think I've ever been that sick."

He nodded at the kettle on the stove. "At the risk of sounding like a wuss, how about some tea and dry toast? I think that's about all I can handle this morning."

"Sounds great. We probably need to hydrate."

He grinned. "That was a lot of fluids coming out."

"Tell me about it." She fingered the robe. "This is nice. Am I the first English speaking female to wear it?"

He leaned against the counter and crossed his arms over his chest. "You were going to let the model thing go."

"I don't remember saying that."

"You should." He looked her up and down. "It's for company, not dates. I don't usually bring women here, remember?"

"But your car is a little small for the wild thing."

He raised an eyebrow. "You're mighty curious about my personal life."

"Men love to talk about themselves."

"We usually go to her place."

"I see. That makes it easier to escape when you feel the need and doesn't push the money thing into their face."

"Exactly."

The kettle began to whistle. At the same time, bread popped out of the toaster.

"Dishes?" she asked.

He pointed to a row of cabinets. It only took her two tries to find small plates. She put the toast on a plate and popped in two more slices, while Todd poured water into a teapot. She glanced over his shoulder and saw fresh tea leaves in a little basket.

"Very fancy," she said. "Yours?"

"Apparently. I e-mailed my housekeeper last night and asked her if I had any tea. She said I did and told me where to find everything."

Imagine having so much stuff, you didn't know what you owned or where it was. Different worlds, Marina thought. Very different worlds.

They sat at the round table by the large window. She nibbled on a piece of toast, then took the mug of tea he offered.

"Interesting house," she said after she'd sipped the steaming liquid. "Kind of intimidating."

"It does leave an impression."

She looked at his face, at the dark stubble shadowing his cheeks and jaw. "How do you know it's ever about you?" she asked. "Nothing about your life is normal. How can you be sure?"

"I'm not. Even you agreed to go out with me after your grandmother offered you a million dollars."

She rolled her eyes. "Oh, please. You know that's just a joke. Although it is fascinating that she does think she has to pay someone to marry you. What does she know that I don't?"

"I'm ignoring the question," he told her.

Marina took another bite of toast and chewed slowly. So far her stomach was staying pretty settled, but she wasn't ready to get wild for a few more hours.

"You have to have been sure sometime," she said. "There have to be some women you trust."

"You don't want to talk about this."

"Are you asking me or telling me?"

His dark gaze settled on her face. "I went to an all-guys boarding school for high school. Ryan and I both did. My first serious girlfriend was a scholarship student at the all-girl school next door. We met at a dance and I fell for her in seconds. She was smart, funny and totally into me."

Marina didn't doubt that for a minute. She had a feeling he'd been the kind of guy a lot of girls would have been totally into.

"Her mother was barely making it, working in an office somewhere. Jenny told her about me. We were each other's first time." His face tightened. "Jenny's mom went to my parents and said that either they would pay her two hundred and fifty thousand dollars or she would bring me up on rape charges. Jenny was only sixteen, so there was a chance the charges would stick."

Marina felt sick again, although this time it had nothing to do with food poisoning. "I can't believe that. How horrible. How old were you?"

"Sixteen. But that didn't matter. My parents paid her off and I learned an important lesson."

She wanted to tell him that he'd learned the wrong thing, that people weren't like that, except she thought for him, maybe they were.

"What did Jenny have to say?" she asked.

"She was upset, or so she said. The week after we broke up, her mother bought her a car. That seemed to help."

He sounded bored and cynical, but talking about the past had to be hurting him. That sort of experience would leave a scar.

"Another woman I was dating came to me and said she was pregnant. I was always careful, but I had no reason to think she was lying. I did the right thing and asked her to marry me. She'd always talked about a big wedding, so I suggested we wait until after the baby was born, so the plans weren't rushed. She freaked at that."

Marina slumped back in her seat and closed her eyes. "Let me guess. She wasn't really pregnant?"

"No. She had a friend who peed on the stick and that's what she showed me. Apparently her plan was to try to get pregnant right away and if that didn't work, to 'lose' the baby right before the wedding. We would both be so devastated by the tragedy that we'd get married anyway."

"I hate that there are people like her in the world," she said. "I know the money makes it difficult, but you have to have had some good experiences with women."

"Some. A few. But I'm never sure. One way or another, I'm waiting for each one to finally admit it's all about the money."

She leaned toward him. "Todd, you're a great guy. You're smart and funny and charming and not half-bad looking."

He smiled. "Wait. I need a moment to bask in the 'not half-bad looking' compliment."

She laughed. "You know what I mean. It's not always about the money. It can't be. There aren't that many horrible people in the world."

"Before Ryan fell for your sister, he was dating a single mom with an adorable little girl. Ryan was convinced he'd found the perfect woman. He was crazy about the kid, wanted them both in his life and proposed. Then I overheard her talking to a friend about how she'd hated having a baby until she realized that most young, rich guys are suckers for a cute little girl. That she planned to stay married to Ryan for a couple of years, then divorce him and live on the child support he would offer to pay."

Her heart ached for Todd. "So what do you do? Never trust? Never care too much? Never put yourself out there?"

"It's working so far."

"But that's so lonely. Don't you want to be in love?"

"Not bad enough to get taken. I can get a woman whenever I want. If I need another heartbeat in the house, I'll get a dog."

Sadness nearly overwhelmed her. On the surface, Todd had everything, but in truth, there were big holes in his life. He was powerful and in charge—the sort of man who thrived on doing. He was also surprisingly kind and caring. And he would never trust a woman enough to truly give his heart.

"What are you thinking?" he asked.

"That we're both seriously twisted. You can't trust anyone else and I can't trust myself."

"I don't believe that," he told her. "You have it all together. Don't you date nerdy guys who are going to change the world?"

"Most of the time. They're brilliant and interesting and…" She bit her lower lip. They were supposed to be talking about him, not her.

"And safe?" he asked, his voice low.

"Maybe. Sometimes. I just…" She took a sip of the tea. "My mom fell in love with my dad the second she saw him. She was seventeen and to this day, she still adores him. My dad isn't a bad person, but he's not the greatest husband and father. He leaves. He just up and disappears for months at a time. We never know when he's going or how long he'll be gone. Every time he walks out, her heart breaks. But she won't tell him he can't come back. She won't let herself love anyone else. She lives a half-life, only truly happy when he's with her."

"You're not like that," he told her. "You're tough."

"You don't know that and neither do I. I'm terrified I'm just like her. That I'll fall for a guy who'll break my heart and I'll let him. I'll say it's okay. Falling in love, really falling in love, seems too much like handing over control of my life. It's not on my to-do list anytime soon."

"So instead of taking a chance, you date guys you're not at risk of falling in love with."

She looked at him. "Do you really want to spend much time pointing out my flaws, because I think you're in kind of dangerous territory."

"I'm willing to risk it. Am I right?"

"Maybe."

"You're always the object of affection, never the one at emotional risk."

"You're making me sound mean and I'm not. I just don't want to fall for anybody until I'm sure I won't be destroyed."

"You can never be sure."

"I refuse to believe that," she said. "One day I'll take a chance."

"Will you?"

She wanted to believe she would. That one man would be worth her step of faith.

"Obviously we both need therapy," she said. "Maybe we could get a group rate."

He laughed. The sound made her feel good inside. Then she yawned.

"Sorry," she said as she covered her mouth. "I didn't get enough sleep last night."

"Me, either." He rose. "Come on. Let's go to bed."

She stared at him. A thousand thoughts raced through her mind. Bed? With him? As in sex? She wanted to be shocked and insulted. She wanted to stand up and slap him. But as images of them together, naked, touching, filled her brain, she found herself just as interested in saying yes.

Todd held up both hands. "Sorry. Poor word choice. Let me start over. Let's go upstairs where we can each sleep in our own beds. Better?"

She nodded, because that was what he expected, but inside, she felt a sharp stab of disappointment. What was up with that?

He waited until she'd risen, then put a hand on the small of her back and guided her out of the kitchen.

"We'll meet up later," he said cheerfully, "and figure out if we ever want food again."

"Sounds like a plan."

At the top of the stairs, they each went their separate way. But as she closed the door of the guest room she couldn't help thinking how much she was wishing he'd meant what he said the first time.

Later that afternoon, Marina stepped out of the shower and reached for a towel. Todd might not invite a lot of lady friends to his place, but he kept the guest room well stocked. In addition to the toothbrush and toothpaste she'd found earlier, there was also shampoo, conditioner, body wash and an assortment of moisturizers.

After slathering on a yummy citrus-scented lotion, she dressed, gave her hair a halfhearted blow-dry and headed downstairs.

She was starving and tea and toast wasn't going to cut it. She figured she could do drive-through on her way home. But first she had to find her host and thank him for everything.

The kitchen was empty, as was the family room. She heard a faint noise, like someone typing on a keyboard and headed in that direction. She located Todd in a panel-lined study that looked like a set out of *Masterpiece Theater.* He was dressed, as well, and looked just as good as he had that morning.

Little tingles broke out all through her body. She felt a distinct flicker of heat and several other unwelcome physical responses.

"How are you feeling?" he asked when she walked into the room.

"Good. I slept more and now I'm starving."

"Me, too. So we both survived our food poisoning."

"Looks that way."

He stood and walked around the desk. "You ready to head home?"

She nodded, even though what she actually wanted to do was throw herself into his arms and beg him to take her. Obviously she was still suffering the ill effects of the bad food.

"Big date tonight?" he asked.

"Not really."

He picked up a folded piece of paper from his desk and offered it to her. "Because I remember you saying you loved Mexican food and there's a great place nearby that delivers. Want to have something to eat before you go?"

She hesitated. Her head told her to get out while she

was emotionally in one piece. The rest of her body—especially the exquisitely female bits—suggested she stick around and see how this might play out.

"We could watch a movie," he said. "I'll even let you pick."

She grinned. "How can I resist that kind of an invitation? What are the odds we'll agree on any movie?"

"There has to be at least one. Something funny."

"But smart, not silly."

"I have that."

"I never thought I'd eat again," Marina admitted three hours later as she stretched out on Todd's sectional sofa in his media room. "But I'm kinda hungry."

Todd sat slumped down with his stocking feet propped up on the suede covered ottoman in front of the sofa.

The fabric on the furniture and the carpeting were the only things soft about this high-tech space. There was a screen that looked as if it belonged in a movie theater, enough speakers to levitate a house, players and recorders and a collection of movies that had made her mouth water. It was man toy heaven.

"A taco, two enchiladas, chips, salsa and a salad weren't enough for you?" he asked as he glanced at her.

She grinned. "Apparently not. I'm kind of in the mood for dessert."

"Then let's go see what's in the kitchen."

He stood and stretched. They were both casually dressed—her in the clothes she'd worn the previous day, him in jeans and a loose T-shirt. As he raised his arms above his head, the hem of his T-shirt crept above the waistband of his jeans, exposing a sliver of skin and his belly button.

It shouldn't have been the least bit erotic. They'd spent the whole night throwing up and doing other disgusting things only a few dozen yards apart from each other. Yet as she watched him, she felt more than a little bit of wanting deep inside.

"You ate a bunch, too," she said as he led the way out of the media room and toward the staircase. "More than me."

"Feeling defensive about your very unladylike appetite?"

"Maybe. I was hungry."

"I won't tell anyone."

She elbowed him in the side. "It's not like I ate with my hands or anything."

He looked at her and raised his eyebrows. "You had tacos. Of course you ate with your hands."

"You know what I mean."

At the bottom of the stairs, she forgot where the kitchen was and went right. He went left and they slammed into each other.

"Sorry," she said as she took a step back.

He grabbed her upper arms and held her steady. "You feeling all right?"

"I'm fine. Just a lousy sense of direction."

His eyes stared into hers. She suddenly felt both vulnerable and incredibly alive. She wanted him to move those hands, to touch her everywhere. Even as her brain screamed out that this was potentially dangerous, she found herself taking a step closer.

She saw the exact moment he felt it, too. There was a sharpening of his features, a subtle tension in his body. Hunger darkened his eyes.

He dropped his hands and stepped back. "Dessert," he said. "We were going to get you some dessert."

"Right. Anything but ice cream."

He groaned. "We're scarred for life."

"I don't think so. I will bravely overcome my fear of cream anything to indulge in chocolate chocolate chip again. It's just the kind of person I am."

He led the way to the kitchen. So neither of them was willing to act on the attraction. Smart, she thought, even as she wrestled with disappointment. Still, there were complications. They were practically related and it wasn't as if he would disappear from her life once the wedding was over. Did she really want to spend the next fifty years sitting at the same table as Todd and have a single night of passion between them? Talk about awkward.

So she ignored the way he moved as he opened the freezer and pulled out an assortment of goodies. There were individual slices of cake, a pie that only needed to be defrosted, then heated, and brownies. In the pantry they found boxes of cookies and some chocolate chips that could work in a pinch.

"What will it be?" he asked.

"Brownies. I'll be putting frosting on mine. I noticed a can in the pantry."

"Because there's not enough sugar in a regular brownie?"

"Exactly."

"Women," he muttered as he pulled the tray of brownies out of the freezer. "We're going to have to microwave these to defrost them."

"I'm an expert at that sort of thing."

She reached for the brownies as he handed them over. But their timing was off and the plastic-wrapped tray slipped through her fingers to crash onto the floor. They both bent over at the same time and bumped heads. Marina slipped and landed on her butt.

"We're a hazard together," she said as she started to laugh. "A complete disaster. I thought both of us getting food poisoning was the worst of it, but apparently not."

He laughed, then sank down next to her on the floor. "You're not like other women."

"I could work on a charming European accent if you want."

He narrowed his gaze. "Let it go."

"Never."

He reached over and tucked a strand of hair behind her ear. "I never thought getting as sick as we did would be fun, but this has been. You don't need to rush home tonight if you don't want to. You could stay."

She knew how he meant the invitation. She could stay in the guest room. It was a polite and well-meaning invitation.

"A sleepover," she teased.

She looked at him, expecting to see an answering

smile. Instead she found heat, desire and a need that made her weak. Then he blinked and it was gone.

Her insides clenched, her heart began to beat faster and her throat when dry. "Todd?"

"I'm trying to be smart here, Marina. I can come up with a hundred reasons why this isn't a good idea."

She pressed her lips together. "A hundred. Wow. I can only come up with about eight."

"I might have been exaggerating." He stood and held out his hand. "Come on. We'll defrost brownies and lose ourselves in the sugar."

"Sounds like a plan."

She put her fingers against his palm and allowed him to pull her to her feet. When she was standing, she found they were really close together. She would have stepped back, but he didn't let go of her.

She let herself get lost in the fire in his eyes. It warmed her and enticed her, and she swayed toward him.

"Damn," he muttered, right before he reached for her.

Seven

His mouth was warm and smooth and when he kissed her, Marina felt heat clear down to her feet. Her toes curled, her thighs trembled, her midsection tightened and her breasts pouted because they wanted some attention, too.

He pulled her close and she let him because she needed to be pressed against the hard planes of his body. She wrapped her arms around his neck and leaned in, making sure they touched everywhere.

He explored her mouth, kissing lightly, gently, but with enough passion to keep her breath locked in her throat. There was a promise in his kisses, a promise that there would be a whole lot more in the near future. As the anticipation was nearly as amazing as what he was already doing, she was willing to wait.

As he continued to tease, rubbing his lips against hers, nibbling, pressing, but not quite taking, she explored the hard muscles of his shoulders and upper back. She ran her fingers through his hair, then raked her nails lightly across his nape.

Wanting poured through her, pooling low in her belly, and her most feminine center ached to be taken.

Finally he tilted his head and touched her lower lip with the tip of his tongue. She parted instantly, welcoming him inside. At the first intimate stroke, a shudder raced through her. Passion grew until her skin felt too tight, too sensitive, too impossibly needy.

She clung to him through deep kisses that touched her soul, through his hands moving up and down her back, until he cupped her rear and she instinctively arched toward him only to encounter the impressive hardness of his desire.

She gasped as she imagined him filling her over and over again. She wanted with a desperation that made her rub herself against him, like a lonely cat. Hunger made her frantic. She'd been very comfortable not dating, not getting involved, not having a man in her life. Suddenly she was starving for contact, for skin on skin nakedness. But not just with anyone…only Todd could scratch this particular itch.

Some of her need must have gotten through to him. Or maybe it was the quick pace of her breathing and the way she clamped her lips around his tongue and sucked. Whatever the method of communication, he seemed to get the message. He moved his hands to her hips, eased them under her long-sleeved T-shirt and rode her curves up to her breasts.

He caressed her with the skill of a man who loves women. Even through the fabric of her bra, she felt the gently but purposefully caress of his fingers. He cupped her, then used his thumbs and forefingers to tease her nipples into a frenzy.

Fire shot through her, diving down between her legs and stirring everything up. She couldn't think, couldn't breathe, could only stand there lost in the pleasure of him touching her. Her only conscious thought was to wonder how much better it would be if she wasn't wearing a bra.

Todd took advantage of her inattention to kiss his way along her jaw, then down her neck. He nipped her earlobe, kissed the sensitive area just below, then traced wildly erotic patterns with his tongue.

The combination of sensations was pretty incredible. She felt herself tensing in anticipation of release that couldn't possibly happen. Not like this. Sure it had been a long time, but she had some pride, didn't she? Shouldn't she at least let him take her jeans off before she gave in to passion?

But as he continued to tease and touch and play with her breasts, she found herself getting closer and closer. Apparently he realized it, as well, because he leaned in and murmured, "We need to get you into bed."

Before she could say anything, he'd grabbed her hand and tugged her out of the kitchen and into the hallway. She hurried alongside of him, eager to get upstairs, get naked and fall into paradise.

They started up the stairs.

"Is sex better on five hundred thread count sheets?" she asked.

He stopped, laughed, then pulled her close. "Of course," he said, right before he pulled her T-shirt over her head and kissed her.

She went willingly into his embrace, kissing him back, needing him more than she'd ever needed anyone.

Even as his tongue stroked hers, she felt him reach for the hooks on the back of her bra. Seconds later, the scrap of lingerie drifted down her arms and onto the stairs.

He broke the kiss and bent his head to take one of her breasts into his mouth. There was immediate heat as he sucked deeply, then circled her nipple with his tongue.

She swayed slightly, then put her hands on his shoulders to steady herself. The powerful pull of his mouth caused every nerve ending to quiver in delight. Between her legs there was dampness and heat and anticipation. More, she thought hazily. She needed more.

But for now, this would be enough.

He used his fingers to mimic the movement of his tongue, caressing both her breasts, forcing her into a higher and higher state of arousal until she knew it would take almost nothing to push her over the edge.

"Todd," she breathed, wanting her release, yet wanting to hang on for a little bit longer.

"Tell me about it," he muttered, then grabbed her hand and pulled her up the last few stairs.

They hurried down the hall and burst into a bedroom the size of lecture hall. She had a brief impression of warm colors, massive dark furniture and a big, comfy, inviting bed.

Finally, she thought as he released her hand and yanked off his T-shirt.

They were barefoot, so it didn't take much manipulation on his part to get them both naked. One second she was topless, then next her jeans and panties were pooling on the floor. His jeans and briefs followed. Then he was easing her back on the mattress and she was in his arms and they were touching skin on skin and it was glorious.

He stared at her, his dark eyes bright with passion. She traced his mouth, then smiled when he gently bit down on her finger.

"I want you," he told her. "You're sexy as hell."

"I find you mildly interesting, as well," she said.

He grinned. "Mildly, huh. So I have some work to do."

"Absolutely." Brave words from a woman on the edge, she thought happily.

"I don't mind getting down and dirty now and then." He shifted so he was next to her, on his side, his hand supporting his head. "Where should I start? Here?" He put his hand on her belly.

While that felt nice and all, it wasn't exactly what she wanted. "Um, no."

"Here?" He ran his fingers from her wrist to her elbow.

She shifted slightly. "Not what I had in mind."

He slipped his fingers between her legs and rubbed her swollen flesh. "How's that?" he asked, his voice low and husky.

It took every ounce of self-control to keep her eyes

open. She desperately wanted to fall into a passionate trance and get lost in her orgasm, but not just yet.

"That works," she breathed as he explored all of her, finding her center and rubbing it.

Tension rose up inside of her. Muscles tensed. She let her legs fall open in a blatant and time-honored tradition of invitation.

"Good. What about this?"

He leaned toward her and stroked her nipple with the tip of his tongue.

It was an amazingly perfect combination. It was exquisite, it was magic, it was more than enough to make her lose control.

She did her best to hang on, to at least take three minutes to come. But he began to move his fingers faster and faster, with the perfect amount of pressure. Then he sucked on her breast.

It was incredible. She pulled her knees up and dug her heels into the bed. Not yet, she told herself. Not yet. Not...

It was too late.

She fell into her release, caught in the waves of sensual pleasure that swept through her. Every part of her sighed in relief as he continued to touch her, easing her onward until her muscles gave out in sheer exhaustion.

Lethargy stole through her. She had to force herself to open her eyes and when she did, she found Todd staring at her.

She'd expected a self-satisfied male smile—one that more than hinted at his expertise and how everything had felt so good because he was so darned talented in bed. Instead he looked serious and intense and instead of smiling, he leaned in and kissed her.

She parted her lips for him and felt the lethargy fade. As his tongue teased hers, passion returned and she found herself eager to have him inside of her.

He was hard…she could feel him pressing into her leg. She reached between their bodies and lightly stroked his arousal. But instead of reaching for a condom and then entering her, he slid down her body, kissing first her neck, then between her breasts, along the center of her rib cage, her belly, before coming to rest at the top of her right thigh. He parted her swollen flesh with his fingers.

While she appreciated the gesture, it wasn't required. "I've already…"

Then he did smile. "I know. I was there."

Her mouth curved in response. "It was great."

"I'm glad. Now let's do it this way."

A man on a mission, she thought as she let her eyes slowly close. Far be it from her to tell him his attentions weren't welcome.

Her stomach clenched in anticipation of his touch. She felt a faint breath of air, then a warm tongue began to explore her.

She groaned as he circled around her still-swollen center. A quick, light brush and then he was gone, caressing the rest of her, getting close, but not actually touching her *there*. It was exquisite torture. It was incredible.

She parted her legs even more and drew back her knees. Heat burned through her as he kissed and licked and sucked everywhere but that one place she wanted the most.

There it was again. One brief moment of exquisite contact, then nothing. One hint of what she could be feeling, then only anticipation.

She began to squirm. She got closer and closer, but knew she couldn't find her release until he focused on that one place. Until he finally—

His tongue brushed her again. She nearly screamed from the glory of the contact, then prepared herself for him to move away. She was an adult and she wouldn't whimper. Only this time he didn't stop. He stayed in that one spot, licking and circling, teasing, arousing, pushing her closer and closer until her climax became as inevitable as the sunrise.

He intensified his attention and she was lost.

The shuddering began deep inside of her midsection and worked its way out. Her thighs trembled, her hands shook and then she was launched into a release so powerful, she truly thought she might never experience anything like it again.

He continued to kiss her, teasing her into coming and coming. She gave herself over to him, letting him take all of her, until the tension finally eased and she was still.

Todd sat up and looked at Marina. A flush stole across her chest and climbed to her cheeks. She was limp, but if the smile was anything to go by, also incredibly satisfied.

Her golden-blond hair spilled across his pillow in sexy disarray and when she opened her eyes, her pupils were so dilated, he could barely see any of the blue.

"Wow," she said, her voice thick and husky. "I don't even know what to say."

He'd been complimented before. Most women made it a point to gush and while he appreciated the praise, he'd sometimes wondered how much of it was earned and how much of it had to do with his bank account.

Marina wasn't like that. Somewhere in the process of planning the wedding, they'd become friends. He liked her. He thought she was funny and smart and sincere. How often could he say that about the women in his bed?

Which made this experience different. He couldn't remember the last time he'd made love with a friend.

She put her hand on his arm and urged him closer. "So far this had been a pretty one-sided show."

At her words, he once again became aware of the pressure of his arousal.

He opened the nightstand drawer and pulled out a condom. After slipping it on, he knelt between her thighs. She reached for him and guided him inside.

Immediately he got lost in the sensation of tight, wet heat. She surrounded him, drawing him in, letting him fill her.

Her scent teased him. He could hear her breathing, feel the light stroking of her hands on his back and sides. For once he wasn't thinking about how quickly he was going to have to get away once this was over. For once he could just enjoy the experience and let the rest of it go.

He pumped harder, faster, in and out, losing himself in the growing pressure. She wrapped her legs around his hips, urging him closer. Her body tightened around him and he was lost.

* * *

"This is not a good idea," Marina murmured, even as she held out her wineglass. "Twenty-four hours ago, I was curled up like a dog on the bathroom floor. I should give my stomach time to recover."

"It has," Todd said confidently. "Besides, you were the one who was going to put frosting on perfectly good brownies. Isn't this better?"

The "this" in question was a bottle of red wine. It was after midnight. She and Todd had made love a second time then dozed off, only to wake up starving. He'd pulled on jeans and had given her a T-shirt to wear, then they'd made their way to the kitchen where they'd found mostly defrosted brownies on the counter.

She inhaled the scent of the wine, then took a sip. It was smooth and dark, with absolutely no bite. "Not bad. Let me guess. You have a wine cellar in the basement."

"The house doesn't have a basement, but there is a temperature and humidity controlled wine cellar."

"Naturally." She thought of the lone bottle of chardonnay she kept in her refrigerator…for special occasions, of course. "And if I wanted a bottle of Dom Pérignon?"

He shrugged. "What do you think?"

That he wasn't what she'd expected. That he was a whole lot better and that made him dangerous.

She took the brownie he offered, then followed him to the sofa in the family room. At some point he must have turned on a stereo because she could hear soft music in the background.

They sat facing each other, the night settling in

around them. She felt a sense of intimacy and connection—neither were very smart.

"Todd," she began, not sure exactly what she wanted to say.

"I know."

"How can you? *I* don't even know what I was going to say."

He set his wineglass and brownie on the coffee table, then leaned in and kissed her. "You're going to say that this is a complication neither of us needs. That we have a wedding to plan and that we're about to become related by marriage—again. That staying friends instead of lovers makes the most sense."

"Okay, yeah, that's probably what I was going to say," she admitted, letting herself get lost in his dark eyes. "Not that tonight wasn't great."

"Agreed."

"And that you're not nearly as toady as I thought you'd be."

He raised an eyebrow. "Toady?"

She grinned. "You know what I mean."

"You mean I'm sophisticated and charming. A man of the world, unlike the boy-nerds you usually date."

"Something like that. And I'm refreshingly intelligent and together, with just a hint of sass and a fabulous grasp of the English language, unlike those stick figures you usually date."

"You are all those things," he said and kissed her again. Then he wrapped his arms around her and eased her onto her back on the sofa.

She stared up at him. "We'd agreed this was a bad idea to continue."

"We'll end things tomorrow," he said as he kissed his way along her jaw.

"It is tomorrow."

"Not until the sun comes up. That means we have all night."

She wrapped her arms around him and gave herself up to his seduction. All night sounded just about perfect to her.

"They're arguing about the color of the shutters," Willow said as she carefully pulled an impossibly tiny plant from the soil and carefully placed it in a plastic container. "I'm sorry I ever mentioned shutters. I don't mind handling the remodel, but I hate it when they start e-mailing me separately."

Marina found herself mesmerized by the quick and expert movements of her sister's fingers. Willow poured in the potting mix, tapped it down, made a hole, plucked a slender plant from the tray and settled it in its new home.

"I'm thinking purple," Willow said. "You know—to match the elephants."

Marina blinked. "What elephants?"

Her sister sighed. "I knew you weren't listening to me. What's going on?"

"There are going to be elephants?"

"No." Willow sighed. "Marina, what's up? You're not yourself. Do you feel okay?"

If she ignored the faint protest of sore and stretched muscles, then she was exceptional. She and Todd had made love past dawn. While she was impressed with his ability to be ready time after time, she was also pretty pleased with her own performance. She would guess that she'd had more orgasms in the last twenty-four hours than maybe in all her previous life.

"I'm fine," she said. "Just a little tired."

"Uh-huh." Willow didn't look convinced. She walked to the door of the back room at the nursery and closed it, then put her hands on her hips and stared at her sister. "Start at the beginning and talk slowly. I don't want to miss anything."

"There's nothing to say." Which was a big, fat lie. "Well, not all that much."

"I'm going to stand here and glare at you until you tell me."

Marina smiled. "You're not actually glaring. It's more of a semiscowl."

"Marina!"

"Okay, okay. I'm fine. Everything is fine. It's just…" She felt her mouth curve up in a very satisfied smile. "Friday Todd and I did some tasting at a caterer. When I went back to his place to discuss flowers with a floral designer, I started to feel really bad. We both had food poisoning. I ended up spending the night there, practically chained to the toilet."

"And *that's* what you're smiling about?"

"No. But Todd was great. By yesterday we were feeling better. He asked me to stay—in the guest room. So we had dinner and watched a movie and then, well…"

Willow's eyes widened. "Ohmygod! You had sex with Todd Aston the Third. I'm going to get a million dollars!"

Marina held up both hands. "Number one, I'm not marrying him, so you can let your dreams of the million dollars go. If you're so hot to open a nursery, talk to Kane. He would do anything for you."

Willow shook her head. "No, thanks. I'm going to raise the money on my own. If you're not willing to marry to get it for me, then I'll get a loan or something. Which, by the way, is so not the point. You had sex with Todd?"

Marina smiled. "I did. It was great. He's nothing I'd imagined. I like him."

Willow moved close and hugged her. "That's great. Yea for you."

"It's not great. It's weird and uncomfortable and we're not going to be together that way again."

Willow stepped back and stared. "Excuse me? You're glowing. I've never seen you glow before. No one walks away from glowy sex."

"I will. We both will. We talked about it and this is the most sensible plan. Look, we're already related by marriage through Grandma Ruth. It's going to happen again when Julie and Ryan get married. Todd is in our lives forever. A relationship with him wouldn't go anywhere."

Willow returned to her plants. "Why not? He's single, you're single. That's an excellent start."

"We don't have anything in common. We're from different worlds. On a more basic level, he doesn't trust women at all. Having heard about his past, I kind of don't blame him. And I'm not totally healthy in that area, myself. I have issues."

Willow collected another plant. "You're not Mom. You're not going to lose yourself in a man."

"You don't know that."

"You don't, either. I know you're too scared to try. You've always chosen safe guys. Guys who adored you but who could never, in a million years, actually touch your heart. You've never risked falling in love, so you can't know what you'll do. None of us want to be like Mom. None of us want to give up everything for a man. So don't. Be strong. Be your own person. But take a chance."

It was really good advice. A sensible person might even consider it. But in this case, Marina refused to be sensible. There was too much to lose.

"Even if I let myself fall for him," she said. "He'd never love me back. He refuses to get that involved."

"There's always a first time."

"Not for him."

"You're wrong," Willow told her. "There's a first time for everyone. Look at Kane. But you have to be willing to take the chance. You can't find perfect happiness unless you're willing to risk the pain. Is a half life of being safe really worth never finding your soul mate?"

Marina thought about their mother. Naomi had only ever loved one man and she'd spent her entire life having her heart broken by him over and over again.

"The soul mate thing is highly overrated," she murmured.

"No, it's not," Willow insisted. "But love does require

faith. If you can't have that, you'll never know. What if Todd's the one? Are you really willing to let him walk away? At least Mom spends some of the time happy. When Dad's with her, all is right with the world. If she didn't have those moments of joy, the rest wouldn't be worth it."

Marina wasn't convinced those brief moments were worth anything. Not when the pain was so great and there was no escape. She'd lived her whole life without a soul mate and had done just fine. It would be a whole lot easier to get over what she'd never had than to risk being destroyed by a man determined to never give his heart.

Eight

Todd checked his watch. He'd arrived a couple of minutes early for his meeting with Marina at the bridal shop, but he wasn't worried about her keeping him waiting. She wasn't the type.

He'd wondered if seeing her again after their long night together would be awkward, but now that he was here, he only felt anticipation. Not a good thing, he thought grimly. She wasn't the type to play the no-strings game and he wasn't willing to accept anything else. Even for her.

So he would forget what happened and look at her only as his cousin's fiancée's sister. A distant acquaintance. Someone he liked, but didn't care about. Wasn't interested in. Wouldn't get involved with.

His good intentions lasted right up until she burst into the bridal shop, looking rushed and five kinds of gorgeous.

"I know, I know," she said as she stepped inside and grinned at him. "I'm a minute late. How you must resent me for treating you so badly. Next thing you know I'll be making you hold my purse while I try on clothes and call you snookums."

He laughed with her and their gazes locked. Within seconds the rest of the world ceased to matter. There was only this moment and the woman in front of him.

Wanting made him hard and need made him step toward her. The sensible part of his brain was outvoted. The only thing that made sense was Marina in his arms.

One of them moved first. He didn't know if it was him or her and it didn't matter. But before he could reach for her, a fortysomething saleswoman walked up to them and sighed.

"How wonderful," she said. "I can always tell when a couple is really in love. You two have brightened my day."

It was like being dropped headfirst in a big, icy pool of reality. He stepped back. Marina did the same and then they avoided looking at each other.

Great, he thought grimly. Now things were going to be awkward. He'd never wanted that. Making love with Marina had been the most fun he'd had in a hell of a long time. Not just the sex, although that had been record-setting. But just hanging out with her. Relaxing, being comfortable.

"We're, ah, not getting married," Marina said with a smile that looked more forced than happy. "I'm Marina

Nelson. You've spoken with my sister Julie. She's the bride who's hiding out in China right now and making everyone else do her dirty work for her."

"Oh, of course." The woman looked between them. "My mistake. I'm Christie."

Todd introduced himself and they all shook hands.

"I have some ideas of what your sister might like," Christie said. "She was very specific about all her no's, which makes things easier. I understand you'll be trying things on and then getting her feedback?"

Marina nodded.

"That's fine. Usually we don't allow brides to take pictures until they've actually put a deposit on the dress, but Julie made special arrangements with the owner, so we're good on that. You have a camera?"

Todd patted his suit jacket. "Right here."

"Good. All right, Marina. Let's dress you up like a bride. I understand you and your sister are about the same size and height?"

The two women disappeared down a hallway. Todd found a comfortable chair and a table full of financial and sports magazines. A few minutes later Christie appeared and asked if he would like anything to drink.

He accepted the offer of coffee, then settled in to read. But he couldn't seem to concentrate on the article. Instead he remembered Marina's teasing expression when she'd first walked into the shop and felt a return of the pleasure he'd felt at that moment.

What the hell was up with that? he wondered. Liking her wasn't one of his rules. Wanting more was even worse. He knew the danger inherent in the situation…the betrayal that would follow. It always had. No woman was to be trusted.

But for the first time in years he found himself wanting to break his own rules. To see if maybe, possibly, Marina was different, even though he knew she couldn't ever be.

Marina fingered the incredibly soft fabric of the wedding gown. Except for the basics, like cotton versus leather, she knew nothing about material. Only that whatever this one was, she wanted it in her life always!

Christie came into the dressing room and smiled. "You look beautiful."

Marina grinned. "I know you say that to all the brides, but right now, I don't care. I feel amazing. I love how this dress feels and moves."

Christie fastened the buttons Marina couldn't reach, then held open the dressing room door. "Come see how you look."

Marina had come in wearing jeans and a T-shirt, feeling frazzled, rushed and weird about seeing Todd again. But dressed in this flowing confection of a dress, she felt beautiful and girly and like a princess. Even the borrowed high heels, compliments of the salon, had fit.

She stepped in front of a three-way mirror and gasped. The dress was perfection.

The fitted, strapless bodice clung to her and made her look impressively chesty. At the waist, the dress cascaded down to the floor in layers and layers of fabric, each row shaped and draping like a flower petal, including the three or four foot train.

There was a hint of pearl in the fabric and it made her skin glow. The style would hide Julie's pregnancy, but was still elegant and to-die-for.

"Wow."

She glanced up and met Todd's gaze in the mirror. She smiled and spun in a slow circle.

"You like?" she asked.

She couldn't tell what he was thinking but she definitely liked the way he had to swallow before speaking.

"Incredible. Both the woman and the dress."

Man, did he have all the good lines, she thought, feeling herself react to his words and his presence.

Christie moved in and began tugging on the dress. "The style is flattering to many body types, although if your sister is built like you, then this should work perfectly. She needs one that's ready to go and this one is available. We'll clean it and get it altered right before the wedding. Can you move in it all right?"

Marina took a couple of steps. The dress swayed gracefully. "It's so fabulous."

"Good," Christie said. "Now let me put up the train and we'll see if you can dance in it."

Dance? Marina looked at Todd again. "Can you dance?"

"I'm practically a professional."

"Liar."

"Try me."

Christie looped the train, fastening buttons and hooks until there was an impressive bustle in the back. Then Todd stepped close and swept Marina into his arms.

She told herself none of this mattered, that it wasn't real. She was helping her sister, nothing more. Yet as they danced to an imaginary song, she felt something stir deep inside of herself. Something dangerous and wonderful and more than a little scary.

She made the mistake of looking into his eyes and found herself wanting to get lost there. His fingers tightened on hers. She shifted slightly closer. The layers of the beautiful dress kept her from feeling his body against hers, which was a serious drag.

"So lovely."

The comment came from an only slightly familiar voice. Marina looked up to see her grandma Ruth standing in the entrance to the bridal salon.

"Hello, my dears," the older woman said as she approached. "I know, I know, I'm not to meddle, but when Julie e-mailed that the two of you would be here this afternoon, I couldn't resist."

Todd released Marina and walked over to his aunt.

"Ruth," he said in obvious affection, then bent down and kissed her. "Watching Marina trying on wedding dresses isn't meddling."

"I'm sure Julie will be delighted to have one more opinion," Marina told her, then hugged and kissed her grandmother as she did her best not to feel or look guilty. She stepped back and turned in a slow circle. "What do you think?"

"That you're very beautiful and so is the dress." Ruth smiled at Todd. "Have you taken pictures?"

"Not yet. We were seeing if Julie could dance in the dress."

Was it Marina's imagination or had Ruth's eyebrows gone up just a little?

"An excellent idea," the older woman said. "I'm sure Julie appreciates your thoroughness."

Marina had the sudden thought that somehow her grandmother had guessed she and Todd had slept together. Heat burned on her cheeks as she tried to convince herself that wasn't possible. No one knew. Well, Willow and eventually Julie and maybe Ryan, but no one else.

Marina posed while Todd took several pictures, then she escaped back into the dressing room. She eased into a second gown, this one also strapless, but with a lace bodice and shirring across the waist. The skirt, a stunning, smooth silky material with an inset of embroidery and lace, fell in a sophisticated A-line that spilled into a train.

Ruth stepped into the dressing room. "Another winner. Julie's going to have a difficult time choosing. But that's the problem to have. Here, dear, let me help you with the buttons."

"Thanks. There are a lot of them."

Ruth stepped behind her and began fastening the cloth-covered buttons. "You and Todd looked very special together, dancing. While I always hoped one of you girls would fall for him, I'll admit I thought it was little more than the dreams of an old woman."

Panic welled up inside of Marina. "You're not old," she said by way of a very pitiful distraction.

"Thank you, dear, but that's not the point. I offered you and your sisters the money as a way to spur competition, but I see now I only needed to let nature take its course."

Marina's mouth opened, then closed. Her brain froze and she had no idea what to say.

"We're not a couple," she managed to say at last. "Seriously. We're barely friends. Semifriends, really. Acquaintances. We're helping with the wedding and that's all. We haven't even had our first date yet. That's not until the wedding."

Ruth finished with the buttons and stepped out in front of Marina. "Apparently a date isn't required. You look very beautiful."

Marina muttered something unintelligible, then hurried out of the dressing room as fast as she could on borrowed three-inch heels. Instead of stepping in front of the massive mirror, she hurried to Todd's side and grabbed his arm.

"She knows. My grandmother, your aunt, knows. She knows we had sex and I'm telling you right now, I can't stand it. I'm totally humiliated and you need to be, too."

Todd looked unconcerned. "She doesn't know. She can't."

"Want to bet?"

Ruth stepped out of the dressing room and Marina moved in front of the mirror. They discussed the dress like rational adults and she did her best to keep from blushing. She even managed a smile while Todd was taking pictures.

"I'll send these to Julie," he said.

"Great. I think she'll really love them."

Which all sounded normal, but what she was thinking was more along the lines of *get me out of here*.

Todd obviously didn't believe her, because he continued to joke with Ruth, right up until his aunt said, "I suppose a double wedding is out of the question."

Todd looked at Marina, then back at his aunt. "You mean Willow and Kane?"

"No, dear. You and Marina. There's obviously chemistry. Of course a relationship requires more than that, but passion is wonderful. I had it with your uncle every day of our marriage." She gave a little laugh. "Well, not *every* day, but most of them."

Marina resisted the need to cover her ears and hum loudly so she wouldn't hear anymore. Todd swallowed hard and muttered, "There's an image I'll never get out of my head."

Ruth sighed. "You young people. Never wanting to know about the older generation. You should be happy to know your uncle and I had a wonderful marriage all those years."

"I'm thrilled," Todd told her. "Details not required."

Ruth smiled. "That's all right. I've waited a long time for you to find the right girl and now you have."

Marina swept past him and headed for the dressing room. He followed on her heels.

"I told you," she said as she presented him with her back so he could unfasten the buttons. "But no. You wouldn't listen. You knew best. My *grandmother* knows we had sex. Do you know how humiliating that is?"

"It's worse for me. You never met my uncle, but I knew him all my life. Now I have a picture of the two of them…"

Marina spun to face him. "You're not taking this seriously enough. Ruth knows. She's talking about double weddings. She might tell my mother. I do not want to have a conversation about my sex life with my mother."

He touched her cheek. "Then don't. Look, telling Ruth wouldn't be my first choice, but she guessed. So what? We know what we want and don't want from each other. It's no big deal."

Apparently not for him, she thought bitterly, wondering if maybe he was right. If maybe she was overreacting.

Ruth stepped into the dressing room. "I have to leave, so you two enjoy yourselves. I hope it all works out. Truly I do. Not just because of what I want, but because all that money will really make a difference for your family, Marina. Sweet Willow can buy her nursery at last."

Then Ruth was gone, but Marina barely noticed. Instead her attention was riveted on Todd's face—on the way his features tightened and the distance she saw in his eyes.

He physically took a step back from her. "I'll leave you to get changed."

Then she was alone in the dressing room. Alone and angry and confused.

Why had Ruth had to mention the money like that? For a woman who was so set on getting them together, she'd picked the one way guaranteed to keep them apart. If Todd had a button, it was women wanting him for his money.

She wanted to stamp her foot in frustration. Talk

about unfair. She wasn't the least bit interested in his millions or billions or however much it was. The bet about marrying him was a joke. He had to know that.

Except why would he? Given his past, he would think the worst because the worst had always been true.

"It doesn't matter," she told herself as she stepped out of the dress. "We don't have a real relationship. We're just friends."

Friends who slept together.

But sex wasn't love and there was no way she was falling for him, so what did it matter that he thought badly of her?

Yet somehow it did matter and when she left the bridal salon a few minutes later, it was with a tightness in her chest and a sick feeling in her stomach.

To: Marina_Nelson@mynetwork.LA.com
From: Julie_Nelson@SGC.usa
Let me just say, for the record, that I'm stunned that you would sleep with Todd Aston the Third and not tell me. Even worse, I had to hear about it from my GRANDMOTHER! You slept with Todd? You slept with TODD? While I'm out of the country and we're so many time zones apart that I'll never hear the details?

I know you're telling Willow everything. I hate being left out. In time I'll forgive you, but know for now the sisterly bonds between us are stretched to the limit.

To: Julie_Nelson@SGC.usa
From: Marina_Nelson@mynetwork.LA.com

When did you become such a drama queen? The sisterly bonds? Someone's getting just a little too carried away by all this.

I'm sorry you had to find out from Grandma Ruth. I was going to tell you myself, but I didn't want to put that kind of information in e-mail. Obviously I'm the only one who worries about that sort of thing.

It was one time, or at least one night. It happened by accident. I'll explain the details later. They're actually kind of funny. But the point is, we're not a couple. We're friends who happened to sleep together and we have no plans for it to happen again.

To: Marina_Nelson@mynetwork.LA.com
From: Julie_Nelson@SGC.usa
That's it? That's all I get? How pathetic. I want details. And FYI…people don't accidentally sleep together. It's a conscious act/decision. You're not fooling me here, kid. So what's really going on?

Marina stared at the e-mail before answering. What *was* going on with her and Todd?

To: Julie_Nelson@SGC.usa
From: Marina_Nelson@mynetwork.LA.com
We're just friends. I swear. I like him, which I never thought would happen, but liking isn't anything more. Yes, we slept together, but there won't be a repeat performance and after this wedding is planned, we'll see each other at family events a few times a year and that's all. He's not the one. He's just a guy.

A special guy, she admitted to herself as she sent off the e-mail. But still, just a guy.

"I'm running late," Belinda yelled as Todd stepped into her photography studio. "Have a seat and I'll be with you in a bit."

He smiled at the receptionist, then made his way back to the large open space where she did most of her work.

Belinda, a petite redhead who dressed like a gypsy, stood in front of a camera and stared at the adorably dressed twins sitting on a bale of hay.

The identical little girls wore pink and white dresses and their dark hair had been carefully curled and styled.

"Okay—heads together," Belinda said with a grin, "but no bumping. Just touching at the top."

The girls complied.

"Now think about Christmas morning. What it's like to be awake but know it's too early to go downstairs. Remember how excited you feel. There are so many presents and soon you'll get to rip open that shiny paper and see what you got. It's so fun, but you have to wait. Think about that."

Both girls smiled, their eyes bright, their faces alive with anticipation.

Belinda snapped several pictures.

"She's good."

He turned and saw Marina had walked into the studio.

Their last meeting had turned awkward, thanks to Aunt Ruth. He waited for some feeling of discomfort, or a need to be anywhere but here. Instead anticipation swept through him and made him want to pull her close.

"The best," he said. "How are you?"

"Good. Busy with classes, but that's fun." She looked at the twins. "Adorable little girls."

"I agree."

"Really? You want kids?"

"Sure. A lot. I've always wanted my own baseball team."

She winced. "That's too many. But three or four would be a nice number. How do you plan to get these kids?"

He glanced at her. "I have no problem with having a family. It's having a wife I object to."

"So you'll adopt?"

Her eyes were the color of the sky. A perfect shade of blue. He liked how he could read her moods and how she wasn't intimidated by him. When this was over, maybe they could stay friends…assuming he got his burning need to make love with her again out of his system.

"Adoption is a possibility," he said. "But I would like a couple of biological kids to carry on the family name."

"Inherit the family money," she teased.

"That, too."

"So what will you do? Hire someone to carry the kids? Rent a womb, so to speak?"

He shrugged. "Maybe. It's an option."

Marina's eyes widened and her mouth dropped open. "I was kidding."

"I'm not. Everything is for sale."

"No offense, but that's really icky."

"Why? Surrogate mothers aren't uncommon. I'd have to be careful."

"Sure. What was I thinking?" She folded her arms over her chest. "It's a complicated choice. After all, the biological mother contributes fifty percent of the gene pool. Plus some scientific studies suggest intelligence is inherited through the mother."

"Which explains why a lot of successful guys who are more concerned about a beautiful woman than one with brains or character end up with disappointing children."

Disapproval radiated from her like fog. It surrounded him, trying to chill him, but he was unmoved. It was his life and he could damn well do what he wanted. If that meant kids without a wife, then that was his choice.

"You sound really cold-blooded," she told him.

"I'm being practical."

She drew in a breath, then released it. "Given your past, I understand your reluctance to trust anyone, but there's still a part of me that says you *can* have it all. You can fall in love, get married and have your kids the old-fashioned way. No contracts required."

"Is that what you want?" he asked.

"Sure. There's something wonderful about being a part of a family."

"You don't seem to be in a hurry to find Mr. Right."

Marina nodded. "I know I have my issues, but I'm willing to take a step of faith."

"Cheap talk."

"I'll get there. Eventually."

Would she? He doubted it. They might be very different, but they both had a fundamental lack of trust when it came to love. She was afraid of losing herself, the way her mother had, and he was determined to be more than a meal ticket.

"It takes faith," she told him. "One day I'll find someone who makes the leap worthwhile and then I'll jump."

Todd looked skeptical. "I hope he's there to catch you."

The photographer finished up with the children, then came over and hugged Todd, then introduced herself to Marina.

"I've never been hired from China before," the older woman said with an easy grin. "This could be fun."

"We'll e-mail Julie and Ryan some samples, if that's all right with you," Todd told her. "Marina and I will pick out a few."

"Sure. Great. I have my albums over here. I'll show you a big selection, then point out which ones are available to be sent digitally."

Marina watched the easy rapport between Belinda and Todd. "How did you two meet?" she asked.

Todd groaned, but Belinda laughed. Then she patted him on the cheek.

"Todd's parents hired me to take his picture for his sixteenth birthday. It was all very formal and solemn."

"So humiliating," Todd muttered.

Marina grinned. "That portrait wouldn't be in the sample albums, would it?"

Belinda shook her head. "He'd kill me if I put it

there, but maybe I can scan one of the proofs and send you a copy."

Marina leaned close to Todd and rested her head on his shoulder. "I would love that."

"You send it and I'll never forgive you," Todd told Belinda.

"Of course you will."

They spent the next half hour going over Belinda's samples. Her pictures were incredible. Romantic without being mushy, clear, artistic, yet timeless.

"She captures personalities," Marina said as she pointed at a wedding picture. "Look at the bride's smile. You can tell she's kind of wacky but fun."

"Yeah and he's crazy about her."

Looking at the happy couples made Marina feel a little empty. She wanted what they had—love and trust. Someone she could count on, no matter what. But this day wasn't about her.

"Any of these would be great," she said. "Let's just give Belinda Julie and Ryan's e-mail address and she can send whatever she wants. They're going to love her work."

They returned to her studio to tell her.

"Sure, I'll send a big selection," Belinda told them. "But before you go, let me snap a couple of pictures of you two. Having a familiar subject can be really helpful."

Todd looked at Marina who shrugged.

"I have a few minutes," she said, not exactly sure what Belinda was talking about.

"Good. I'm all set up for my next appointment. That will make this go quickly."

Belinda pointed at a muted backdrop done in blues and grays. There were lights all around and a camera in front of the backdrop.

"Stand in the middle," Belinda told him. "Close together. Let's try a traditional pose. Todd, put your arms around her waist. Marina, put your hands on top of his."

They did as they were told. Marina did her best to ignore the heat of Todd's body and the way his nearness made her thighs tremble. The longer he held her, the more she ached for him.

"Big smiles," Belinda said. "Come on, don't make me do the Christmas morning speech a second time today. It gets old. Think about something great. I know. The last time you had sex."

Involuntarily she glanced up at him only to find him looking down at her. She remembered everything about them being together that night. His touch, his laughter, the way he'd made her respond in ways she hadn't thought possible.

"Perfect," Belinda called. "Keep looking like that. Okay, now think of something funny—like Todd in a chicken costume, complete with a big chicken tail."

Marina felt her mouth twitch as she got the image in her mind. Then she started to laugh.

"Gee, thanks," he told her.

"You'd make a great chicken."

"My life is complete."

Marina was still laughing when Belinda told them they were done.

"I'll e-mail these pictures to Julie and Ryan, as well,"

she said. "I'm holding the date, so if you could let me know in the next week or so, that would be perfect."

"Will do," Todd promised.

"Thanks for everything," Marina told her. "You're amazing."

"Words I live to hear."

Marina followed Todd outside.

"We're still on for the wedding this Saturday, right?" he asked as they stopped by her car.

"You mean the wedding we're crashing? I'm braced."

"We're there to hear the orchestra. That's not crashing. We won't eat anything. It will be fine."

"I've never crashed a wedding before," she said. "That will make this very special."

"You'll like it."

She waved, then climbed into her car. He did the same and drove away first. But before she started her engine, she thought about what he'd said about having kids without a woman in his life. While she admired his desire to have a family, she was also sad at how he was limiting himself by refusing to trust anyone.

Ironically they were opposite sides of the same issue. He trusted himself, but no one else. She trusted everyone *but* herself. They both needed to take a leap of faith, but could they? And if they didn't, would they ever find their heart's desire?

Nine

Late Saturday afternoon Todd drove through West-wood toward UCLA. Marina had called earlier and asked him to pick her up on campus, instead of at her place, for their appointment to listen to the orchestra. She'd given him directions to one of the frat houses.

Now he found the correct street and turned right, then looked for the address. He spotted Marina before he saw the house. She stood on the lawn with a tall good-looking guy and they were gesturing at each other.

As he watched, the guy pulled Marina close and hugged her. She laughed and kissed his cheek.

Something dark and cold coiled low in his belly. He narrowed his gaze as Marina spoke using sign language. She obviously knew the other guy really well. But what the hell were they talking about?

They continued to gesture rapidly, then Marina turned, saw him and waved. The guy looked at him, hugged her again and turned back to the house.

As she walked toward his car, Todd was torn between being unreasonably pissed off and admiring the way her dress outlined her curves. He'd only ever seen her in casual clothes, so the high-heeled sandals, dangling earrings and upswept hair were a change.

"I'm ready for my night of crime," she said as she opened the passenger door and lowered herself onto the seat. "I thought about bringing masks so no one would recognize us, but then I was afraid we'd really stand out."

He ignored the humor and stared at the big house. "You date frat boys?"

"Date? Uh, no. That was David, one of the people I sign for. He's a senior, he has a hot date and his car died a couple of days ago, so I'm loaning him mine. Normally I wouldn't, but he's planning on proposing, so that seemed like a good cause to support."

He turned his attention to her and saw a combination of humor and exasperation in her eyes.

"I just wondered," he said defensively. "Frat guys have a reputation."

"Sure. That was the only reason for going all primitive on me."

"Primitive? Not my style."

Not ever. That would require jealousy and jealousy implied caring. While he liked Marina, theirs was a friendship.

"You're weird, Todd," she murmured. "You know that?"

"Not weird. Charming, handsome, sexy, mysterious."

She eyed him. "I'll give you complicated, but nothing else."

"You just don't want to admit how much you're attracted to me."

"As if."

But as she spoke, her gaze lingered on his mouth. He felt a rush of heat and need that had him shifting uncomfortably on the seat.

He pulled into traffic. "The reception is in Beverly Hills," he said. "We'll go in, smile politely, offer congratulations, listen to the music, then leave."

"Whatever you suggest," she told him. "You're the professional criminal. This will be my first time."

"We're just going to listen to music, that's not against the law."

"Criminals always have an excuse. Does Ryan know about your lawless ways? You guys are business partners—he should probably be protecting his assets. Next thing you know, you'll be pilfering."

He deliberately kept his expression stern. "I do not pilfer."

"Sure you don't. You're practically sainted. If your aunt Ruth could see you now."

Speaking of Aunt Ruth. "Did she call you?"

Marina looked at him. "My grandmother? No. Was she going to?"

So he'd been the only one. "No. Don't worry about it."

"You can't just bring up something like that and then drop it. What happened?"

"She's called me a couple of times since she dropped by the bridal place. There were a few unsubtle hints about us taking things to the next level."

Marina winced. "She wasn't talking about us sleeping together again, I'm guessing."

"Not exactly." Although his aunt had mentioned the whole "passion" issue several times, taking the conversation to a place Todd never wanted to go again.

"You're probably not going to think this is good news, but she also blabbed to Julie, who probably told Ryan."

He glanced at her. "Your grandmother told your sister we had sex?"

"Oh, yeah. I had a couple of very shouty e-mails from Julie. She's afraid she's missing out."

And he wanted a family why?

"What did you tell her?" he asked.

"That I'd share all the details when she got back." She smiled at him. "We're very close."

He had a feeling she was kidding. Or maybe that was wishful thinking on his part. Women did talk and he had no idea what they said to each other. Like every other normal guy on the planet, he didn't *want* to know.

"I'm sorry Ruth is being a pain," he said. "Can you ignore her or should I say something?"

"As I'm not the one she's calling, ignoring works for me. Are you going to have problems ignoring her?"

"No." He loved Ruth, but she didn't get to tell him

what to do. He knew she wanted him married and that wasn't happening.

"That sex thing was probably a mistake," Marina said quietly. "It's good we're never doing it again."

He thought about how great they'd been together. How much he'd enjoyed pleasing her, tasting her and touching her. How easily they'd talked and laughed. How much he still wanted her.

"I couldn't agree more," he said firmly.

The hotel was like something out of a movie, Marina thought as she and Todd strolled down wide, well decorated hallways to the ballroom overlooking the private garden.

They managed to slip inside without anyone asking them questions or accusing them of being there without an invitation, although she felt as if everyone in the room knew they were imposter guests.

"Relax," Todd said as he slipped an arm around her waist. "There have to be at least three hundred people here. No one will notice us."

"Okay, but no eating or drinking. We probably shouldn't even sit down and take a real guest's place."

He smiled a her. "You're not much of a rule-breaker, are you?"

"Only under very specific circumstances. Like the no more than four items in a dressing room rule. That one I'm good to break."

They circled the ballroom, avoiding the tables clustered at one end and staying toward the dance floor. A waiter came by and offered some kind of puff pastry treat. Todd reached for it, but she pushed his hand away.

"We're not supposed to eat," she told him, her voice low and insistent.

He chuckled. "You're making this too much fun."

"We're not here to have fun. This is serious. Okay, they're setting up to play. This is good. We can listen, then leave."

"Coward."

"I'm ignoring you." She watched the small orchestra seat themselves. "You're right—there aren't too many of them. So what are you thinking? The alcove in Grandma Ruth's ballroom?"

"Or that space between the pillars. The sound would be better coming from there."

"Good point. I just wish they'd start."

A well-dressed older couple moved toward them.

"Kitty and Jason Sampson," the woman said as she reached for Marina's hand. "How good of you to come."

Marina froze. They were caught!

But Todd smiled smoothly and responded. "Everything is lovely. Very impressive. Such a happy day."

Kitty beamed. "Isn't it? We're so delighted."

"Of course you are," Todd told her.

Jason leaned down and kissed Marina's cheek, then slapped Todd on the shoulder. "Thanks so much for joining us today. It means a lot."

"We wouldn't have missed this for anything."

The Sampsons left.

Marina waited until they were out of earshot, then

covered her face. "We're going to hell. I can hear them etching our names on our chairs."

"We get chairs in hell?"

She glared at him. "You know what I mean."

"Nothing happened. We were polite and gracious. In five minutes, Kitty and Jason won't remember us. Come on. You can handle this. Look, the orchestra is about to start."

"Maybe. It's not that I *want* to feel guilty," she began.

"Then don't. Come on. We'll lurk in the corner and stay out of trouble."

As he spoke, he grabbed her hand and pulled her to the side of the room. While his touch was totally casual, her body responded as if he'd just ripped off her dress and thrown her down on a table. Make that a bed…in a very private place, because her reaction was anything but outrage.

She melted from the inside out. The need to be with him nearly overwhelmed her, which was five kinds of crazy. They'd only been together that one night. Even though it had been a great time, it shouldn't have made that much of an impact on her.

Still, she found herself wanting to be with him, but not just in a sexual way. She wanted to be in his arms, talking and laughing. Watching him smile, listening to his voice and hearing his unique perspective on the world. She wanted…more.

"Better?" he asked as they stopped in a corner of the room, close to the orchestra but out of the flow of guest traffic. "We're practically acting like spies, hiding behind this potted tree." He fingered a leaf. "Do you know what this is?"

"Not a clue. That's Willow's area of expertise. It looks real, though." She allowed herself to relax. "Yes, this is much better. I can feel my guilt easing."

"Excellent."

He smiled at her. The answering quiver deep inside had something to do about his proximity, but not totally. Some of her reaction was just about him.

What was up with that?

Before she could figure out an answer, a waiter stopped by and offered them each a glass of champagne.

"The bride and groom will be here in a few minutes," he said. "This is for the toast."

Marina pulled free of Todd and tucked both her hands behind her back. "We can't," she whispered.

Todd took the two glasses and thanked the waiter. When the two of them were alone again, he offered one of the glasses.

"We have to," he told her. "Not toasting the bride and groom would be tacky and rude."

She bit her lower lip. "This is a very slippery slope. Okay, we'll raise our glasses, but we can't drink."

He grinned. "Right, because after we put the glasses down, someone else will gladly finish off the contents? Face it, kid. You're in this for a glass of champagne."

Marina sighed. "Maybe we can find out Kitty and Jason's favorite charity and make a donation."

"You're such a lightweight," he told her as he put his

arm around her waist and pulled her close. "I like that about you."

The quiver intensified.

A man who was probably the best man walked up to the microphone in front of the orchestra. "Ladies and gentlemen, will you please join me in welcoming Mr. and Mrs. Alex Sampson."

Everyone cheered as the bride and groom entered the room.

"A toast," the best man continued. "To a couple who defines love. May each day be better than the one before."

He raised his glass. The guests all did the same. Marina winced, then raised hers and took a tiny sip of the illicit champagne.

Todd leaned close. "Dom Pérignon."

"Really?" She took another sip. It was really nice. And honestly, if the families could afford that high-end champagne for the crowd, then maybe two stolen drinks weren't that big a deal.

"I'll accept the champagne," she murmured, "but we're not staying for dinner."

"Absolutely not. Just for one dance."

The orchestra began to play. The bride and groom stepped onto the dance floor and moved together.

Marina ignored them and instead focused on the smooth music. It was definitely more elegant than a DJ, but not really stuffy.

"Good choice," she told him. "I like the orchestra. Now let's go."

"Not so fast." He took her glass from her and set it

on a small table next to them. Then he led her toward the dance floor.

"What?" She tried digging in her heels, but it was a hardwood floor and that was not going to happen. "We can't dance."

"Why not? Everyone else is."

Sure enough several of the guests had moved into the center of the room and had joined the bride and groom. Marina decided that one dance wouldn't hurt. It wasn't as if they were eating anything. So she relaxed into Todd's arms and found out that he had yet another talent she'd never considered. This was even better than their spin around the bridal shop dressing rooms.

"You're good," she said after he'd twirled her around and then neatly caught her. "Lessons?"

"Years of them."

He pulled her close as the music slowed in tempo.

She rested her head on his shoulder. He had one of his hands on the small of her back. They pressed together in a way that was both sensual and enticing.

"We'll leave after this song," he said, speaking directly into her ear.

"Okay."

"You want to get something to eat?"

"Sure."

"Takeout?"

She raised her head and stared at him. Passion turned his eyes to the color of night.

He touched a finger to her mouth. "I know what

you're going to say," he told her softly. "That we agreed we couldn't do this again. That it would be a mistake for a lot of reasons. If that's what you want, I won't ask again. I've spent the past week telling myself why I have to let this go, but I can't. I want you, Marina."

They were words that would have cracked a wall a whole lot tougher than hers. "You had me at 'takeout,'" she whispered. "Let's go."

They went to his place because it was closer. The seventeen-minute drive seem to last forever, possibly because Todd spent much of the time nibbling on her fingers. The combination of teeth and tongue and lips was amazingly arousing. More than once she'd been tempted to tell him to pull over and they could just do it in the car.

She held back because it was daylight, she wasn't into being an exhibitionist and because a night in jail wasn't on her to-do list for that day. Of course Todd hadn't been, either, but she did try to be flexible when offered a wonderful opportunity.

They reached his house and piled out of the car. He opened the front door, pulled her inside, slammed the door shut behind her, flipped the lock and dragged her into his arms.

She went willingly, already anticipating the heat of his kiss.

He didn't disappoint. His mouth was firm and hungry and he tasted like great champagne. Even as they touched and strained and did everything they could to climb inside each other, he swept his tongue into her mouth and began that passionate dance.

He circled her, teasing, exciting. She met him with moves of her own and then closed her lips around his tongue and sucked gently. He groaned. She felt his hardness press against her belly. She was already wet and swollen. Her breasts ached. Deep inside she clenched in anticipation of what was to come.

He pulled back slightly and nudged her backward. "Bed," he murmured against her neck. "Up. Go."

The instructions would have been funny if she hadn't been so eager. She forced herself to break free of his erotic kisses and hurried toward the stairs.

Before climbing, she kicked off her shoes. He did the same.

Halfway up, they stopped and kissed again. As he stirred her soul, he reached for her zipper and pulled. She pushed off his suit jacket, then began to loosen his tie. He pulled his shirt free.

While she wasn't usually overly aggressive in bed, Marina didn't think of herself as shy. So she took a step back, shrugged out of the dress and let it fall to her feet.

Underneath she wore a lavender lace bra and matching panties. Todd's breath caught audibly. She reached behind herself, unfastened her bra, let that fall, as well, then turned and ran up the stairs.

It took him a second to follow, but when he did, he caught up quickly. At the second-floor landing, he lunged for her, grabbing her and pulling her to a stop. She laughed and spun toward him.

He was standing a step lower. He tore off his tie, unfastened his shirt and tossed it down, then leaned in and took her right nipple into his mouth.

He sucked and licked and circled until she could barely keep standing. She had to hold on to his shoulders and even so, her legs shook. The deep tugs caused an answering response low in her belly.

When he moved to her other breast, she felt herself starting to lose her balance. He must have sensed it, too, because he put his arms around her waist and lowered her to the top of the carpeted stairs.

She went willingly, wrapping her arms around him and enjoying the feel of his hot skin.

He raised his head. "We *will* make it to bed," he told her.

"I'm in favor of that plan."

He smiled. "But first…"

He reached for her panties and pulled them off in one quick movement. Then he shifted down a couple of stairs, urged her to part her legs and kissed her between them.

The intimate caress took her breath away. She had to brace herself on her arms to keep from falling over and even that wasn't enough. Not with her already shaking in need.

He was as good as she remembered. Exploring, circling, stroking, licking, driving her to the edge, only to back off just enough to make her whimper.

Over and over he touched her with his tongue and his lips. He drew her higher and higher, pushing her forward, then letting her fall back. He made her pant. He nearly made her scream.

She lost track of the world and everything in it. There was only this moment and this man and what he was doing to her.

Her muscles clenched tighter and tighter. She could feel herself swelling, pushing close. Her orgasm was tantalizingly out of reach. Close, so close, but not yet there.

Then he began to flick his tongue over her center in an age-old rhythm. At the same time he inserted first one finger, then two. He filled her, pushing up as if to caress her from the inside, as well.

One stroke, two…and then she was lost.

Her release claimed her with an unexpected force. She lost control and cried out. She came again and again, riding the magic of his tongue, his fingers, his whole body. Pleasure claimed her, marked her, then eased her back into reality.

When she finally surfaced, he sat next to her, smiling.

She sat up and sighed. "Go ahead. Gloat. You earned it."

"I will in a second. Meet me in my bed, okay?" He stood.

"Where are you going?"

"It's a surprise."

He hurried down the stairs. She watched him go, still basking, then realized she was sitting naked on his stairs and she had no idea if this was housekeeper day or not. Which got her moving.

She found her way to his large bedroom and had

barely pulled back the covers when he walked into the room carrying two champagne flutes and a bottle of Dom Pérignon.

She laughed. "You did say you always had some on hand."

"I did."

While he opened the bottle, she climbed into bed. He poured them each a glass, took off the rest of his clothes and joined her.

"To unexpected surprises," he said, touching his flute to hers. "You more than qualify."

She opened her mouth, then closed it. She couldn't speak, couldn't move, could barely breathe. It was as if she'd been flash-frozen.

And then she knew why. Looking at Todd, at his handsome and now familiar face, listening to his voice, sitting in his bed after he'd just taken her on an amazingly sensual journey, she suddenly realized what she'd been ignoring all along.

He was perfect.

Well, not perfect. The man had flaws. But he was everything she'd ever been looking for. Caring, warm, smart, into family, affectionate, challenging, determined and not the least bit intimidated by her big brain.

Perfect.

And somewhere along the way, she'd fallen in love with him.

Ten

A night of incredible lovemaking managed to distract Marina from her unexpected realization. The next morning she ducked out early, claiming a very legitimate meeting with Willow. She was terrified that she wouldn't be able to keep acting normally around Todd. How could she when her brain was practically rotating from shock?

In love with Todd? How? When? She wasn't supposed to fall in love with anyone, and should the unexpected happen, did it have to be with a man who would never, ever, under any circumstances, trust a woman?

She made her way home where she showered and changed. As promised, David had dropped off her car in the night and left the keys in a planter by her front door. She collected them on her way out and drove to the bridal salon where she and Willow would pick out a couple of bridesmaid dresses to e-mail Julie.

"Nothing yucky," Willow said after Marina pulled in next to her in the salon parking lot and climbed out of her car. "Nothing too frilly, and nothing you have to be tall to look good in. I don't know if you've noticed, but I'm not tall."

Marina pretended surprise. "Since when?"

"Very funny. You know what I mean. So many clothes look fabulous if you're as tall as a giraffe but the rest of us mortals end up looking dumpy. I refuse to be dumpy at my sister's wedding."

Marina grinned. "No dumpy dresses, I promise."

"You'd better. I don't want to be outvoted by the two tall sisters."

"Trust is an important part of our relationship."

Willow narrowed her gaze. "I don't trust anyone with legs as long as yours." They walked into the salon. "I saw the wedding gown pictures. It looks great."

"I'm sure Christie will bring out the dress Julie picked," Marina said. "It's strapless, so I was thinking we could go that way, or do spaghetti straps. Nothing long."

Willow rolled her eyes. "Thank goodness. I have so many long dresses from other weddings. And the bride always said 'you can take it up.' Right. Because there are so many places I can wear a lime-green flocked short dress. Speaking of green, I know that's one of the colors, but come on. We're blond. We're doing shades of rose, aren't we?"

"Oh, yeah. Green reminds me too much of recent attack of food poisoning. I'm not wearing it."

"See. This is how it should be," Willow told her. "Sisterly solidarity."

Christie walked toward them. "Morning ladies. You must be Willow. I'm Christie."

They shook hands.

"Ready to try on bridesmaid dresses?" Christie asked. "I've been e-mailing Julie and she has a few suggestions."

Marina looked at Willow who groaned.

"Good suggestions or bad suggestions?" Willow asked, her voice small.

Christie smiled. "Good ones. I think you'll be pleased. Oh, Willow, did you want me to bring out Julie's dress so you can see it?"

"If you don't mind, that would be great."

"I'm happy to." Christie looked at Marina. "Maybe we can do the preliminary fitting, if you have time this morning."

"I'm available."

"Excellent. Now if you two will come with me, I have the dresses Julie liked picked out."

They followed her to a room on the side that was filled with bridesmaid dress samples. Two dresses were displayed on the wall. One was strapless, fitted to the waist, then flared gently to the straight hem. There was an overlayer of some sheer fabric that was scalloped at the hem. The second dress was a slip style, with a little bit of lace at the bodice and tulip hem.

Willow fingered the material on the second dress and smiled. "I think both of these work. What do you think?"

Marina nodded. "Neither are scary. I give Julie points for that."

"Good." Christie pointed to a set of dressing rooms on the far wall. "There's one for each of you inside. Why don't you try them on. I'll be back in a few minutes."

"Which means Julie e-mailed our sizes," Willow murmured when they'd slipped into the dressing rooms. "Does her level of organization ever worry you?"

"Not too much." Marina pulled off her T-shirt and unfastened her jeans. "They have shoes here that we can try on. Just to see how the dresses look in heels."

The door to her dressing room opened. Willow stepped inside and closed the door behind her.

"Okay," she said flatly. "What's wrong?"

Marina stared at her. "Nothing. Why? I'm fine."

"You're not fine. You're…" She frowned. "I don't know. I can't put my finger on it, but fine isn't applying. Are you upset? Did something bad happen? Do you need Kane to kill someone?"

"While I appreciate the offer, and I'm sure he does, too, I'm good. Really."

Willow folded her arms over her chest. "I'm not leaving until you confess everything."

"There's nothing to…" Marina sighed. "I'd been so determined to act normal, too."

"You didn't quite make the goal." Willow's mouth twisted. "What happened? Is it Todd? Did he hurt you?"

"No. Of course not. He didn't do anything wrong. It's just…"

Willow moved closer and touched her arm. "You don't have to talk about it if you don't want to."

Marina managed a smile. "Oh, sure. Say that now. I just… We…" She swallowed. "I'm in love with him."

Willow continued to stare at her. "And?"

"And nothing. Isn't that enough? I'm in love with Todd Aston the Third. How crazy is that?"

Willow grinned, then hugged her. "Not crazy at all. It's great. You're in love. You're single, he's single. You're amazing, he might be someone the rest of the family can tolerate. What's the problem?"

Marina sank onto the bench in the room and covered her face with her hands. "I'm terrified. What if I'm just like Mom? What if I get lost? What if I let him treat me horribly and I pretend it's enough because it's better than being without him?"

Willow sank down next to her. "What if you don't?" she asked as she put her arm around Marina. "What if you're strong and grown-up and you just let yourself be happy?"

While she appreciated the support, happy didn't seem like much of an option. "He has issues."

Willow rolled her eyes. "Of course he does. All men do."

"His are complicated. He doesn't trust women. At all. Ever. No female trusting by the rich guy."

"Sounds simple to me," Willow said. "Fine. He doesn't trust. I'm sure other women have taught him that. But what have you ever done to make him not trust you? Nothing. So it may take some time and a little work, but you'll bring him around."

Marina wished it was that easy, but something in her gut told her that Todd wasn't going to be convinced by a lack of action on her part.

"Have you always been this optimistic?" she asked.

"I think so," Willow told her. "I'm the middle child. It's my job to see both sides of things. Although in this case, I'm only seeing yours. Have a little faith. I doubt your feelings are one-sided. You're pretty amazing. He's lucky to have you in his life."

"I don't think I'm the problem. He is and I don't know how to fix that."

"You don't have to. That's his job."

Marina looked at her sister. "I'm not like Mom, am I? Falling for a guy who can't commit?"

"You're nothing like Mom. You are your own person. Have a little faith in yourself."

Faith sounded easy enough, but Marina wasn't sure how to put it into play.

"You okay?" Willow asked.

Marina nodded. "We have dresses to try on."

A few minutes later they met by the large three-way mirror.

"This is not flattering," Willow grumbled as she tugged on the spaghetti straps of her dress. "The tulip hem thingy makes me look short."

"You are short," Marina teased. "But the dress isn't the right one. We both looked better in the strapless one. I hope Julie doesn't mind that the waist is so fitted."

Willow grinned. "You mean she'll be bitter because her tummy is growing? Hmmm. I hadn't thought of that. But it's okay. She can be bitter for a while. She's getting a baby." She smoothed the front of her dress. "After Kane and I get married, we're going to try for children right away. I'm really excited. I feel like I had my first taste of pregnancy the first couple of weeks I was on the pill."

"Bloated?" Marina asked sympathetically. "That's why I'm not on it. Plus, I felt yucky."

"Me, too. But the yucky part passed. Good things, too, because of the whole condom problem."

Marina stared at her. "What condom problem?"

"You know. That they're not a hundred percent. If used perfectly, in controlled studies, they're like ninety-seven percent effective. But in real world use, it's a lot lower than that."

Willow kept on talking, but Marina wasn't listening. Less effective? As in more chance of getting pregnant?

All she and Todd had used were condoms. She wasn't on anything else and he'd never asked. Not that there was a whole lot more he could have done, but still.

She touched her stomach and tried to relax. So they weren't a hundred percent. She and Todd had only made love a few times. Nothing could have happened. Not really. Could it?

Two and a half long hours later, Marina finally escaped the bridal shop. She'd had to suffer through the wedding gown fitting, which Willow had stayed for. In the end she, Marina, had gotten away only to drive to a drugstore and buy two different pregnancy tests. She was positive she was fine, but a little scientific evidence never hurt.

Now she counted out days on her calendar and had to admit that maybe she was a little late. Just by a couple of days, but still.

Her chest tightened until she found it hard to breathe. Pregnant? She couldn't be. Not that she didn't want kids, but not now. Not like this.

She remembered all the horror stories Todd had shared. If she were pregnant, he would think she was just like the other women in his life. He would never trust her.

Scared, shaking and terrified of the outcome, she opened both boxes and took the test. When the needed time has passed, she stared down at two plastic sticks and groaned.

One said she was pregnant, the other one didn't.

"Just so how my day is going," she said, fighting tears of frustration. "I have to know."

She grabbed the first of the boxes and dialed the 800 number for customer service.

"Hi," she said, when a woman answered. "I took one of your pregnancy tests a few minutes ago. I also took another brand. Your test says I'm not pregnant and theirs says I am. Who should I believe?"

"Oh, no," the other woman said. "That's not good. How late are you?"

"Just a couple of days."

"Okay, you have a couple of choices. You can buy more tests and see what they say, or you can wait. I know it's hard, but that would be my advice. Wait about a week and take the tests again. Your final option is to make an appointment with your doctor."

Marina thanked the woman and hung up. Going to her doctor wasn't an option. He was practically a friend of the family and her mother worked in his office. That was a little too close to home for this situation. She could find another doctor, but by the time they fit her in, at least a week would have passed anyway. Waiting and taking the tests again made the most sense.

But being sensible didn't ease the knot in her stomach to make her breathe any easier. Pregnant? Was it possible?

She was torn between the maternal thrill of a baby and the horror of knowing what Todd would think about her. That she'd tricked him.

Needing to talk to someone, she picked up the phone and called Willow.

Her sister's cell went right to voice mail, which meant Willow was probably with Kane and they were practicing for making babies of their own.

Restless and still needing to talk, Marina walked to her laptop and turned it on.

To: Julie_Nelson@SGC.usa
From: Marina_Nelson@mynetwork.LA.com
Hi. It's the middle of the day here, so I'm thinking it's the middle of the night there. Which is a serious drag because I really need to talk. Not that we will, and I don't want you to call. It's about a billion dollars

a minute and I'll be in class most of tomorrow. It's just...

Okay—don't be drinking your morning coffee when you read this. I'm late. As in...late. So I got a couple of pregnancy tests and took them. One says I'm pregnant, one says I'm not. The lady at the company suggested I wait another week and retest, which really makes sense. Except wait a week to know? How is that possible?

I want kids. I really wouldn't mind being pregnant—except for Todd. He's not a trusting guy and while I don't blame him, I can't begin to imagine what he would say if I told him I was pregnant. He would think I was trying to manipulate him or trick him. It would be awful.

Even worse...and you can't tell anyone about any of this, but especially what I'm about to say. I think I'm in love with him.

Marina paused in her typing, then sighed.

No. That's wrong. I know I'm in love with him. I've been in love with him for a while now. Maybe from the beginning. I'm excited and scared. I mean, what if I'm like Mom? But what if I'm not? What if I can't be strong? So that's a good possibility. But this is Todd. Would he ever trust me enough to have a real relationship? Is he even interested in a real relationship? And if he could be, being pregnant will ruin everything.

So that's how my day is going. E-mail me back

when you can. I feel better now that we've "talked."
Thanks for listening.

* * *

Marina didn't sleep much that night, which made her
morning class on the physical aspects of Inorganic
Chemistry class tough. She did her best to clear her
mind of all that was currently going on in her life and
pay attention to the lecture. She seemed to do okay,
because Jason, one of her deaf students, only frowned
at her twice.

When class ended, she made arrangements to meet
him in the lab later that week, then walked toward her
car. As she moved through the crowd of students, her
mind swirled and dipped and raced in a hundred different directions.

What if she was pregnant? How would she tell Todd?
What if she wasn't? Would she be sad?

She felt her emotions being ripped in two. She loved
Todd and would be thrilled to be having a baby with him.
But with his past, she doubted they could ever get past
his inherent mistrust of all women, including her. So the
most sensible thing to hope was that there was no baby.
Except she couldn't quite bring herself to want that.

Sleep, she thought as she walked across the parking
lot. She needed sleep.

What she got was a familiar expensive convertible
pulling up next to her. The driver's window rolled down
and a very angry-looking Todd stared at her.

"Get in," he said flatly. "We have to talk."

Eleven

He knew. She could read it in the coldness in his eyes.

Marina wasn't surprised. There was no way Julie wouldn't have told Ryan, and Ryan and Todd were as close as brothers.

"I'll follow you to your place," she said, knowing there was a very good chance that any conversation with Todd right now wasn't going to go well. Better to be able to leave and not have to wait for him to drive her anywhere.

He opened his mouth, but before she could speak, she added, "I'll follow you there. You should at least trust me that much."

"Why?" he asked bluntly. But he also closed the window and drove a few feet forward so she could back out her car.

Twenty minutes later she drove onto the familiar circular stone driveway in front of the massive house she'd actually grown to like. But as she climbed out her car, she felt an uncomfortable combination of apprehension and panic. Based on all that she knew about him, Todd wasn't going to handle any of this well.

They walked inside without saying anything. She figured that she should probably be the one to start the conversation, but she didn't know how. Nor did she know what he knew. Which might be a good place to start.

She followed Todd into his study and set her purse on one of the leather chairs in the book-lined space.

"Did Ryan give you a recap or just forward my mail?" she asked, suddenly remembering her confession of love. Surely Julie hadn't shared that with her fiancé.

"He gave me the facts." Todd's dark gaze dropped to her midsection. "That you think you're pregnant."

She couldn't figure out what he was thinking from his tone. So far, his body language seemed controlled enough, so she should be feeling better. Except she wasn't. There was a coldness, a bitterness, that seemed to steal all the warmth from the room. Despite the pleasant temperature, she found herself shivering.

"I don't know if I am," she said. "He told you about the two pregnancy tests?"

Todd moved behind his desk, then turned to face her. "Let me be clear. I've been manipulated by women far more experienced than you, Marina. You will not win this game."

She felt as if she'd been slapped. "I'm not playing a

game. How could I be? I'm not like that and you know it. You know *me,* Todd."

"Do I? You're the one who's in this for a million dollars."

She stared at him. "Don't be ridiculous. That's just a crazy idea of Ruth's."

"She offered to take the money off the table, but you told her no."

Coldness eased down her spine. "I was kidding. It was a joke."

Nothing in his expression hinted that he believed her. The walls seemed to close in a little.

She took a step toward him. "This is crazy. We've become friends. We've laughed together, we'd talked about our hopes and dreams. I'm not some manipulating bitch out for the money. Dammit, Todd, I didn't trap you. You wanted us to make love, too. You were a more than willing participant."

He opened a desk drawer and pulled out a pad of paper. "If you continue to claim to be pregnant, I'll want the condition confirmed by an independent test performed by a doctor of my choosing. I will be there for the test, as will my attorney."

"Claim to be pregnant?" she asked, her voice low and shaky. "I'm saying I don't know. How much more honest can I be?"

He ignored that, too.

"If you are pregnant, I want paternity determined by a DNA test upon birth. If I am the father, we'll have to negotiate some kind of custody arrangement." He stared at her. "I wouldn't count on winning that battle if I were you."

It was like being locked in a freezer. The chill made it nearly impossible to breathe.

She closed her eyes as she remembered his words about wanting children, but not a mother. Was that really his plan? To take her baby?

"This isn't about me," she told him. "None of this is. This is about your past. You're making me pay for what those other women did to you."

"Did my aunt offer to withdraw the million dollars?" he asked.

She couldn't win. He wouldn't let her. "Yes."

"Did you tell her to keep it on the table."

"Yes."

There was no point in explaining she'd been kidding. That she'd never imagined even liking him, let alone falling for him.

"It's like asking for the moon," she said, even as she knew she was wasting breath and energy. "Sure, I said I'd take it but it was like accepting an offer to raise the Titanic. It's not going to happen. The money isn't real."

She took another step toward him, although with a giant desk between them, it was a pretty useless gesture.

"I wanted to give my sister a great wedding," she said. "Just like you wanted to give that to Ryan. We had to work together. At first I didn't like you very much, but then we became friends and it was great. That's all, Todd. Don't make it ugly now."

"Give me one reason why I should trust you."

"You can't argue trust. It has to be earned over time. Tell me one thing I've done to violate your trust."

"I can give you a million of them. You getting pregnant only confirms what you wanted all along."

Horror swept through her. "It was a joke," she began, then stopped. What was the point?

She grabbed her purse and pulled out her cell phone. Ruth's number was in her address book. She hit Send.

"Hi, it's Marina," she said, when Ruth had answered. "I need to tell you I'm not interested in the million dollars. Whatever happens, I don't want it."

Her grandmother sighed. "You never did want it, dear. I knew that."

"Todd doesn't."

"Oh, yes. He can be stubborn. But he'll come around."

Marina stared at his stern expression, at the starkness in his eyes. "I'm not so sure about that."

"I know he seems like he's too much work, but he'll be worth it in the end. Have a little faith."

"I'll try." She hung up.

Faith. Was there enough of that in the world?

"It doesn't mean anything," he told her. "You know you can get even more money from me."

And then she got it. She couldn't win. That was the point.

"If it wasn't the pregnancy concern, it would have been something else," she said, more to herself than him. "You're determined to never trust me and people always find what they go looking for. If you expect the worst, you'll find it."

She drew in a breath. "Someday I'll appreciate the irony of this situation. I've been so worried about being like my mother. I've been terrified I'll lose myself in a man. I never stopped to think about the danger of falling for someone who couldn't love me back. In my head, I was the one with the big problem."

She shoved her cell phone into her jeans pocket and grabbed her purse. "But I'm not. I was willing to risk it with you. I was scared and worried, but still willing to take on that next step. I never stopped to think all my fears didn't matter. Because you're not willing."

His expression didn't change. She wasn't sure why she was explaining herself, except maybe for some kind of closure.

"The only way to convince you I'm not in it for the money is to not be pregnant and never see you again," she said. "I can't do anything about having or not having a baby, but I can get out of your life. If I really am pregnant, we'll work something out. Something fair. You're not going to simply take my child. If I'm not, then we only have to deal with each other at the wedding and then stay out of each other's lives."

She walked to the study door, then turned back. "I know you're scared, Todd. I'm scared, too. But after falling in love with you, I'm willing to face my fears. Maybe I'm not the one for you. Maybe you don't want to care about me, and that's fine. But if you never care about anyone, the bitches of the world win. They might not have you, but they've sure made sure no one else will, either. It's a hell of a way for you to live."

* * *

He waited until he heard the front door close before walking out of the study. The emptiness of the house pressed down on him, but was nothing when compared to the fury he felt at her betrayal. If there was one woman he was going to trust, it would have been Marina. Only she'd turned out to be just like the rest of them.

Pregnant, he thought grimly. Fine. If she wanted to play that game, he would play it right back. He would take the baby and start the family he'd always wanted. She would be compensated, but nothing else.

She was, he acknowledged, a good genetic candidate for his child's mother. Intelligent, healthy, determined. He would hire a nanny and be a father.

It was a plan and he always felt better when he had a plan. But not today. He had a hole in his chest and it burned.

He wanted to throw something. He wanted to put his fist through a wall. He wanted her not to be like them. He wanted to trust her.

Which he couldn't.

He might have given her a second chance if she'd confessed and then begged for his understanding. If she hadn't said she loved him. Because that was the biggest betrayal of all. To use the one thing he truly wanted to manipulate him. That he could never forgive.

Marina knew she would probably drown in her tears. They came and came, pouring down her face as sobs ripped through her body. The pain was more intense than anything she'd ever experienced. It was as if she'd been cut off from the very air she needed to survive. Only she didn't die. She just hurt and cried and prayed to feel better.

Willow held her and soothed her with soft sounds. Not words. There were no words.

"How do I stop loving him?" Marina asked, her throat raw, her body battered. "Tell me how."

"I don't know," Willow admitted softly. "But we'll figure out a way."

Nearly a week later, Todd walked into the florist to finalize the order for the flowers. While he wanted to make sure the wedding looked good for Ryan and Julie, most of his attention was on the fact that he was going to see Marina again.

He'd expected her to call and she hadn't. So what did that mean? She'd claimed to love him and then she'd disappeared. If she loved him, shouldn't she be trying to get him back?

He wanted her to be trying and it really pissed him off that she hadn't once been in touch with him. As he'd been the point of contact with the florist, he'd been forced to call Marina to set up their appointment. Even more annoying, he'd been disappointed when he'd gotten her machine.

He'd done the right thing—leaving a message rather than trying again later. But she hadn't phoned him back and now, as he stood surrounded by flowers, he found himself looking forward to seeing her again.

He knew he shouldn't. He knew she was screwing with him, but that didn't stop the anticipation from rising inside of him.

She walked in, right on time for their appointment.

Even as he held himself still and didn't say anything, his body reacted to her nearness. She was beautiful, in a stern, pale kind of way. His fingers itched to get lost in her long gold-blond hair. He ached to touched her all over, to listen to her voice, to hear her laugh. He wanted to lean in and inhale the scent of her body.

Damn. What was wrong with him? He knew better. Look at what she'd done.

Except what had she done? Thought she might be pregnant? As she'd pointed out, he'd been more than willing to sleep with her. They'd used protection, but it didn't always work. Weren't they equally to blame for what happened? Did he really believe that Marina was trying to trick him?

"I have a class in an hour," she told him. "So why don't you go head and make the final selection on the flowers?" She handed him a few printed out e-mails. "These are Julie's ideas for her bouquets. I'm sure Beatrice can come up with something beautiful."

"You're not staying?" he asked, knowing he sounded like an idiot. Oddly he'd counted on them spending the afternoon together.

"No. I can't miss class. I know the wedding is next week, but everything else is taken care of. Julie and Ryan will be back this weekend."

She glanced around, as if checking to make sure they were alone, then she lowered her voice. "The mixed message has been resolved. I'm not pregnant."

"You took the tests again?"

"I didn't have to."

There wasn't a baby. Nothing about her expression told him what she was thinking, but he was shocked to feel the ache of sadness sweep through him.

Sad? Why should he be sad? Because he'd secretly wanted a baby with Marina?

"I'm sure you're relieved," she told him. "I know I am. Not that I wouldn't have loved to have a baby. Just not with you."

Her words did what they were supposed to. They cut through him, wounding.

"Under the circumstances," he began.

She shook her head. "I'll accept you being upset. Anyone would be. I'll even accept that you have issues, but there is no excuse for what you said and how you treated me. You threatened to take my child. You accused me of lying deliberately for financial gain. You made judgments and decisions before you knew all the facts. You were wrong about me, Todd. So very wrong. I was never in it for the money."

She squared her shoulders. "The thing that hurts the most is that I think you knew you were wrong, too. I think you secretly did believe me, but you couldn't admit it. So you attacked. That's not something I can get over. I suppose the only bright spot in all of this is that I was wrong about you, too. I was wrong to think you were special. I was wrong to think you were the kind of man I could fall in love with."

And as she had before, she walked out and left him alone.

But this time was different. This time as she left, he realized the enormity of what he'd lost. That despite the pregnancy, his past, her worries and all that had happened between them, that he'd fallen in love with her.

But he realized it too late. As he'd once told her— what had happened was unforgivable.

Twelve

Tuesday after work, Todd sorted through the mail. There was a large, stiff envelope with no return address on the bottom of the pile.

He opened it and removed several photographs. The pictures they'd taken at Belinda's studio. Samples, to send to Julie and Ryan. Apparently Belinda had decided to send him copies.

He pulled out the eight-by-ten pictures and studied them. Marina stood in his arms, staring up at him, her mouth curved in a smile. He stared down at her with an intensity that made him wonder what he'd been thinking.

There was an ease in their pose, and a connection. The camera had captured what he'd never allowed himself to see before—how he and Marina seemed to belong together.

There was something else in the pictures. Something in her blue eyes. Love.

He flipped through the six photographs, then carried them into his study and sat behind his desk. After turning on the lamp, he laid out pictures and let the images speak for themselves.

There was a hint of laughter in one, sexual need in another. A smile that spoke of a shared secret.

The pain slammed into him with the subtly of a lightning bolt. It cut through him, leaving him exposed and bleeding. Something dark and ugly surrounded his soul and began to squeeze the life out of him.

He'd lost her. He'd been so sure he would never want anyone that he'd made the decision to let her go before he'd even known what it was to have her. He'd assumed she wouldn't matter, couldn't be special. He'd cast off her gift of love without being aware that it could change him forever.

Now, alone, he felt the loss of her. He ached to hear her laughter, to see her smile, to touch her, hold her. He wanted her to need him—not just in bed, but in her life. He wanted her to miss him, to grow old with him. To love him.

He returned the pictures to the envelope. She'd made it pretty damn clear that she wasn't interested in him anymore. That she didn't love him.

He closed his eyes for a second, then opened them. Marina wasn't someone to give her heart lightly. Was it possible that she'd just been able to turn off her feelings or had she been bluffing because anything else hurt too much. Was there still a chance?

He pushed to his feet and realized it didn't matter about chances or hopes or wishes. He'd always been a man who worked his ass off to get what he wanted. If he'd been willing to give that much to something as meaningless as a business, what more would he be willing to do to convince the only woman he'd ever loved to take a chance on him?

Marina was making coffee when she heard a knock on her front door. She instantly thought it was Todd, crawling back to beg her to give him another chance. The visual would have been funny, if her reaction hadn't been so incredibly sad. Even knowing what he was and how badly he'd handled the situation, she desperately wanted to give him another chance. Which made her a huge weenie.

But it didn't stop her heart from fluttering in anticipation as she pulled open the door. And while the person standing there wasn't Todd, it was nearly as good.

"Julie! You're back!"

Marina reached for her sister just as Julie grabbed for her. They hugged and screamed and danced in front of the open door, then Marina stepped back to study the changes of the past six weeks.

"You're barely showing," she said, staring at her sister's nonexistent bump. "But you look so happy."

It was true. Julie's face glowed with contentment.

"I am happy," her sister told her. "Ryan and I got back last night and I wanted to come see you first thing. How are you?"

Marina led the way into the apartment. "I'm good. Fine."

Julie didn't look convinced. "You can't be fine."

"Okay—how about I'm adjusting? Would that work?"

"Maybe." Julie hugged her again. "Are you sorry about the baby?"

"Yes and no. I was excited at the thought of being pregnant. Terrified, but excited. Then when Todd freaked, I knew having a child with him would be a big mistake. He's not ready to trust anyone. I can't have a relationship with a guy who's so willing to think the worst of me. I certainly can't have a baby with him. So not being pregnant is a good thing, right?"

Marina did her best to speak calmly, to be logical and rational and sensible about the whole thing. But in truth, her heart hurt. She missed Todd, she missed the baby, which was insane and she didn't know when she was going to be able to get back to her old self.

"Oh, Marina," Julie murmured. "I'm so sorry. About all of it. I shouldn't have asked you two to work on the wedding."

Marina took her hand and led her to the sofa. They plopped down at opposite corners.

"You had nothing to do with this," Marina told her honestly. "Todd and I are totally responsible for what happened. I thought I was safe from anyone like him. He's so not my type."

"Apparently he is," Julie told her.

"Tell me about it. The thing is, we were attracted, we acted on that attraction and I screwed up. I thought it was more than it was. It ended badly, but at least I know the truth about him. I won't spend my time missing a man who can never be what I need."

"So you're over him?" Julie asked, sounding doubtful.

"I'm working on it. The good news is if I fell in love with him, I can fall in love with someone else. It will just take a little time."

"As easy as that?"

"I don't think it will be easy." She thought about Todd, about how he made her laugh and how they were more alike than she ever would have guessed. "I miss him. I'll miss him for a long time, but I'll recover, and then I'll move on."

To what? Another man? She couldn't imagine ever caring about anyone the way she cared about Todd. Worse, even though she would never admit it to another living creature, she finally understood her mother. In truth, she, Marina, would also settle for a small piece of Todd rather than having no part of him at all. Thank goodness no one was giving her the option.

"What about the wedding and the rehearsal and the rehearsal dinner?" Julie asked. "Will that be too awful for you? Would you rather not come?"

Marina shook her head. "It's your wedding. Of course I'll be there. I love you and I want to see you and Ryan get married. Plus, hey, I have a whole lot invested in the event."

"But Todd…"

"I can handle it," she promised, hoping it was true. "It's one evening and one day. I'm tough. Don't worry about me. Just focus on yourself and your happy day. You're marrying Ryan."

Julie smiled with so much love, she lit up the room. "I know. I can't believe I was so lucky to find him. Thank you for all you've done. Thank you for making my wedding perfect."

Marina had to blink several times to fight tears. "Don't thank me yet. You haven't seen anything. You did say you wanted a jungle theme for the reception, right? Because we found the cutest little stuffed giraffes for wedding favors, not to mention a 'sounds of the jungle' CD to play at the reception."

Julie swallowed hard. "You didn't. You wouldn't."

"You'll have to wait and see."

The rehearsal dinner was held on the Thursday before the wedding. Marina spent most of the afternoon in hot curlers in a feeble attempt to get her long hair to be something other than straight.

She usually didn't bother, but today she felt compelled. Probably because she was going to have to spend several hours in Todd's company and she was bitter enough to want to look good enough to make him feel bad. Not exactly her proudest moment.

She was also scared about seeing him. At the florist, she'd been able to keep the meeting short and maintain control. While the wedding rehearsal itself didn't worry her, the dinner was another matter. It was just going to be family—Julie, Ryan, Willow, Kane, Todd and herself, their mom, Ruth plus Todd and Ryan's parents.

That meant a small table and lots of conversation. Everyone would notice if she was too quiet or if she and Todd weren't speaking. It could be awkward and embarrassing. Plus her mother didn't know anything about her relationship with Todd...unless Ruth had shared that information with her, as well as Julie.

Marina groaned at the thought, then slipped on her dress and zipped it up the back.

The dark blue fabric brought out the color of her eyes and the fitted style made her feel especially skinny. She'd already finished her makeup so all that was left was her hair.

She took out all the curlers, then bent over at the waist and began to finger-comb the curls. When they were loose and, hopefully, sexy-looking, she stretched out her arm to grab for the hairspray, but instead encountered a hand.

She immediately screamed, jerked into an upright position and took a jump back.

Todd stood next to her dresser in her bedroom. Her messy bedroom with the unmade bed and clothes scattered everywhere. Although when compared with how fast and hard her heart pounded in her chest, she wasn't sure that mattered.

She had a brief impression of how great he looked in khakis and a silk shirt, then remembered her hair and clamped both hands on top of her head.

"What are you doing here?" she asked. "How did you get in? Couldn't you have knocked?"

At least she was dressed, but jeez. Talk about a shock.

"I knocked several times, then tried the door. It was open. You okay?"

No, she wasn't. She risked a glance in the mirror and saw her hair didn't look too bad, so she lowered her hands to her sides.

"You shouldn't leave your door unlocked," he said.

"You drove all the way out here to tell me that? Fine. I shouldn't. I don't normally. I don't know why I did today."

Distraction, she thought. She'd been distracted at the thought of seeing him, and now that he was standing in front of her, she knew why.

She still loved him. Despite everything he'd said and all that had happened and how much she should know better, she loved him. Right this second, she wanted to throw herself into his arms and have him tell her that they would work it out. That what had happened before had been nothing more than an icky misunderstanding. Not that Todd would ever say "icky."

"Why are you here?" she asked.

"I wanted to talk to you," he told her. "There are some things we have to clear up."

Right. The rehearsal dinner. "I'm fine with it," she said, hoping she would be. "Yes, it will be awkward with our family there. I've been thinking about everything and I think we can pull this off. It's not like we were dating for years. No one really knows. Well, my sisters and Ruth, but they won't say anything. We planned the wedding together, nothing more."

His dark gaze settled on her face. "Is that all that happened?"

"It's all I'm going to admit to."

"I'm giving a toast tonight. At the dinner. I would appreciate it if you'd listen to it and tell me where I can improve it."

He wanted her advice? Even worse, she was pathetic enough to be willing to give it.

"Fine. Read away."

He pulled a piece of paper out of his shirt pocket and unfolded it. "The Bible tells us that love is kind. Scholars tell us that love can change the course of history. Scientists tell us that love is chemical. Poets tell us that love is eternal. But true love is so much more than that. It's about believing and risking. It's about committing to always being there for one person and believing that person will be there for you. Love is about hanging on through the roller-coaster ride of life. Love is having faith, in yourself and the person you love. For Julie and Ryan, love is who they are."

His words wrapped around her like a hug. She wanted to both laugh and cry, but mostly she wanted to go to him and tell him that no matter what, she would always love him. That's what love was for her. How had he known?

Instead she said, "It's lovely. They'll be deeply touched."

He took a step toward her. "I mean it. For a long time I didn't know what to say about them getting married.

I thought Ryan was a fool for trusting Julie. Eventually she won me over and I was happy for him. But not envious. I never wanted what he had…until now." He smiled wryly. "Not Julie—the in-love part."

"Good to know," she managed to say even though her throat felt tight. What was he saying? That he cared? That he wanted to care? That she mattered?

"You know my past," he said. "You know why I hold myself back, never really getting emotionally involved. You know what I'm afraid of." He shook his head. "I can't believe I just admitted I'm afraid."

Neither could she. "I do know why."

"When you said you were pregnant, I thought you were just like them," he said, staring into her eyes. "I was angry, but more at me than at you. I was angry at myself for wanting you to be different. For wanting to believe you hadn't tricked me. I said a lot of things I shouldn't have said. I was wrong. Because you're not like them."

Her eyes filled with tears, but she blinked them away. He took a step toward her.

"Marina, when you told me there wasn't a baby, I was devastated. I want to have children with you. I love you. I want to marry you and grow old with you. I want to live with you in that damn house of mine and have you change everything in my world. I want to believe in forever."

She was already on the emotional edge, barely able to believe he was actually speaking these words to her.

Then he stunned her by dropping to one knee, taking her hand in his and asking, "Can you forgive me? Can you give me another chance? Will you take that step of faith and believe in me? Will you marry me?"

She didn't mean to burst into tears, but she did. She also managed to nod and that must have been enough because then Todd was standing and pulling her close. She went into his embrace and knew she would always feel safe when she was with him.

He held her tightly against him. "I love you," he whispered into her ear. "I think I've loved you from the first. It was safe to be friends and so I let down my guard. One day I woke up and you were a part of me. I'm so sorry for what I said, how I reacted."

"It's okay. I understand." She looked at him and smiled through her tears. "I love you, too."

He wiped her face with his fingers. "I'm glad you didn't change your mind."

"I wanted to, but I couldn't. I seem to be a one-man woman."

"Thank God."

She laughed and so did he. Then he kissed her. At the first brush of his mouth, her whole world righted itself.

"We need to get to the rehearsal," he said when they came up for air. "But first…"

He pulled a small box out of his slacks front pocket. "This belonged to my grandmother. If you don't like it, we can pick out something else."

He opened the box and she gasped. Nestled in the velvet lining was a sparkling diamond ring. A huge, round center stone was surrounded by other diamonds. The light glinted off the facets and nearly blinded her.

"It's beautiful," she whispered, "but it's really..."

"Big?" He grinned. "We Astons don't do anything by halves. It's about eight carats total."

"Wow."

"Too much?"

"I'll adjust."

He slipped the ring on her finger and it fit perfectly.

"It was meant for you," he said just before he kissed her. "I love you, Marina."

"I love you, too." She gave herself up to his embrace, then pulled back. "Does this mean there's going to be a Todd Aston the Fourth?"

"Probably."

"I can live with that." She glanced down at her ring, then pulled it off her finger.

He nodded. "After the wedding?"

"If that's okay. I don't want to take away the spotlight from Julie and Ryan."

"I'm good with that. We have our whole lives to celebrate."

He set the box on her dresser and she put the ring into the box. Then they walked out together.

"I have some very specific ideas about our wedding," he said as she collected her purse. "Color schemes. Place settings."

She laughed. "So you think we should plan it together?"

"We did a good job on this one. We're a great team."

"Yes, we are."

* * * * *

TAME ME

by
Caroline Cross

CAROLINE CROSS

Bestselling author Caroline Cross, winner of numerous awards, including the respected RITA® Award from Romance Writers of America, hopes that her books bring others a little of the pleasure she feels when she reads her own favourite authors.

Born and raised in the Pacific Northwest, she shares her life with her husband, two terrific daughters, a hundred-pound lapdog named Maddy and a circle of fabulous friends.

Dear Reader,

I'm thrilled to have this chance to wish Mills & Boon Happy 100th Birthday! As someone whose idea of a perfect day includes curling up with a great romance, it's an honour to be part of a century's worth of terrific storytelling. I can't thank them enough for including me.

Tame Me, the third book in my MEN OF STEELE series, is my eighteenth published romance. I love writing tough, sexy heroes and the heroines who, ahem, tame them. Yet even though over the years I've been lucky to receive a number of industry awards, including a RITA® (the romance community's equivalent of the Oscar) writing is still rarely easy for me. Between that first thrill of creation – ooh, I love this hero and heroine, I can hardly wait to unravel their story! – and the Snoopy dance of joy that comes with typing "The End", lies hours and hours of teeth-grinding and hair-pulling caused by that same hero and heroine refusing to behave the way I expected – and leaving me to deal with the consequences.

That was exactly what happened with *Tame Me* when Gabe, my ultra-capable, ex-Special Ops, take-no-prisoners tycoon, set out to rescue destitute socialite Mallory Morgan and nothing went quite the way either of us had planned...

Happy reading!

Caroline

This book is dedicated with love to four terrific
women I'm lucky to call my friends –

To Susan Andersen,
who makes me a better writer in every way and
who – thankfully – always knows what my
characters think even when I don't have a clue.

To Barbara McCauley, whose optimism and
generous spirit are a constant inspiration.

To Melinda McRae, who not only listens,
but knows all sorts of unexpected things.

And to Kris Nelson, my long-lost sister…
finally found.

One

Once upon a time when she'd still had a life, Mallory Morgan would've described Gabriel Steele as tall, dark and delicious.

That was before he'd cost her everything. Now, as she opened her flimsy apartment door and found him parked in the dingy hallway outside, the words that came to mind were hard, heartless and not-to-be-trusted.

"Mallory." As always his voice was quiet but commanding, the perfect match to his lean, powerful body and reserved green eyes.

"What do you want, Gabriel?"

"We need to talk."

"Do we?" To her relief she sounded calm and in

control, something that had eluded her earlier that day
when a chance meeting between them at Annabelle's,
one of Denver's trendier restaurants, had resulted in her
behaving badly—and paying a price she could ill
afford. "Gosh, let me think." Tipping her head to one
side, she pretended to consider for all of two seconds,
then straightened. "No."

With a flick of her wrist, she sent the door swinging
shut. It would just be too bad if it smacked him in his
autocratic chin.

He didn't so much as blink. Probably because the
cheap panel moved barely an inch before bumping against
his big booted foot. "Look, I get that you're angry—"

Her free hand tightened on the scarlet satin of the
robe that she'd thrown on over her bra and jeans at his
unexpected knock, bunching the thin, slippery fabric at
her throat. "What was your first clue? When I crossed
out your reservation and refused to seat you even
though the dining room was half-empty? Or when I quit
my job rather than apologize?"

"Don't be insulting. I caught on with your pig at the
trough comment."

"Then I believe we're done. Because I've certainly
got nothing more to say."

A grim smile touched his lips. "You don't want to
talk? Fine. You can listen then." Like the poster boy for
overbearing men, he slapped his palm against the wood
and pushed.

Instinctively she started to push back, only to check
herself as she realized he was already widening the

gap between jamb and door as if she didn't exist. Deciding she'd be a fool to engage in another battle she was sure to lose, she abruptly changed tactics.

"Well, since you insist…" Letting go of the doorknob, she gave a nonchalant shrug and took a giant step back. "By all means, come in."

To his credit, he didn't gloat. But it wasn't much consolation when the instant he crossed the threshold and the door shut behind him, she realized she'd miscalculated once again. No matter how big a hit her dignity had taken, she should have kicked, cried, screamed—done whatever she could to keep him out.

Because with Gabriel in it, her already minuscule studio apartment seemed to shrink. He not only took up all the available space, but also all of the air, making her feel small, breathless and far too…aware. Of his height, his power, his body heat. Of the jolt she felt when he looked at her.

It was hard to believe she'd once thought nothing of flirting shamelessly with this man. Not that it had meant anything—and not just because she'd had a carefully crafted reputation as a frivolous party girl to maintain. But because, her own shortcomings aside, she'd known early on that *he* was far too formidable for any involvement beyond a little lighthearted fun.

Still, whenever they'd bumped into each other at one or another of the Denver A-list's glittering soirees, she'd delighted in the subtle sizzle of mutual awareness that would envelop them, the way the air seemed to heat just a little with their proximity.

Inevitably, they'd wind up dancing, and she'd delight in leaning in close, in whispering outrageous suggestions in his ear, in watching the dangerous smile that would tug at his mouth when she trailed a fingertip along his jaw. The only thing better had been the proprietary way his hand would tighten on her waist when she rubbed her thigh against his as they circled the floor. That, and the amused glint of warning that would spark in his eyes, igniting a sharp little thrill she'd feel down to her toes.

All part of that other life, she reminded herself sharply. The one before Gabriel and his bedamned Steele Security had gone after her father and she'd lost her home, her friends, the last of her illusions and most of her self-respect.

Not to mention a fortune so large that up until it disappeared, her most pressing concerns had been along the lines of whether she should spend the weekend shopping in Paris or skiing in Gstaad.

It already seemed like a hundred years ago. And a distinct contrast to now, when she was already sick with worry about whether she'd be able to find another job that would allow her to both eat and keep a roof over her head.

That, however, was nobody's business but her own. Sure, Gabriel could barge in here, looking like a fallen Armani angel with his inky, razor-cut hair, beautifully tailored clothes and calf-length black leather coat, displaying the style she'd once jokingly dubbed "elegant badass." He could disturb her peace and stir up memories of a life she'd spent the past months trying to put behind her.

But he couldn't touch the core of her. She'd had years to perfect her defenses, to learn how to keep people in general at arm's length—and males in particular off balance.

The realization calmed her, allowed her to steady her bottom lip, which, infuriatingly, was threatening to quiver. Quietly blowing out a breath, she released her grip on her robe, knowing full well the effectiveness of a little insouciant sexuality as she reached up with both hands, gathered the long, unruly mass of her hair and tossed it behind her back.

"So?" She crossed her arms beneath her breasts, doing her best to look bored. "Are you just going to stand there? I thought there was something you simply had to say to me."

"Yeah. So did I." His expression gave nothing away as his gaze flicked from her eyes to her throat to the creamy V of her exposed cleavage before settling squarely back on her face. "I was wrong."

"You? Wrong?" She waited a beat, then smiled insincerely. "Surely not."

He didn't smile back. "I'd rather hear you talk. Why don't you tell me what the hell you're playing at, Mallory?"

"Excuse me?"

"I realize the past months must've been tough, but—"

"Tough?" Her voice started to climb; she wrestled

it back down. "Please." She flicked her fingers dismissively. "I was a debutante, and everyone knows that once you've learned how to waltz in high heels and make a perfect curtsy, you can handle anything. Having my home foreclosed on, my belongings auctioned off, my car repossessed, the family name dragged through the dirt by the press? No sweat. Learning the city bus routes, now, that's been a real challenge—"

"Don't," he said flatly. "I'm not trying to downplay the seriousness of the situation, and you know it. There's no excuse for what Cal did, ripping off the Morgan Creek investors, then bolting the way he did. But that doesn't explain what you're doing working at Annabelle's—"

"Formerly working at Annabelle's, thanks to you," she murmured, ignoring his reference to her father.

"—or living here, like this." He made a dismissive gesture that encompassed the kitchen with its single scarred counter and old hot plate as well as her living room-bedroom, where the nicest thing in the space was the pair of mismatched TV trays she'd lugged home from the Goodwill nine blocks away.

"I know, isn't it ridiculous? Just because I have limited funds, no job experience and a woeful lack of references, employers and landlords seem reluctant to take me on. Who would've figured?"

This time the jab hit home and that sensual mouth tightened, if only for an instant. "The last time I checked," he said evenly, "you had a trust fund that the courts and the banks couldn't touch."

"Ah, yes, my trust fund." Knowing she was on dangerous ground, she made a moue of regret—and shrugged, making no effort to stop the robe as it slid dangerously low on her shoulders. "The sad truth is, between travel and partying and my inordinate fondness for Jimmy Choos, Dom Pérignon and silk lingerie…it's gone."

"Are you serious?" He stared hard at her, clearly not certain whether to believe her or not.

She looked steadily back. "As a heart attack."

"And…this?" With a twirl of one long forefinger he indicated the shabby little room with its Texas-shaped water stain on the wall between the two narrow windows.

Before she could stop herself, she raised her chin a notch. "The best I can do."

He went utterly still, his impossibly green eyes seeming to spear right through her as he appeared to weigh her words. Then he uttered a single searing expletive and turned away, his coat billowing out as he paced three strides into her living room before running out of space.

"Get your things together," he commanded, his back still to her. "Whatever you'll need for tonight. I'll send someone for the rest tomorrow."

He couldn't have surprised her more if he'd fallen to the floor and declared he couldn't live without her. "What?"

He pivoted. "I said, pack a bag. You're not spending another night here."

Okay. This had to be a dream. She might feel wide-awake, but the truth was she'd fallen asleep on the lumpy little pullout sofa and everything that seemed so real—the chill of the worn linoleum against her bare feet, the faint, heady scent of Gabriel's aftershave, the jump of nerves in her stomach that his presence always provoked—was just a product of her imagination.

She cocked her head, wondering what would happen next. "And where, exactly, am I supposed to go?"

"My place."

Wrong again—definitely *not* a dream. Because no matter how wild and crazy her subconscious got, no matter how alone or desperate or frightened she felt, she would never consider moving in with him a solution to her problems.

It would be like agreeing to share a cage with a tiger.

Fascinating for maybe half a second. Totally terrifying after that.

So why, just for a moment, did she want more than anything in the world to take him up on his offer? Why did she want to close her eyes and step into the hard circle of his arms and say, yes, Gabriel, please take care of me?

Habit, she told herself angrily. Twenty-eight years of careless living, of always taking the easy path, of giving away her power and allowing others to dictate her fate.

Something she'd sworn on the day she'd been evicted from the estate that had been in her family for ninety years she'd never let happen again. A vow she refused to forsake, no matter how many jobs she lost or how many meals she had to skip to make ends meet or how long she had to live in a place like this.

If that meant thwarting Gabriel, who was, after all, responsible for lighting the fuse that had resulted in her life being blown up, it was simply an added bonus.

"Thanks so much," she said with patent insincerity, "but I'll pass."

She'd always considered him astute—on several occasions more than she might've wished—and he didn't disappoint her now. "You don't want to come home with me? Fine. Pick a hotel. You can stay there until I arrange something else."

She thought about her last experience at a hotel and shuddered. Still, she couldn't deny she was curious. "You'd do that? Put me up somewhere at your expense? Even if I tell you I'm not about to forget your part in everything that's happened?"

"Yes."

"Even though no matter how nice you pretend to be, I'm not going to sleep with you?"

"Yes, again—and I don't recall asking you to."

"Then why? What's in it for you?"

He shrugged, broad shoulders moving easily beneath the supple leather of his coat. "Peace of mind. It doesn't take an expert to know this place isn't safe. The building entrances aren't secure, there's no dead bolt on your door and I'd bet a year's profit an anemic five-year-old with a toothpick could jimmy your windows. Factor in that this is one tough neighborhood, which you're about as equipped to handle as a kitten dropped into a kennel of pit bulls, and there's no way I'm letting you stay here."

If it had been anybody else, she'd have considered

that last statement the height of bravado. But not Gabriel. In her experience, he said what he meant, then followed through.

Too bad that nobody—not even him—always got their way. "That's not up to you," she said flatly. "It's up to me. And I'm not going anywhere."

"Mallory." He spoke in the ultrapatient way adults reserve for recalcitrant children. "Be reasonable."

"No." One little word. So much power. "I don't want your help, Gabriel. I don't need it. I can take care of myself."

"You actually believe that?"

Of course she didn't. Not yet. Not entirely. But she'd beg for change on the street before she'd admit it to him. "Yes. Absolutely."

He stared at her, his expression once again guarded, displaying not a trace of surprise that she'd say something so outrageous. Trapped in the tractor beam of his gaze, with no clue what he was thinking and no words as a distraction, she found herself waiting.

For what, she wasn't sure.

Yet as the silence dragged on, her mind began spinning scenarios. If he wanted to, she mused, he could toss her over his shoulder and simply carry her out of here. Or—the old familiar thrill of awareness slow-danced down her spine—he could walk over, tug her close to that hard, elegant body, tumble her onto the couch and—

"All right, then. I guess we're done."

His flat, uninflected voice startled her out of her

reverie. Yet it still took a good long moment for his actual words to sink in.

That was it? They were done? Really?

For one appalling moment, she didn't know whether to laugh or cry. Then her common sense, which she'd done her best to shun most of her life, kicked in.

Are you crazy? He's throwing in the towel. For heaven's sake, hurry up and hustle him out the door before he changes his mind.

"Well, fancy that," she said with a calculated touch of mockery. "Finally. Something we can agree on."

A nerve jumped in his jaw. "Watch yourself, sweetheart," he advised, even as he took that first wonderful step toward the door. "You know what they say about little girls who poke at predators."

"No. I can't say that I do." She forced herself to stand her ground as he approached, telling herself she was glad this was almost over. He'd go his way, she'd go hers, and in a day, a week, a month, he'd be nothing more than a hazy memory of another life. "Nor, for that matter, do I care—"

With no warning, he crowded close. Startled, she sucked in a breath and tried to scoot out of his way, but it was too late.

He caught her chin in one big hand, tipping her face up to his. "You should," he murmured. "Because the adage goes that eventually the predator strikes back. And eats sweet little things like you—" her stomach flip-flopped at the silky note of warning in his voice "—for lunch."

She swallowed. Hard. Yet somehow her voice sounded almost steady as she fluttered her eyelashes at him and said, "How entertaining. Now let go of me."

"Not yet. There's one other thing we need to get straight."

"Oh? And what is that?"

"When we do have sex—" his gaze flicked to her mouth, lingering before he slowly raised his eyes to hers once again "—it won't have a damn thing to do with payback. Trust me, Mal. You'll be every bit as hot for me as I am for you." And with that he released her as abruptly as he'd caught her and stepped away.

By the time she recovered her breath, he was gone.

Two

Impertinent. Infuriating. Impossible.
And damn near irresistible.

That pretty much summed up Mallory Morgan, Gabe thought blackly, as he stepped out onto the cracked sidewalk fronting her run-down apartment building. Flipping his coat collar up against the chill March breeze, he checked for traffic on the litter-strewn street, then strode across to his SUV parked on the opposite curb.

He gave the vehicle a cursory look and handed a twenty to the sturdy little Latino kid who'd offered to keep an eye on it for him. "Thanks, *mi'ijo*."

Since their deal had been for ten upfront and ten if

the boy stuck, the youngster's delight was understandable. "*Muchas gracias*, mister!"

Gabe inclined his head. "You earned it."

"*Sí.* So if you come back to Lattimer Street and you need anything, you ask around for Tonio, okay? I take very good care of you."

"I'll keep it in mind."

"*Bueno!*" The kid flashed him a quick grin, then sprinted away as a bus stopped at the far end of the block. Darting around a trio of tattooed street toughs who stood smoking before a boarded-up storefront, he waved as a tired-looking young woman trudged down the steps. "Mama, mama! Guess what?" he exclaimed as he raced toward her through the gathering twilight.

It appeared Gabe had just made somebody's day.

Too freaking bad it was the wrong somebody.

But then, what did he expect? He, who was known for his shrewdness, his finesse, his ability to think outside the box—and yes, dammit, to always be three steps ahead of an opponent—had just behaved with all the subtlety of a Mack truck. He'd invaded Mallory's space, demanded answers, barked orders, bullied when he should've cajoled.

He'd even made a more balls-than-brains promise about their sexual future, for God's sake.

The only thing that kept the day from being a total bust was the very lucrative contract he'd inked at lunch to assess vulnerabilities and tailor protection strategies for the Lux Pacifica hotel chain's overseas executives.

When it came to everything else, however… With

an impatient shake of his head, he put the SUV in gear
and set a course for the warehouse district where the
Steele Security offices were located. It was slow going
due to the Friday night rush hour traffic, affording him
plenty of time to think.

There was no excuse for the surprise he'd gotten when
he'd walked into Annabelle's and realized the caramel-
haired hostess all the men seemed to be admiring was
Mallory. Just as there was no rational explanation for how
strongly he'd disliked seeing her smoky gaze go from
pleasant to hostile at the sight of him.

Given that in the four years he'd known her he'd
never seen Mallory get worked up about anything—
from being drenched with champagne by a hapless
waiter at a Denver symphony opening to strolling onto
a balcony at Meg Bender's Halloween party and finding
her father getting it on with one of her girlfriends—her
ire had gotten his attention. So had her scathing denun-
ciation of him.

But not, as Annabelle's horrified manager had
assumed, because he was angry or offended.

No, what had set him back on his heels, what had
tested his normally abundant patience as he'd been
forced to go ahead with what had seemed like an inter-
minable business luncheon, was the desolation he
thought he'd glimpsed under Mallory's anger. That,
and the suspicion that her transformation from lighthearted nymphet to go-to-hell working girl meant
somewhere along the line he'd made a major miscalculation.

He didn't make miscalculations. Major or otherwise.

That wasn't to say he considered himself infallible. It was just that from his youngest days, after his mother had died and he'd found himself in charge of a brood of eight at the ripe old age of fourteen, mistakes had been a luxury he couldn't afford. That hadn't changed during his years with the military's Special Operations Command.

As for his current circumstances, he hadn't gone from penniless stand-in parent to powerful millionaire businessman due to faulty judgment. No. All that he had, the success, the sterling reputation, the respect of his peers, had come from shrewd vision, meticulous planning, superior instincts and razor-sharp situational awareness.

Not that you'd know by today's performance, he conceded as he finally pulled into Steele Security's underground parking garage.

In his world, where outcome was everything, the fact that Mallory remained ensconced in her squalid little apartment suggested that his decision to chase her down before he'd fully vetted the situation wasn't the smartest move he'd ever made.

Still, honesty forced him to admit that things hadn't gone irredeemably to hell until she'd actually opened her door to him.

To say he'd been caught off guard was an understatement. It had felt more like he'd taken a shot between the eyes with a sledgehammer. Because dear God, the sight of her…

Wrapped in that flimsy siren-red robe, with her feet bare, that streaky brown-and-gold hair mussed and a faint flush tinting her petal-smooth cheeks, she'd looked as if she'd just tumbled out of some lucky man's bed.

Lust had slammed him like a punch to the gut.

By itself, that shouldn't have been a factor since he never allowed his libido to rule his head. But when moments later she'd made a valiant effort to control her trembling lower lip, something inside him had shifted.

What, he couldn't say. But whatever it was, the combination of it and that blast of desire had taken him completely out of his game.

His jaw bunched at the reminder. Climbing out of his vehicle, he punched in the code for the security door and let himself in to the building core, choosing the stairs over the elevator. Once on the main level, he bore left, his long legs eating up the distance as he strode down the wide, airy corridor. He passed by his own spacious office in favor of his brother Cooper's, glad to see the lights were still on.

He ducked his head in the open doorway. "Did you get that information I asked for?"

The younger Steele—number four in the nine-man birth order—glanced over from where he sat slouched in his tilted-back office chair. He was the picture of relaxation with his sneaker-clad feet propped on his desk, an illusion contradicted only by the rapid movement of his fingers over the computer keyboard propped on his lap.

"Do women swoon when I walk into a room?" he responded serenely. "The answer to both questions, big brother, is yes. Of course."

"And?"

"And you're giving me a crick in the neck standing over there. Why don't you come in, take a load off, tell Uncle Cooper what's put the stick up your ass."

Gabe snorted inelegantly. "That'll be the day." Despite his words, he did walk farther into the room, although not to take Cooper up on his invitation. He was here to collect intel, not dispense it. "Well? You going to tell me what you found out or not?"

The younger man shrugged. "Nothing much has changed. The warrant for Cal Morgan's arrest remains active, although my contact at the Feds says it's currently not worth the paper it's printed on. As long as Morgan stays in San Timoteo, they can't touch him, much less a dime of all that stolen money. Which, FYI, my friend now puts at twenty million, meaning that you, once again, win the office pool."

"Terrific." He shrugged out of his coat and tossed it with more force than was necessary onto one of the navy suede chairs in front of the desk. "There's nothing I like better than accurately predicting the extent of a disaster."

"Not your responsibility," Cooper said calmly. "You know damn well it would've been a whole lot worse if we hadn't been brought in when we were."

The hell of it was, Gabe did. And it wasn't that he was the least bit sorry Steele Security had been the one to expose Caleb Morgan's crooked dealings, he admitted, pacing restlessly toward the bank of windows at the far end of the room.

They'd done what they'd been hired to—check out Morgan Creek Investment. And they'd done it the way they did everything, thoroughly and completely.

It hadn't mattered that it wasn't their usual sort of job. Or that their client, a prospective Morgan Creek investor, had only expected them to give the company a quick once-over to placate his elderly mother, who swore that while on a recent trip overseas she'd been unable to locate the Taiwanese shopping mall featured in the company's literature.

The son was now sending his mother flowers weekly, since she'd saved him a bundle when it turned out the mall really didn't exist.

While Morgan, who'd fled the country the day after Steele had clued in the authorities, was most likely sipping mai tais on the veranda of his newly acquired tropical estate, living a life of luxury made possible by the pirated millions he'd socked away in untouchable offshore accounts.

No, if Gabe did have a regret, it was that they hadn't brought the bastard down sooner. While it wouldn't have changed what Morgan had done, it no doubt would have limited the extent of the ensuing damage. As it was, between unpaid taxes and first-position creditors, there hadn't been much left but crumbs for his bilked clients to recover.

And then there was Mallory. Who, until five hours ago, Gabe had assumed was off in St. Croix or Monte

Carlo or some other exotic locale, licking her wounds in luxurious seclusion. Not living all on her own in one of Denver's worst neighborhoods, trying to scrape by on some minimum wage job.

And there it was, that unexpected, unacceptable miscalculation.

"What about Morgan's daughter?" he asked abruptly, swiveling around to stare expectantly at his brother. "What did you find out about her?"

Cooper's busy fingers stilled. "You mean, in addition to the fact that she gave you a shellacking at lunch today?"

"How the hell did you hear about that?"

Cooper rolled his eyes. "How do you think? Family grapevine, bro. Some woman Lilah went to school with saw what happened at Annabelle's and couldn't wait to call Lilah and tell her all about it. Lilah told Dom when he took her to her doctor's appointment, and he told me when he stopped by to pick up the Lederer file on their way home."

"Geezus." The intrabrother communication network had always been good, but the addition in the past year of Gen and Lilah, his sisters-in-law, had definitely kicked it up a notch.

"Yeah. Pretty scary, huh?"

"You could say that. Is Lilah all right? No surprises at the doctor's?" Leaving the windows, he walked back toward Coop's desk.

"As far as I know, she's as good as a woman six months gone can be. Dom, on the other hand, may not make it."

"No news there." Their brother, Dominic, a former

Navy SEAL, had been the embodiment of the brash, tough, never-let-'em-see-you-sweat warrior until he'd signed on to rescue a pretty blond socialite from the banana republic where she was being held prisoner. Now he and Lilah were married and expecting their first child, and he was as overprotective as a five-star general with a troop of one.

"I guess that's true," Cooper conceded. "But still…Lilah mentioned today how much she's enjoying working on some big charity ball, and you could practically see Dom's teeth start to gnash. It seems like the closer she gets to her due date, the harder it is for him to pretend he doesn't want to haul her off somewhere and wrap her in a nice safe protective bubble." He sighed. "If it wasn't so funny, it'd be pathetic. He used to be such a player."

Gabe's dark mood lightened fractionally at his brother's mournful expression. He shrugged. "Love makes people crazy." One of the excellent reasons why it wasn't for him.

"I'll say." Sliding the keyboard onto the desk, he turned his attention back to Gabe, his melancholy vanishing as quickly as it had come. "While we're on the subject of crazy, was the divine Ms. Morgan really working as a waitress?"

"Hostess," Gabe corrected.

"And she actually called you an egotistical, scumsucking sonofabitch?"

"She may have. I wasn't exactly taking notes."

"And?"

"That about covers it. As noted, she called me a few choice names, refused to seat me, then left when her boss tried to smooth over the situation."

"Huh." Cooper eyed him consideringly. "So what did she say when you went after her later? Was she still pissed?"

"Who said I went after her?"

"Please." Cooper sniffed. "You canceled your afternoon appointments, you asked for a Morgan family update, and it's been obvious ever since you walked in here you're tweaked about something. Plus Dom says you two have always had a thing for each other…"

A vision of Mallory's robe drifting south and exposing her smooth, velvet-skinned shoulders flashed through Gabe's mind.

"So yeah," Cooper concluded. "You went after her."

He thrust the vision away. "You're right. I did. And yes, she wasn't exactly thrilled to see me, which given the circumstances is no great surprise. As for the rest of what we discussed…"

He thought about Mallory's attempt to act indifferent about her situation while foolishly insisting she was doing just fine, and once more felt frustrated, impatient, annoyed—and yes, although he couldn't quite figure out why—touched.

"It's none of your business."

"Aw, come on. Don't tell me you're going to stonewall your favorite sibling."

"Hell, no. But then, last I checked, Deke's still in Borneo."

"Ouch." Cooper gave him a faux-wounded look. "You could've just said no."

"Like you've ever let that word stop you? Give me a break." Leaning over, he planted his hands on his brother's desk. "And as much as I'd love to share my innermost feelings, hear all about your and Dom's riveting take on my love life—" with each word his voice acquired a little more bite "—it's after six and I have plans for tonight. So what do you say you just tell me what I want to know, and we leave the rest for another time? Say, the next time you girls have a slumber party?"

Cooper made a reproachful face. "No need to get surly."

Silent, Gabe continued to stare down at him.

"Okay, okay," he said hastily, raising his hands in mock surrender. "Here goes. Up until six months ago, our subject was holed up at the family estate, even though the staff had been let go months before that. Then, when the Feds finally came in, seized everything and locked the place down, she checked into the Markham Plaza. She was there for several weeks, until her credit card was declined and they found out it was no mistake. Word is she tried to make good with a check, but it bounced, too, and the management not so kindly asked her to leave."

Straightening, he consulted his computer monitor. "Her credit report shows two different apartment management firms checked her history the following week. Considering that she had an extensive collection of plastic, but that every single card was closed due to late or no payments, several with substantial balances, I'm guessing they passed on renting to her."

Considering where she'd wound up living, Gabe imagined he was right.

"The interesting thing is, except for a small portion of one account, everything else was paid off a few weeks later. And she was making the bare-bones payment on that last outstanding debt until roughly sixty days ago, when she also started to fall behind on her rent."

Gabe frowned, trying to make sense of it. "What about bank accounts?" he asked, pushing upright and starting to pace.

"Checking account was closed due to overdrafts. Nothing else popped, but then I didn't have enough time to do much more than skim the surface. Does it matter?"

"Probably not. It's just that I thought—" incorrectly, it appeared, although it was still the main reason he hadn't seen fit to check up on her before "—she had a trust fund, a substantial one. She says it's long gone."

Cooper frowned. "You don't believe her?"

"I didn't say that. But I want to be sure." Despite the overwhelming evidence that Mallory was operating without a safety net, this time around he wasn't assuming anything.

"I'll have another look."

"Thanks."

"Anything else?"

"No. I'd say that does it for now."

Cooper drummed his fingers on the desk. "I take it that means you're not done with Mallory? Even though, from the sound of things, she ranks you somewhere below foot fungus on the list of things she could live without?"

"What's your point, Coop? Assuming you have one?"

"I do." Never shy about stating his opinion, he met Gabe's narrow stare straight on. "Look, I know how committed you are, not just to making this business a success, but to doing your best to ensure that the work we all do matters. That whenever possible, we do what we can to make peoples' lives safer and better.

"Because of that, I think you need a reminder that no matter what this woman said to you, no matter how hard she may have tried to guilt trip you, she's not your responsibility—and you definitely don't owe her anything."

"Believe me." Gabe smiled sardonically. "That's not the problem here."

Cooper looked surprised. "No? Then what—"

"Leave it alone, little brother. I appreciate your concern, but I've been successfully conducting my own affairs for a whole lot of years now. If I decide I need help, from you or the rest of the family, I'll be sure to let you know. In the meantime—" shooting his cuff, he glanced at his wristwatch "—the clock is ticking and I'm sure I've got a stack of things to take care of before I can get out of here."

"That's it? You're just going to walk?"

"Pretty much." Reaching down, he snagged his coat off the chair and deliberately steered the conversation in a different direction. "You going out to Taggart and Gen's for dinner tomorrow?"

To his credit, Cooper knew when to throw in the towel. "Are you kidding? Free, home-cooked meal along with Rockies Cactus League ball on the tube?" He sat back and again propped his feet up. "I'm there. What about you?"

"Yeah, I'm in, too." He headed toward the door. "You want to share a ride?"

"Sure."

"I'll call you tomorrow, we can hash out the details." Reaching the doorway, he paused. "Hey, Coop?"

"What?"

"Thanks for the information. I appreciate it."

"Easy for you to say," the younger man groused, but without any heat. "You're not the one left hanging."

"I think you'll survive," he said drily. And with that, he headed down the hall toward his own office and what was sure to be a fat folder of items needing his attention, reassured by the knowledge that Cooper's bad temper wouldn't last past the next five minutes.

Knowing as well that while his brother's concern for him had been misplaced, the younger Steele had been right about one thing.

Gabe wasn't done with Mallory. Not by a long shot.

Three

"Are you all right, Miss Morgan?"

Mallory dragged her gaze from the rectangle of paper clutched in her trembling hand to stare blankly at the man seated across from her. "What?"

Mr. Cowden's thin, intelligent face softened. "You seem a bit shaken," the owner of Finders Keepers, the search firm she'd been contacted by the previous day, observed not unkindly. "Can I get you something? A glass of water? Some coffee?"

"No. I… It's just…" Embarrassed to find herself babbling, she pressed her lips together and struggled for composure. "Please, could you explain to me again where this came from? You said it's a behest from a relative?"

"Yes. According to the letter we received, the funds originated with—" he glanced down at the paper centered atop his glossy walnut desk "—one Ivan Mallory Milton. Your cousin, it seems, although most likely a distant one since it states here he was ninety-one at the time he expired. The family connection—" he adjusted his glasses and scanned further down the document "—was apparently through your maternal grandmother."

"But I've never even heard of him."

"Well, yes, that's actually rather common with this sort of distant connection. And truthfully, as you might imagine, quite often inheritances go unclaimed for just that reason. In this case," he said, tapping a finger against the paper, "it seems that Mr. Milton first realized the relationship after reading a newspaper article about your family."

Mallory winced. Given her father's notoriety and the extensive press coverage he'd received, she didn't imagine that anything her late cousin had read would have been complimentary. Not that that appeared to have made a difference.

"The information was found among his belongings after he passed away, and since he had no other heirs, it was determined these funds should come to you. Although these days, with the popularity of the Internet, it is rather unusual for us to be contacted through the regular mail this way…."

Even as she told herself she should pay attention to what Mr. Cowden was saying, Mallory's gaze drifted back to the cashier's check.

Sure enough, right after Pay To The Order Of was her name, followed by the fabulous, wonderful, miraculous sum of four thousand, seven hundred, twenty-one dollars and forty-six cents.

A year ago, that amount wouldn't have qualified as her monthly shoe allowance. Now it meant she could take a deep breath for the first time in months. And she owed it all to someone she'd never met, and never would.

Thank you, dear departed cousin Ivan.

Not, she thought hastily, that she was glad her long-lost relative was dead. But if the old guy had to go, she certainly couldn't fault his timing.

"Miss Morgan?"

With a start, she realized her companion was staring at her quizzically, as though he'd stopped speaking some time ago and was waiting for a response. "I'm sorry," she said hastily. "It's just this—" she smoothed her thumb over the crease in the paper caused by the overly enthusiastic grip of her fingers "—I can't quite take it in. It's such a surprise."

"But a welcome one, surely." Smiling, Mr. Cowden came to his feet.

"Oh, yes." It was so welcome she couldn't quite believe somebody wasn't going to pop out of the woodwork at any second, claim there'd been a mistake and snatch her windfall away.

"I can't tell you how much that pleases me," he went on as he came around the desk. "And how glad I am that we were able to be of assistance. Frankly," his blue eyes gleamed cheerfully, "this is always my favorite part of the job."

"I can understand why." With a smile of her own, she carefully folded the check and slid it into the inner compartment of her purse for safekeeping. Since it was obvious from Mr. Cowden's behavior that he considered their business done, she stood, as well. "Do I owe you something? Isn't there a fee for you finding me?"

"Yes, of course there is, but it's already been taken care of by Mr. Milton's representative." He held her coat for her, then ushered her through the door into the outer office. Minutes later, after signing a paper acknowledging receipt of the money, and a round of thank-yous, good lucks and goodbyes, she found herself standing outside on the sidewalk in the midmorning sunshine.

For one glorious moment, elation got the better of her and she actually did a twirl. Four thousand, seven hundred and twenty-one dollars! She couldn't seem to wipe the smile off her face as she waltzed up the street toward the bus stop, her feet barely touching the ground, her mind filled with possibilities.

Where, oh where, to start? Tres Chic for a facial, a massage, a full day of beauty? Heaven knew, her pores would thank her. Or Mr. Kenneth's to pamper her hair with some highlights and one of his signature haircuts? Should she make a trip to Marchant's and pick up that to-die-for Moreno handbag she'd seen in the window last week? Or spring for a new pair of Merrazi wedges since a toddler with attitude had stomped on the toe of her favorites her first day at Annabelle's?

Maybe the order of the day was to go out for a leisurely lunch. Or, even better, treat herself to an elegant dinner. It would feel good to get all dressed up. Although most of her clothes had gone for consignment, she still had a few nice things. She could catch a cab to Gambiolini's and request her usual table, then while away a few hours sipping a glass or two of pricey red wine, flirting with Phillippe, her favorite waiter, indulging her months-long craving for the house specialty, shrimp tettrazini.

Except somebody she knew was bound to be there. Did she really want to deal with the whispers and repressive stares or, even worse, the humiliation of being treated as if she were invisible?

Okay, so maybe dinner out wasn't the best idea, she decided, as her bus pulled up. No matter. There were all sorts of other ways she could amuse herself. Like getting her good wristwatch back from the pawnshop, she thought as her bus pulled up and she instinctively checked the time on its drugstore replacement.

Climbing on board, she flashed her pass at the driver, walked back to her accustomed seat in the middle, and continued to dream.

She could rent a car and make the trip to Aurora to make sure her favorite jumper was doing all right with his new owner. Top Flight had always been a challenge, part of the reason she'd loved him, and it would be good to know that he'd settled into his new surroundings.

For that matter, she could drive up to Breckenridge

and spend a few days skiing and being pampered at The Pinnacle, one of her favorite little ultraluxury spa resorts. Although she supposed she should probably call first. It wasn't unusual for them to be booked an entire season in advance.

Of course, before she went anywhere or called anyone, she needed to pay her overdue cell bill—something else she could now afford to do. Just think! For the first time in what felt like forever, she wasn't going to have to worry that her phone service, an absolute essential to job hunting, not to mention her sense of safety, was about to be cut off.

Heck, once her account was cleared she'd even be able to use some of her precious minutes on nonessential calls, such as letting Gabriel know—again—that she didn't want or need his help. Even better—the thought of it had her sitting up straighter—she could send him the money to pay for the locksmith who'd shown up the day after their encounter to install locks on her doors and windows.

She still wasn't sure what she resented most about the gesture. The hit to her pride that with a snap of his elegant fingers he could dispatch someone to take care of something she herself had been unable to afford? Or that she could no longer crawl into bed without thinking about him because, for the first time since moving into the place, she was actually getting some sleep instead of constantly jolting awake at each and every little noise? Even though the night after the locks had gone on she'd bolted awake to hear someone fruitlessly trying to force her front door?

Or was the agitation she felt when she thought of him caused by something else entirely? Perhaps a secret fear that hiring the locksmith had been his parting gesture? Could it be that deep down she was really afraid he'd taken her at her word and intended to respect her request that he stay away?

Absolutely not, she thought, squaring her shoulders. Sure, she was surprised he hadn't been back to harass her. But why shouldn't she be? He didn't seem like the sort of man to back down from anything. And his parting shot *had* seemed to indicate that as far as he was concerned, they were far from finished.

Which was just plain crazy, given that they'd never started. Certainly they'd been friends of a sort, and she couldn't deny that they'd always had chemistry, but they'd both chosen never to cross the line into something more. And while she'd obviously had her reasons for keeping him at arm's length—he *so* wasn't the type for a superficial dalliance—he'd quite clearly kept his distance for reasons of his own.

Reasons she'd never really thought about.

And wasn't about to start now, she told herself firmly. For too many years she'd been like a leaf in the stream going wherever the current took her, coasting over bumps, sliding around obstacles, letting outside elements determine her path.

Well, she was done with that. Like it or not, it was up to her whether she wound up over her head in some stagnant pool or learned how to keep herself afloat.

That was why, she realized, coming back to earth as

she stared out the window at a cityscape that was getting drearier with every passing block, she wasn't going to spend cousin Ivan's money on anything foolish like designer shoes or salon haircuts or pricey vacations. For the very first time since she'd found herself stranded outside the Plaza with no one to call and nowhere to go, she had a cushion, however small, between herself and life on the street.

She wasn't about to blow it. No, except to take care of her overdue rent and phone bill and purchase some urgently needed groceries, the new, improved Mallory was going to sock that money away and continue to watch every last nickel, dime and penny.

She was certain she wouldn't have to do it indefinitely. After all, a mystery relative unexpectedly bequeathing her money had to be a sign that her luck was changing. So tomorrow she would again scour the papers for jobs, hit the streets, renew her quest to join the ranks of the gainfully employed.

And surely, if she just tried hard enough, by this time next week she was bound to be somebody's favorite new employee.

Stripper. Nursing home attendant. Fast-food worker.

That pretty much described her current career path, Mallory thought dejectedly as she climbed off the bus well after dark a week later.

Pulling her coat a little tighter against the chill from the snow that had begun falling in the past hour, she began to pick her way home through the freezing slush in her too-thin pumps, sincerely wishing that she'd had the foresight to wear boots when she'd left that morning.

Of course, at the time, the weather had been warm and sunny, matching her mood as she set out to apply for half a dozen promising employment possibilities.

Now, twelve long hours later, after riding eight different buses, walking dozens of blocks, and an eternity of waiting, talking, smiling and praying, not one job offer had come her way.

But then, the positions she'd applied for had actually paid a livable salary, instead of minimum wage for part-time hours too sparse to cover the barest necessities like rent or food. As an added bonus, they also hadn't required her to breathe heavily into a phone or take her clothes off in front of strangers.

And so far, with the exception of the hostess gig at Annabelle's, which she'd so foolishly thrown away, those seemed to be the only kind of offers she could generate.

Not that she was feeling sorry for herself or anything, she thought, jumping a little as a door slammed in the distance and an unseen man screamed an obscenity. Okay, so maybe her inability to find decent employment was making her feel even more useless than normal. And she couldn't seem to stop thinking about how close to living under a bridge she'd be if not for last week's windfall.

And yes, her feet were freezing, the too-quiet, seemingly deserted street was creeping her out and the thought of spending another night eating boxed mac and cheese all alone in her drafty apartment made her feel beyond bleak, but—

"Well, look what the cat dragged in."

Her head snapped up as a tall, menacing figure materialized out of an unlit doorway in front of her. She slid to a stop, her heart jamming into her throat as the interloper stepped squarely into her path.

Time slowed, then ceased, while her thoughts splintered. *Run!* screamed through her along with *ohmigod I'm going to die* at the same time an oddly detached little voice murmured, *Gee, doesn't that voice sound sort of familiar?*

Then the man took a threatening step closer and the snow-dappled light from the streetlamp on the corner touched his face and her heart lurched back to life.

"Have you lost your *mind*?" Dragging desperately needed air into her constricted lungs, she didn't think, just reacted, lunging forward to smack Gabriel in his big, broad, not-even-breathing-hard chest. "Of all the mean, rotten, low-down dirty tricks! You scared me half to death—"

"*Good.*" His warm fingers braceleted her flailing wrists. "You should be scared, dammit!" Even in the dark, there was no mistaking his grim expression. "What the hell are you doing out here at this hour?"

"Gosh, let me think. Oh, I know—I live here!"

"Well, here's a news flash," he shot back, effortlessly reeling her closer as she tried to pull free. "You won't be living anywhere if you don't have better sense than to tiptoe around after dark with your head bowed like some scared little mouse. God, Mallory! Don't you have enough sense to know that in a neighborhood like this, any display of weakness is an invitation to be mugged—or worse?"

"You mean like having to fend off some know-it-all wannabe stalker?"

He leaned into her, so close she could feel the warm wash of his breath on her icy skin. "Believe me, sweetheart. If I were stalking you, there wouldn't be any wannabe about it."

Maybe it was the delicious tickle of terror evoked by his words. Or the sight of that hard, chiseled mouth mere inches from her own. But in a flash, awareness roared to life, crowding out her anger. She registered his heat, his size, the strength of the hands dwarfing her own.

Her throat went tight. And try as she might to tell herself it was a delayed reaction to the fright she'd received, no way did that explain the overwhelming urge she had to crowd closer and give herself over to his potent masculine power—

"Dammit, you're shivering." Abruptly, he released her. Relief streaked through her, only to be snuffed out as he whipped off his coat and wrapped it around her. "Come on." His voice was as hard as the arm suddenly looping her waist, urging her forward. "Let's get you in out of this cold."

She thought of her apartment, and the idea of being trapped in that small, intimate space with him had her digging in her heels. "I'm fine. Really. And you can drop the concerned act because I'm absolutely not inviting you in—"

"No problem. My car's right here."

"What?" She tried to struggle as he unlocked the door of a big black SUV, only to find that his enveloping coat was as confining as a straitjacket. "No, Gabriel. While I understand your compelling need to put your hands on me—" she gamely tried to infuse some of the old flippancy into her voice "—it's been a really long day."

"We need to talk." He opened the door and planted his free hand on the roof of the car, neatly boxing her in. "So either we go inside to your place where it'll be just the two of us or you get in the car and we drive to some nice, public restaurant. You decide."

It was no choice at all, and he knew it. Yet it was also clear he wasn't going away. "Fine. We'll go to the restaurant." Giving him a narrow-eyed stare, she allowed him to help her up onto the seat. "But this had better be brief."

He said nothing to that, simply shut the door, walked around and got in on the other side.

Five miles and what felt like another world later, they were seated across from each other at a booth in a cozy little diner that came complete with checked curtains on the windows, a bell over the door and an array of mouthwatering scents wafting from the kitchen.

"Hungry?" he asked as the waitress arrived with her pad.

Mallory shrugged, ignoring the sudden grinding of her empty stomach. "Not really." Dinner out simply didn't figure into her budget. Not when she had food at home, and the twenty dollars in her wallet was supposed to last her through the end of the week.

He studied her a moment, then turned to the waitress. "Two coffees, the chicken fried steak for me and a chef salad for the lady." Switching his attention back to Mallory, he ignored her look of disbelief. "I'm buying," he informed her matter-of-factly. "Now, what kind of dressing do you want?" When she simply continued to stare at him, he gave a slight shrug. "Make it Thousand Island," he told the bemused server.

"Make it blue cheese," she contradicted. If she was going to eat, she might as well get what she liked. "And I'd rather have tea instead of coffee, please. And separate checks, if you would." She'd just have to skip lunch during her job hunt the next few days.

The waitress, a stout, pleasant-faced woman in her forties, wisely refrained from comment. She asked a few order-related questions, brought their drinks, then hustled off to post their order and take care of the rest of her tables.

Mallory gave the tea time to steep, then wrapped her hands around the cup and took a sip, hoping to counteract the exhaustion that was suddenly sweeping through her.

Gabe looked over at her, far too astute for comfort. "You all right?"

She sat up a little straighter. "You mean, except for having been so rudely snatched off the street?"

"Yes. Except for that."

"I'm fine."

"You mentioned that it had been a long day. Where were you, anyway?"

She might be tired but she wasn't dead, and she certainly wasn't discussing her failure on the employment front. She fluttered her eyelashes. "Where else? I was off meeting Raoul, my secret lover."

"Ah." He took a sip of his coffee. "He must be a real prize to send you home on the bus."

She shrugged. "What can I say? He's French."

"My sincere condolences." His tone was perfectly solemn, but those jewel-tone eyes suddenly gleamed with a touch of laughter.

It was unexpected. And shockingly attractive. Just like him, she thought, studying that symmetrical, good-looking face. The strong cheekbones, level eyebrows and sensual mouth were enough to turn any woman's head. But it was the self-assurance, the surety of purpose, the wicked intelligence that held her gaze.

She felt the pull of his appeal clear to her toes. It didn't mean anything, of course. She was simply experiencing the ever-present hum of awareness she felt whenever she was near him.

And if perhaps there was something more? If, as their gazes meshed in that moment of shared humor, she inexplicably felt connected to him?

An illusion, she told herself sharply. One she couldn't afford to indulge. Lifting her cup to her mouth, she used the movement as an excuse to look away. "Why were you waiting for me tonight, anyway?"

There was a moment's silence. "I came to give you

this." Pulling out his wallet, he extracted two hundred-dollar bills and three twenties—the exact amount of the money order she'd sent him to pay for the locksmith—and held it out.

"Then you wasted a trip," she said, making no move to take it. "I'm grateful for the thought, but as it happens I recently received an unexpected windfall so I can afford to pay for—"

"No." For a second his mouth tightened with exasperation, then his expression smoothed out. "I'm not taking your money, Mallory. Not for a meal I coerced you into ordering. And certainly not for hardware and labor—" before she could stop him, he picked up her purse, opened it and tucked the cash into an inside pocket "—for a job you didn't have any control over."

"That's not true," she said instantly, telling herself she'd just leave the money in his car later if he refused to see reason now. "I could've refused to let your man in."

"Yes, you could. But it wouldn't have made any difference. As I believe Sonny told you, he had his orders."

"He said if I didn't let him install the locks, you'd make sure he got fired."

"Ah." Gabe steepled his fingers. "Well, there you have it."

There was something in his voice, and she eyed him suspiciously. "It wasn't true?"

"Let's just say it would be tough to do since Sonny owns the business."

"Ohmigod," she breathed. "You two played me. Doesn't it bother you that I think you're that ruthless?"

"Not if it makes you safer."

The easy statement stole her breath. At the very least she ought to be angered by his high-handedness, disgusted by the deception, indignant at his interference. Instead, she was stunned by the idea that he actually seemed to care what happened to her. God knows, her own father hadn't.

That's right. The thought put a little starch back in her spine. *So instead of getting all fluttery inside and doing a Sally Field, this would be an excellent time to remember that no matter what Gabriel does, you still have to learn how to take care of yourself.*

Misreading her silence, he raised a hand. "Just so there's no misunderstanding, since you always seem to think I've got an ulterior motive, I'm not saying that just to get into your pants." His eyes glinted, but this time it wasn't humor lighting them up. "Not tonight anyway."

She tried to ignore the flicker of heat generated by his threat—or was it a promise?—that there'd be another time, and focus on all the questions that still remained between them. Yet before she could do either one, the waitress arrived with their food.

It smelled fabulous, and with a slight jolt, she realized three things simultaneously.

Call her a wimp, but she'd had all the responsibility she could handle for one day. Being a grown-up was hard work, and between having to weigh every dime she spent, looking for a job and questioning every word that came out of Gabriel's mouth, she was just plain worn-out with it. Surely, the world wouldn't come to an end if she took a time-out and simply enjoyed herself for a measly half hour.

She supposed it also wouldn't tilt off its axis if she allowed Gabe one small victory and let him pay for her meal.

The last was that she was a lot hungrier than she'd thought.

So it seemed only fitting, after the waitress served her salad, to slide the mound of lettuce across the table, then reach up and intercept Gabe's plate. "I'll take that, thanks."

The woman didn't so much as blink. "You bet, honey," she said, making a hasty retreat.

Not missing a beat, Mallory slid her fork into the creamy mound of mashed potatoes, slipped it into her mouth and practically moaned with appreciation. "This is wonderful." She took another blissful bite before finally venturing a glance to see how Gabriel was taking the theft of his food.

To her surprise, he was watching her with the strangest look on his face.

One that vanished with the droll twitch of his lips. "Glad you're enjoying it," he said drily as he reached for the salad dressing.

It was the last thing either of them said for quite a while.

Four

"Wow." With a murmured sigh of pleasure, Mallory stretched her feet toward the stream of warm air blasting from the SUV's heater. "That second piece of pie may have been a mistake. I feel like a boa constrictor that swallowed a goat."

Gabe took his eyes off the road to glance over at her. Her heavily lashed eyes were closed, her shining hair tumbled, while her fine-boned profile was a perfect silhouette against the snow-lit night beyond the windows.

She didn't look a thing like the minx who'd hijacked his dinner, then devoured it with such hedonistic pleasure that at one point she'd even licked her spoon.

Instead, she was a dead ringer for a patrician young queen who'd taken a night off from some palace intrigue. Or—his gaze flicked to her mouth—an ultra-exclusive, high-priced courtesan taking a break from the scores of men vying for her attention.

The lust that had dogged him all night pounced, jaws snapping closed like a vise.

He wanted to touch her, dammit. He wanted to skim his palm over her silken jaw, rub the pad of his thumb against those soft, full lips, bury his face in the curling mass of that burnished hair.

Bury himself in her hot silky sex.

Except any one of those moves might accurately be construed as an attempt to get into her pants. Which he, in his infinite wisdom, had promised wasn't on this evening's agenda.

He yanked his gaze back to the street, his mouth twisting at the irony. He'd had, after all, abundant opportunity in the past to make a move on her. Yet he'd always chosen to pass, for reasons as varied as they were numerous.

He'd been too busy working. She'd been too busy playing.

He'd had younger brothers to raise, a business to run, a host of responsibilities. She'd had none.

He'd preferred his sexual liaisons to be straightforward, a pleasurable exchange between two responsible adults with no strings and no messy complications.

There'd never been anything uncomplicated about Mallory. Then or now.

"Gabriel?" Her voice cut through his thoughts. As if on cue, in a quicksilver shift of mood she suddenly sounded serious, the levity of the previous moment gone.

"What?"

"Why did you come so see me tonight? Really?"

"I told you. The check—"

"No." Cutting him off, she tucked a knee underneath her and shifted on the seat to face him. "If that was your only purpose you could have dropped the thing in the mail or called to tell me you'd destroyed it. You didn't have to show up in person."

"Okay." He inclined his head. "You got me. I wanted to make sure you were okay. I told you before that you don't belong in this neighborhood, and earlier tonight, on the street, you proved my point."

She ignored the provocation of that last statement. "All right. But why do you care? Why now, when I've been living here for months?"

"It's no great mystery, Mallory. Until we ran into each other last week, I didn't know you needed help. Now I do."

"And you feel compelled to provide it?"

"That's not exactly how I'd put it, but yes."

He heard her breathe in, then carefully exhale. "Is it because of my father? Do you feel guilty for exposing him?"

For a second he was tempted to dance around the question. After all, as Gabe had personal reason to know, kids made all sorts of excuses for parents, defending behavior that was often indefensible.

But on this issue, at least, he felt he owed her the truth. "Hell, no," he said flatly. "You may not want to hear this, but it's my firm opinion that your father ought to be in prison. Not off living the high life, working on his tan at a lot of other people's expense."

"Oh."

Braced as he was for a much more vocal protest, her one-word response caught him off guard. Still, he figured they might as well get past this hurdle now.

Pulling up to the curb in front of her building, he switched off the engine and turned to face her, "Oh what, Mallory? Oh, I really am the cold-blooded bastard you thought I was?"

That lush courtesan's mouth unexpectedly curved up for an instant. "How about, oh, I still don't get it? Because if you're not here because of my father and you don't want sex, then what's the draw, Gabriel? Why do you care what happens to me?"

"Why shouldn't I?" He made a note to kick himself later for the whole sex debacle. "We're friends, or at least, we were—"

"No." She shook her head. "We weren't. Maybe it's not exactly my area of expertise—" her voice took on that familiar note of self-mockery "—but even I know that friends spend time together, and talk, and know about each other's dreams and quirks and even some of their secrets. You and I... We were more social acquaintances with a long-standing jones for each other."

He should've been gratified by her acknowledgment of the attraction between them. So why, instead, did her dispassionate dismissal of a broader connection grate like a handful of sand scrubbed across glass? "There's more to it than that. But my point is, while your father deserves the worst the system can throw at him, you…you were just an innocent bystander in all this. Yet somehow you wound up taking the hit for him, and no matter how you view it—a miscarriage of justice, a monumental screwup—it never should've happened."

"So that makes me…what? Collateral damage?"

If he hadn't been so caught up in choosing his next words, her utter lack of inflection might have warned him he'd made a major misstep. "Sure, I suppose you could say that. The label isn't important. What matters is that it's not acceptable. You shouldn't have to lose everything while he skates."

"And you're here to fix that?"

"Yes." Flashing on her reaction every other time he'd tried to offer his assistance, he thought it wise to add, "If you'll let me."

"I see." She slid her feet back into her discarded pumps, her face hidden by the gently curling mass of her hair as she leaned forward. "Well, here's your answer." Straightening, she swiveled to face him, her eyes dark with something he couldn't identify—and anger so blatant a blind man couldn't have missed it. "Go to hell."

She snatched up her purse, shoved open the door and had her feet planted squarely on the pavement outside almost before he could decide what to do.

Almost, but not quite. "I don't think so." He was out

his door and around the vehicle so fast she didn't manage to get more than a few feet before he caught up with her.

"What the hell is your problem!" he demanded, catching her by the elbow and swinging her around.

"You!" she shot back. "You arrogant, self-satisfied jerk!" Sucking in a breath, she yanked her arm free. "In what universe do you think I'd *ever* agree to be your pet project?"

"*What?*"

"Either you're hard of hearing, or just so full of yourself that nothing can penetrate that incredibly thick hide, so let me spell it out. I don't want your pity or your charity. And I am not, nor will I ever be, some wrong you need to right!"

"Is that what you think?" He couldn't remember the last time he'd completely lost his temper, but he could feel it beginning to go. And it seriously pissed him off. He ruled his emotions. They didn't rule him.

"Yes!" She started to whirl away, then thought better of it. "And just so there's no mistake—" she jerked her handbag open, fumbled around for something inside "—I don't need your damned money, either!" Crumpling the bills that had appeared in her hand, she hurled them at him.

He didn't think, he acted. Trained to always take control of an attack, he snatched the money out of the air, wrapped an arm around her waist and yanked her close.

Mistake. The warning went off in his mind like a Klaxon the instant he felt her plastered against him, all slim curves and yielding flesh. He drew in a breath, but that was a mistake, too, as her scent filled his head, a faint trace of exotic flowers and something that was exclusively, erotically Mallory.

Like a bomb going off, temper exploded into something much, much hotter.

He tossed the money to the ground. Fisting his hand in the heavy silk of her hair, he tipped back her head and claimed her mouth.

If she resisted, it was for the barest second. Then with a shaky little sound that made every muscle in his body tighten, she crowded closer, wound her arms around his neck and hungrily kissed him back.

God, those lips. Sleek, plump, soft, so soft. How often over the years had he wondered how she'd taste, how she'd feel?

Now he knew. And he, who prided himself on always being in control, wasn't.

He wanted to plunder, possess, eat her up.

And touch. Limited by their layers of clothing, he settled for sliding his hand out of her hair to cup the curve of her jaw, trail the pad of his thumb down to the shallow notch at the base of her throat. Her skin felt like satin, and his breathing sped up as he imagined her naked. He knew with a certainty he didn't question she'd be silk soft all over.

He raked his teeth against her bottom lip. She shuddered, then the damp tip of her tongue strafed his upper lip and every Y chromosome in his body stood up and howled.

Bending his knees, he slid his arm from her waist to the firm undercurve of her ass, boosting her up to give himself better access. With another needy little sound she clamped her thighs against his hips.

It was all the encouragement he needed to slide his tongue into the hot sweetness of her mouth. She widened her lips, inviting him deeper, meeting each thrust of his with a welcoming one of her own until he felt as if the top of his head was going to blow off. And still the kiss grew hotter, more demanding, an act of possession that had some primitive part of his brain calculating the number of feet to the SUV's wide backseat.

Yet even as he pictured himself laying her down, stripping away her clothes, the protector in him registered the sound of a door opening somewhere up the street. It was followed by a chorus of adolescent male voices raised in a mixture of taunts and laughter that was slowly drifting closer.

As a former military officer, he knew all about young men, rampaging hormones, the pack mentality. Add in that these youngsters were more likely to be gangbangers than Boy Scouts and he had to wonder—

What the *hell* was he doing? Since when did he forget his surroundings to make out on a darkened sidewalk in a bad part of town?

A week ago the answer would've been never. But not anymore.

Not since Mallory had somehow managed to turn him inside out and upside down.

That was no excuse for him behaving like a

hormonal teenager himself, however. Much less acting in a way that could draw unwanted attention her way, jeopardizing her safety.

He brought his head up, breaking their contact, and abruptly set her on her feet. "Mal." His voice was harsh with the cost of his reacquired restraint.

"Hmm?" She stared blankly at him.

He steadied her as she swayed. "Come home with me."

"What?" Although her voice was still a velvety rasp, her passion-dazed eyes were starting to clear.

"It's late, it's cold, you shouldn't be here by yourself." He ignored the little voice that urged him to just shut up, throw her over his shoulder and cart her back to his cave. "Come home with me," he repeated. "We can sort things out in the morning."

"I—" She took a jerky step back. "No. I—" She dampened her lips with her tongue and to his chagrin it was all he could do not to groan out loud. "*Ohmigod. I can't believe I just did that. That I let you…*" She made a strangled sound and retreated another step, nearly tripping over her forgotten handbag, which at some point she'd dropped on the ground.

He reached out to catch her and she wrenched away. "Don't," she said sharply, scooping the purse from the snowy slush and clutching it to her breasts like a shield. "I…I need to go."

The hell of it was, unless she was going to miraculously change her mind and get in the car, she was right.

Not that she appeared to require his permission. Turning on her heel, she fled toward her building, wrenched open the main door with its useless lock and disappeared out of sight inside, leaving him alone in the night.

He waited until the lights in her unit went on, standing his ground as the small group of teenagers finally sauntered by, jostling and talking trash to each other, yet giving him a wide berth. Intuitively they seemed to know it would be an extremely bad idea to tangle with him.

Not until the boys rounded the corner and the street was quiet once again did he turn and start for his car. He was almost to the curb when something on the ground caught his eye.

Bending down, he saw it was the money Mallory had tossed at him. He picked it up and straightened. Smoothing the bills out, he saw that in her anger she'd only managed to hurl about half of the cash he'd returned to her back at him.

He supposed he ought to be glad she hadn't tossed the whole damn purse at him.

The errant thought brought a faint smile to his mouth. It grew nominally wider as he considered the implication of the dazed look that had been on her face when he'd had to set her away from him. No matter what she might say in the future, she wanted him.

And he wanted her. Not for forever, he thought as he folded the cash and slipped it into his breast pocket. Forever was a very long time, and at this stage in his life, after devoting most of the past twenty years to his brothers' welfare, he didn't see himself signing on for more than right now with anyone.

But that didn't mean he was just going to walk away from what he wanted, either.

Five

"Now let me see…" An insincere smile on her flawlessly made-up face, Nikki Victor-Volpe looked away from Mallory to contemplate her immaculately manicured fingertips. "You worked on Bedazzled in some capacity for how long…?"

"Nine years," Mallory replied steadily, even though she knew perfectly well that Nikki already knew the answer. Both of them had volunteered to work on the event during their junior year at the exclusive private prep school they'd both attended, where a public service stint was a graduation requirement.

But even if Nikki had suffered a temporary brain lapse—not, Mallory supposed, completely out of the realm of possibility considering the amount of empty space in the blonde's expensively coiffed head—the information was also in the extensive application she'd had Mallory fill out.

The one visible in the opened folder on Nikki's lap.

Mallory reminded herself that being made to jump through Nikki's little hoops didn't matter, not compared to how much she wanted this job. The Bedazzled Ball was the most prestigious of Denver's charity events, a mammoth black-tie affair that raised a huge amount of money each year for a worthy local cause.

While most of the work was done by volunteers, the job of event coordinator was a paid position. And though the coordinator put in mostly part-time hours up until the months directly preceding the event, the job came with a prorated salary since it was normally filled after the previous year's ball.

Now, with only six weeks to go until the big night, the position had suddenly become available. While that was unusual in itself, the fact that someone on the steering committee had thought of Mallory as a potential replacement and had instructed Nikki, the committee secretary, to call and ask if she'd be interested, was a miracle.

One she intended to try her best to capitalize on. That's why she'd spent hours at the library yesterday reading everything she could about the charity. It was the reason she'd changed clothes six times this morning before settling on exactly the right outfit and shown up at Bedazzled's downtown offices for her interview forty minutes early.

Because not only did she really, really want this job, she *needed* it. For the obvious reason—she was desperate for gainful employment—but also because it would give her some much-needed experience to add to her résumé, a chance to do work that was actually meaningful, and a shot, however slim, at landing a similar, hopefully longer-term position in the future.

It was just an added bonus that it might also help her forget the blinding speed with which she'd turned into a sex-crazed nymphomaniac at the first touch of Gabriel's lips.

His hot, hard, drugging, lay-me-down-and-do-me lips.

Oh, God. Heat twisted through her despite the chilly temperature of the conference room where she and Nikki sat. Without even closing her eyes she could recall the weight of his hand in her hair, the warm roughness of his palm sliding over her throat, the heady taste of his tongue moving against her own. And the singular sensation of the dense, steely muscles in his chest and abdomen flexing against her front as he'd lifted her up, pressing her against his—

No, no, no. She absolutely wasn't going there. Not here, not now, not again. It was bad enough that she seemed to be incapable of purging her mind of those thigh-clenching memories. But what did it say about her character that the episode could intrude into her thoughts at such a crucial time?

Maybe that you were right all those years to fear your attraction to him? Because now you know what before you only suspected—that one touch, one taste, one embrace won't ever be enough?

No. Absolutely not. Unconsciously sitting up a little straighter, Mallory did her best to dismiss that last idea. If she was hung up on what had happened, it was simply because he'd caught her at a vulnerable moment. Exhausted by another long day, punch-drunk from having eaten her weight in carbohydrates, she'd been feeling relaxed, a little sleepy, almost…happy. And then with a few offhand sentences he'd reduced her to some sort of obligation, demolishing her already mangled pride.

Big surprise that she'd gotten mad. Or that when he'd grabbed her the way he had, all the emotion she'd been holding in the past few months, the fear, frustration, disappointment and loneliness, had simply bubbled up, turned into a soupy sea of lust and swept her away.

Yes, it was beyond mortifying that he'd been the one to put an end to the kiss—and that to do it he'd had to practically peel her off his front.

But so what? She'd endured worse. Hadn't her mother walked out when Mallory was nine to make a new life with a man who didn't want kids? And then there was her darling father, who'd done what he had without a thought to her happiness, much less any concern about what would happen to her when he left.

But that's not Gabe. He does care. That's why he came looking for you, has tried to make your apartment

*safer, keeps offering to help you out. Isn't a large part
of the reason you can't let this go because it rankles
that what he seems to care about most is doing the right
thing, not you specifically? And that, far more impor-
tantly, there's a part of you that still wants to take the
easy path, to lean on him and let his broad shoulders
carry some of your responsibilities?*

Maybe, she answered reluctantly, unwilling to
concede there was any truth to what she was thinking,
but at the same time unable to dismiss it out of hand.

Yet just the possibility that on some level she wanted
to let Gabriel take care of her was alarming. And yet
another reason she needed him to keep his distance—
which she'd done her best to insure in the note she'd
sent him along with the rest of his cash.

And if they did cross paths? She intended to treat
him the way she once had—as a distantly amusing acquaintance, nothing more. No matter what he said or
did, she intended to smile, make polite conversation and
go her own way, her dignity, her virtue, her heart intact.

The reminder steadied her. Suddenly feeling back in
control, she refocused her attention on the interview
where it belonged. "I worked on the ball for nine years,"
she said to her former classmate. "Starting in high school."

"Oh, yes, that's right." Nikki nodded as if it was
news to her.

"At one time or another, I've headed all of the major
committees. Entertainment, venue, refreshments, publicity. I think that gives me a good overview of what
needs to be done, when and by whom."

"I suppose it does." The other woman tapped her right index finger against her cheek. "We did make some changes last year, however. I don't believe you were here then, were you?"

"No, I wasn't."

"Didn't you resign from your committee?"

"Yes." Although it wasn't easy, Mallory kept her voice even. "I did." This time last year the first rumors of trouble had started to swirl around her father. Certain that it was all just a mistake, and shocked by how quickly people she'd known her whole life had been to believe the worst, she'd decided to take a break from Denver until he got things straightened out.

Which of course, he never had.

She lifted her chin the merest fraction. "But I've always been a quick study, and I assume that everything I'd need to know is in your former planner's files. And that if I missed anything—" she forced herself to smile "—you or someone else who worked on the event last year would be happy to set me straight."

Nikki sniffed. "You're certainly right about that."

All right, so the conversation didn't exactly seem to be going great. Mallory told herself not to panic. There was still a chance she could turn things around.

Swallowing her pride, she leaned forward. "If you'll just give me an opportunity to show what I can do," she said earnestly, "I promise you won't be sorry, Nikki. I'll work harder than anyone else you might be considering."

The blonde pursed her lips, then suddenly gave the

exasperated sigh of someone forced to perform a truly oppressive task. "I guess you should know that April, the former coordinator, didn't just leave. She was fired."

"Oh." It was a startling piece of news simply because, as far as Mallory knew, it was the only time in the charity event's fifty-five-year history that it had happened.

"'Oh' is right. When she started, we all thought we were so lucky because she seemed so efficient and organized and she kept agreeing to take on tasks that have always been handled by the volunteers. But as we recently discovered, she was in way over her head right from the start, and when things started to pile up, she just set them aside and pretended they didn't exist."

"What sort of things?"

For the first time in the interview Nikki actually looked a little uncomfortable. "Well…there happen to be lots of little items. Deposits and payments that were never sent to various suppliers, an incomplete list of this year's sponsors, and it seems none of the programs or merchant flyers have been put together, much less sent to the printers. Then there's also the fact that at present we don't have anyone contracted to provide the music for the big night."

Mallory considered. While it sounded as if it would be a huge amount of work to get everything back on track, so far none of the obstacles seemed insurmountable.

"There's also a problem with the venue for the fashion show."

"What's that?"

Nikki shrugged. "We don't have one."

Mallory stared at her in disbelief. "But it's always held at the Botanic Gardens."

"Not anymore. Apparently they changed their policy years ago about allowing outside fund-raisers, but we were an exception because Mrs. Wentworth sat on both boards. When her health forced her to step down last year, that changed. Only April didn't bother to mention it."

For once, Nikki was absolutely right, Mallory decided. It was a huge problem since most of the sites that could accommodate such an event—and all of the best ones—would already be booked by other organizations.

Still, if she put her mind to it, she was sure she could come up with a solution. And when she did, it would surely improve her odds of landing a more permanent position in the future.

She took a breath and sat up a little straighter. "I realize it won't be easy," she told Nikki, "but I'm sure I can handle it."

"I take it that means if the job were offered to you, you'd take it?"

"Yes." Mallory sat back and prayed. "Yes, I would."

"Oh, all right then." Nikki shut the file with a snap.

Mallory stared at her in surprise. "Does that mean…I'm hired?"

"I suppose so." The blonde smiled humorlessly at her. "Since the board already agreed the job was yours if you wanted it."

"They did?" She tried to take it in, too stunned to even be mad about Nikki's apparently needless inquisition.

"Yes. Although I'm sure it's only because they've been unable to find anyone else on such short notice. All the really qualified people are working on other projects."

"Right." She'd gotten the job. *She* was Bedazzled's new event coordinator. Between this and cousin Ivan's behest, she could finally start to look toward the future instead of expending all of her energy on just trying to survive.

It was all she could do not to leap up, grab Nikki and dance around the room. Probably not a great idea in light of the other woman's hostility.

"So." Nikki gave an exasperated little huff. "How soon can you start?"

Mallory didn't hesitate. The quicker she got to work, the harder it would be for them to change their mind. "Right now if you'd like."

"I suppose that would be for the best. Since April left, nobody seems to have a clue what anyone else is doing. Of course, you'll have to fill out some paperwork first." She reached out, reopened the file, riffled through it and extracted a handful of papers. She thrust them at Mallory. "Here. It's the standard stuff, W-2, medical and emergency forms. I assume you don't need any help?"

"I think I can manage."

"I'll leave you to it, then." Tossing back her hair, she stood. "When you're done, come and find me and I'll show you your office, get you some keys and a current copy of the event schedule. As you'll see, there are a lot of things on the calendar, starting with a party this weekend out at the O'Keefe's in Lone Tree."

"Thanks." She felt a brief pang about the logistics of getting out to the exclusive neighborhood, then decided she'd worry later. For now she intended to enjoy the moment.

Nikki shrugged. "It's not like it's my choice, Mallory. I'm just doing what I was asked to. If it were up to me, no matter how much we need to fill this position, you wouldn't have been considered, much less chosen. And I'm sure once other people find out you've been hired, they'll feel the same way. Your father cheated a lot of people, and I'm not the only one who hasn't forgotten."

"I'll keep that in mind," Mallory murmured.

"You do that," Nikki said coolly as she sashayed out the door.

Mallory stared after her for a moment, then looked away, giving herself a mental shake. Compared to everything else she'd been through, Nikki's attitude qualified as a minor bump in the road, she told herself firmly. Sure, the injustice of being blamed for dear old dad's misdeeds rankled, and the thought of being thrust back into her social circle in the guise of paid employee was more than a little daunting, but she'd survive. The important thing was that she'd gotten the job.

The reminder brought on a fresh wave of exhilaration. Once more she had to conquer the urge to jump to her feet and twirl around like some giddy little teenager. Still, it was the kind of news that wouldn't feel completely real until she shared it with someone.

She had her purse open and was reaching for her cell phone when she realized that the only person who might actually understand her elation was Gabe.

She snatched back her hand. Good grief! Where had that come from? Because it most certainly wasn't true. And even if it was, he was the last person on earth she'd call since he'd no doubt take it as a sign that despite everything she'd said, she secretly wanted him in her life.

Which she didn't. She couldn't, she told herself firmly, as she picked up a pen and began filling out the first of the forms Nikki had left with her, ignoring the slight squeezing sensation around her heart.

For her own peace of mind, from here on out Mr. Killer Lips Steele had to be just another part of a past she might finally be starting to put behind her.

Gabriel knew by the slight tingle of awareness that slid down his spine the instant Mallory arrived at Saturday night's Bedazzled cocktail party.

Taking a sip of his wine, he finished listening to what the delicate blonde at his side was saying, then lifted his head. Aided by his height, he casually surveyed the crush in Melissa O'Keefe's enormous living room.

He wasn't surprised to see Mallory standing just inside the hall entrance. Tonight her streaky caramel-brown hair was piled on her head in an updo that drew attention to the slenderness of her neck, while her lissome curves were draped in a slim-fitting, silvery-pink sheath that was somehow both restrained and drop-dead sexy.

She looked good enough to eat.

An unfortunate train of thought, he realized, as his body reacted to the image that sprang to mind of her tousled, naked and stretched out for his delectation.

He glanced away. Taking another swallow of his wine, he returned his attention to his companion—and found her watching him with an arrested expression on her classically beautiful face. He raised an eyebrow. "What?"

"I wondered why you offered to be my date tonight," his sister-in-law, Lilah, said. "Now, I know."

He met her astute blue gaze with a steady one of his own. "And if I said I had no idea what you're talking about?"

She smiled. "I wouldn't believe you."

"No?"

She shook her head. "No." Gently rubbing a spot on her very pregnant stomach, she glanced pointedly back toward the doorway. "That *is* Mallory Morgan, isn't it?"

He followed her gaze and saw the subject of their conversation was now talking to two of the charity's founders and most influential board members, the white-haired DeMarco sisters, who also happened to be longtime Steele Security clients. "Yes, it is."

"I thought so. The two of us have been playing phone tag the past several days."

"How come?" Annalise, the older of the elderly

DeMarco sisters, smiled at something Mallory said, while Eleanor, the younger, had a more reserved, wait-and-see look on her face.

"It's a long story, but it boils down to my having volunteered to find a new site for the fashion show we always put on, and her being the new event coordinator. Which, by the way, has caused a small furor all on its own."

Gabe abruptly shifted his gaze back to her. "In what way?"

"Let's just say that several of my fellow volunteers have concerns about her being hired."

"Which are?"

Lilah gave a slight shrug. "Pretty much what you'd expect. Can she be trusted to do the job? Is she really qualified? Are they going to have to hide their purses when she's around?"

"You're kidding about that last one, right?"

"I wish I was. But unfortunately, rich people, like everyone else I suppose, tend to be pretty unforgiving when it comes to their money." She paused to take a sip of her sparkling water. "There's also a lot of speculation about just how she wound up with the job." She tilted her head a fraction and considered him. "Clearly someone with influence vouched for her, but nobody seems to know who."

Gabe shrugged. "Don't look at me. Like I said, I'm just here to enjoy the company of my favorite pregnant sister-in-law."

Something glinted in Lilah's big blue eyes, but

whatever it was she chose not to pursue it. "Don't give me that. We both know that you're really here because Dominic asked you to watch out for me while he's in London."

"Well, sure," he said, promptly stepping into the path of a passerby before the man could inadvertently jostle her. "And what's wrong with that?"

"Absolutely nothing. Except that if he doesn't stop worrying all the time, he'll be in the hospital before I am. And don't pretend you don't think his behavior is a little over-the-top," she went on before he could so much as part his lips to protest. "I talked to Cooper the other day, so I know you've all taken to calling him Dr. Demento behind his back."

Gabe might have smiled if not for the genuine concern he saw on her face. "He'll be fine, Li," he said quietly. "It's just that he's an action-oriented guy, and having a child involves a lot of waiting. Add in that he's wired by nature and training to protect you, yet he sees himself as responsible for you being in this situation in the first place, and I'm not surprised he's acting the way he is."

"Crazed?" she suggested drily.

"Exactly. This is just a suggestion, but you might want to consider trying, just for now, to be a little less self-sufficient." Never much of a drinker since he didn't like feeling even mildly impaired, Gabe exchanged his half-full wineglass for water as a waiter passed by bearing a tray. "Maybe if Dom had more to do, he wouldn't feel so out of control. At least that's the way it used to work when he was a kid. The busier he was, the less trouble he got in."

For a moment she just looked at him, then slowly she nodded. "You know, I hadn't thought of that. Not in that context, anyway. But you may be right. Maybe I've been trying so hard not to worry him, I've made him feel as though I don't need him. And nothing could be further from the truth." She smiled sweetly. "You're actually rather perceptive. For a man."

"Thanks." His own mouth curved up. "I think."

They enjoyed a moment of companionable silence, and then found themselves the center of attention as a changing parade of people came up to exclaim over Lilah's pregnancy, ask about Dom's absence, discuss the recent fluctuations in the weather, the upcoming ball, and even, on two occasions, speculate on whether the new coordinator was up to her job.

It was a good hour before they found themselves alone again, and had a moment to simply watch the crowd around them. Or at least, Lilah did. Gabe found his own gaze drawn unerringly back to Mallory.

She'd moved deeper into the room and was currently standing with an older couple, an interested look on her vividly pretty face at whatever they were saying.

And then, she suddenly turned and looked over at Gabe as if they were connected by some invisible tether, and for an instant it was as if they were the only two people in the world.

The moment didn't last, however, as almost immediately she stiffened. Lifting her chin, she deliberately turned her back on him.

"We went to the same high school, you know," Lilah volunteered quietly beside him. "Taylor Union. Mallory was a few years behind me, but even back then… She had quite a reputation."

He turned to look at her. "For what?"

"Wild behavior. I can't say I paid much attention, but I think I remember something about a midnight horse race that destroyed a fairway out at the Fairlawn Country Club. And I have a very clear memory of Gran and her friends talking during my first spring break from college about how disgraceful it was that Cal Morgan just let her do whatever she wanted. As I recall, she'd flown herself and a handful of friends to Rio for Carnivale. I'm not sure, but I don't think she could have been much more than sixteen."

Gabe tried to imagine it. But he just couldn't. It was about as far from his experience of scrambling to make ends meet and trying to keep the family together while they bounced from one military base to another, as Paris was from Fort Dix. "Sounds like an interesting childhood."

"Does it?" Lilah pursed her pretty lips thoughtfully. "I suppose, growing up the way you did, with so much responsibility, it might."

"But?"

"Oh, I don't know. I just think that's awfully young to have so much freedom and absolutely no rules or guidance." She paused, then sucked in her breath.

"Dear God in heaven," she said with a dismayed groan. "That sounded just like my grandmother."

"Nope," he said emphatically. "Not even close."

Her grateful look prompted them both to laugh.

Sobering, she touched her fingertips to his forearm. "I guess what I mean is… Doesn't it strike you as sort of sad that she didn't have anyone to place restrictions on her, if only for her safety? And make you wonder what kind of parent lets a girl that age go traipsing off to South America without any supervision?"

An egocentric bastard like Cal Morgan, he found himself thinking. But before he could say as much, Lilah suddenly grimaced and pressed a hand to the small of her back. "Uh-oh."

He tensed. "What?" All joking aside, he didn't want to think what Dom would do if anything happened to his wife.

"All the sparkling water I've had tonight just caught up with me," she said serenely, seemingly unaware that she'd just given him a momentary case of cardiac arrest. "If you'll excuse me?" Without waiting for an answer, she pressed her glass into his hand and took off in the direction of the powder room.

Filled with a combination of exasperation, relief and awe—he'd rather face a truckload of terrorists any day than be a pregnant woman—he watched as she made her way across the room and disappeared into the hall, her normally light, graceful walk transformed into something that was anything but by her altered center of gravity.

Then his gaze swung back toward Mallory, only to find that she was gone, too. A quick look around had him homing in on her slim back and taut fanny just as she disappeared out a set of French doors leading out to the terrace.

He was halfway across the room before he'd made a conscious decision to go after her. Keeping to the same brisk pace, he stepped out onto the flagstones of a wide, multilevel patio dotted with huge pots of bright flowers and a dozen wrought iron tables. In sharp contrast to the last time they'd been together, the night was balmy, ripe with the scents of freshly mown grass and incipient spring.

Nodding to several seated acquaintances, he went down the wide, shallow steps to join her at the railing where the patio overlooked the pool.

She turned to glance at him as he walked up and he saw her tense. Okay, it was hardly unexpected given the way they'd last parted, the terse little missive she'd sent him afterward, or the way she'd reacted inside when their gazes had met so briefly.

That was why apologizing was already part of his plan. He'd do whatever he had to do to get them back to the tentative truce they'd briefly enjoyed over dinner the night he'd kissed her.

Not that he expected her to make it easy, he admitted, as she deliberately turned her back to stare out at the pool.

"Well, surprise, surprise," she said. "If it isn't Denver's own Mr. Here, There and Everywhere One Wishes He Wasn't."

"It's nice to see you, too, sweetheart."

"Of course it is." There was the slightest pause, and then she glanced sideways at him. "It's hardly a secret that I'm irresistible." Holding his gaze, she idly began to wind a glossy tendril of hair around her finger.

An untrained observer might have missed the subtle shift in her manner. But not someone for whom the slightest change in a person's inflection could sometimes be the difference between life and death. Curious, he said mildly, "No argument from me there."

"Oh, dear." She turned more fully in his direction, and looked up at him through the dark fringe of her lashes. "How tragic for you. I do hope my fatal allure isn't the reason you're here tonight."

"And why's that?"

"Promise you won't be crushed?"

"I'll try to survive." Of everything he'd anticipated from her—the cold shoulder, outright anger, a flat refusal to acknowledge him at all—a reemergence of her old flirtatiousness hadn't even made the list. But then, as he really should've figured out by now, Mallory was rarely predictable.

But then, neither was he.

"Yes, well, the thing is," she sailed on, "as much as I cherish your unselfish devotion, I'm afraid I'm otherwise engaged this evening."

He raised an eyebrow. "Really?"

"Yes."

"Let me guess. Raoul?"

It took her a moment to get it. When she did, her

eyes narrowed for the merest instant. Almost immediately, however, she recovered. "Ah, yes, Raoul. How I wish I could say yes. But the truth is, the poor darling is still recovering from our latest incredibly athletic encounter. No, I happen to be here in an official capacity. You may not have heard, but I've been hired to take over as Bedazzled's event coordinator."

"As it happens, my sister-in-law did mention that earlier. Congratulations."

"Thanks." It was the perfect place for her to point out yet again that she could take care of herself. Yet true to form for tonight, she took a different tack. "Just who is your sister-in-law?"

"I believe you know her," he said casually. "Stunning blonde, impressively pregnant?"

She straightened. "Lilah Cantrell is your sister-in-law? Since when?"

He felt a stab of satisfaction as she confirmed his hunch that she'd been paying more attention to him tonight than she'd let on. "It's Lilah Cantrell Steele these days. She and Dom celebrated their first anniversary in February."

"Gosh, I guess I missed the wedding. Of course, a year ago… I would've been Down Under for the Sydney Regatta, cheering on those hunky Aussies. Such lovely blokes." She gave a fond little sigh, then cocked her head as if thinking. "No, wait. That was March. In February it would've been New York for fashion week."

She waved her hand dismissively. "In any event, it's

good to know someone was finding true love while I was off being useless and spending pots of money." She flashed a brilliant smile that didn't come close to reaching her eyes.

He reached out instinctively, touching his hand to her shoulder. "Mallory—"

"Oh, look," she said brightly, glancing up toward the house at the same time she moved just out of reach. "Isn't that Lilah now, heading this way? She must be looking for you. And I really must circulate."

"Actually," he interrupted, stepping over and blocking her path so she couldn't leave without dodging inelegantly around him, "I'm sure she's looking for both of us. She mentioned something about needing to talk to you about the fashion show, and I told her I'd find you and arrange it."

"And just how do you propose to do that?" she said, just as Lilah, whom he'd always considered to have impeccable timing, arrived to join them.

"I wondered where you'd disappeared to," his sister-in-law announced, a knowing gleam lighting her eyes in the instant that her gaze met his. "Not that I'm surprised," she went on, turning conspiratorially toward Mallory. "The Steele men simply can't seem to resist smart, beautiful women." She smiled, and her genuine friendliness was impossible to miss. "Hi. I'm Lilah. I'm sure we've been introduced before, but it's nice to finally get to say hello. Particularly after the way we've been missing each other on the phone."

Clearly surprised by the other woman's warmth, after a brief hesitation, Mallory smiled back. "Yes, it is."

"I was just about to suggest," Gabe jumped into the conversation, "that Mallory let us give her a ride home. That way you two will finally have a chance to discuss your business and she won't have to wait for a taxi." He shifted his gaze from Lilah to Mallory. "That is what you're planning, right?"

"Yes, but it's really no problem—"

"Don't be silly," his brother's beautiful wife interjected, her inherent kindness coming to the fore exactly as he'd counted on. "It'll take forever for a cab to get here, if you can get them to come out at all on a Saturday night. Besides—" she sliced him a look that let him know that while she was going along, she knew very well what he was up to "—I'd love a chance to visit. Frankly, there are times when even the nicest man can be a little tiresome."

"Great. It's settled then," Gabe said, judging it to be an excellent time to make himself momentarily scarce. "I'll go get the car while you two say your goodbyes, and meet you out front."

And with that he gave both women a gallant smile and headed inside.

Six

"So I guess you're not speaking to me," Gabe remarked into the silence that filled the SUV.

Staring out at the distant lights as they drove back toward the city after dropping Lilah off at her home in the Denver foothills, Mallory parted her lips to say *that's right*.

Then she caught herself.

No. She'd already been much more gracious than he deserved, chatting with Lilah about the fashion show debacle and exchanging ideas about what they might do about it, just as if she wasn't perfectly aware of how he'd maneuvered her into accepting this ride.

More to the point, it was clearly a trick question. Regardless of what she said, she'd be trapped into defending her answer. And once she did, she knew exactly what would happen.

He'd say something charming or aggravating or arrogant or insightful. What, it didn't matter. And she'd feel angry or enchanted or amused or alarmed, the particulars of which also wouldn't matter.

Because just like back at the party, the whole time they were talking her heart would be racing and her stomach jitter-bugging. Worse, she wouldn't be giving the conversation her complete attention because no matter how hard she tried to concentrate, part of her would be wondering whether a second kiss between them would be as explosive as the first.

Given that she'd already decided there wasn't going to be a second kiss, her continuing fixation on the subject was mystifying. Granted, his unexpected presence at tonight's event had taken her by surprise. And in retrospect, she could see that her decision to resume her old party girl persona with the hope of re-establishing a proper distance between them had been a miscalculation.

She simply should have ignored him. And if that hadn't worked, she should have behaved like the rational adult she was and pointed out that in light of her new job, she clearly didn't need his assistance.

But she hadn't. Instead, she'd gotten sucked into having a conversation with him and look where it had landed her. Once again they were alone in a car in the dark. Only unlike a week ago when she'd so foolishly lowered her defenses, this time around her awareness of him was on heightened alert. She found herself listening intently to his every breath, her pulse jumping each time he moved, her body humming with the effort of remaining aloof.

Even more confounding, there was a reckless part of her that had an alarming desire to slide across the seat, climb into his lap, bury her fingers in his hair and take another taste of that hot, chiseled mouth.

Forget mystifying. It was mortifying. And another excellent reason to remain silent, no matter what.

"Well, if you're not going to talk, I will," Gabe said out of the blue, as if he'd read her mind and decided it wouldn't do for her to think she was actually in control of the situation. "Because I want you to know that I'm sorry about what happened the last time we were together."

Pursing her lips, she forced herself not to react even though she suddenly felt as if he'd jabbed her with a knife. Sure, *she* regretted that kiss, but the idea that *he* might had never even occurred to her.

"Not for kissing you," he went on, just as if he really were clairvoyant. "But for letting you think that my interest in you isn't first and foremost about you as a person. That may not have been the case initially, but it is now, and it's important to me that you know it."

Well…damn. How exactly was she supposed to respond to that? Or, more to the point, how could she not? "I—that's…thank you."

The words seemed woefully inadequate the moment

she said them. Yet the truth—that he'd just slid past her guard and said the one thing she'd wanted to hear before she'd even known it herself—was far more than she was willing to reveal.

"I just thought you should know."

Once again, silence descended. Feeling totally inadequate, thinking there must be something more she could add, Mallory looked out the window, hoping for inspiration. And felt a niggle of surprise instead as she realized that at some point during their conversation they'd left the highway and were now winding through a sprawling community of large, modern homes set well back from the road.

"Where are we?" she asked.

"My place," he answered, turning into a wide, well-lit driveway leading up to a contemporary wood and stone house with, of all things, a basketball hoop attached to the three car garage.

One door of which had started to rise.

"What?" She swiveled to face him. "No. Absolutely not, Gabriel. I agreed to a ride, not a tour of your own personal Bat Cave. And if this is what your little declaration was really about, you trying to lull me into thinking you can be trusted—"

"Relax, Mal," he said, a steely note of temper edging into his voice. "I didn't bring you here for sex, if that's what you're thinking." Pulling into the garage's cavernous interior with the ease of long practice, he switched off the car engine and hit the button to lower the door behind them. "Not that I'd say no if you decided you were up for it." Beneath his attempt to smooth things over, something darker lurked in his voice that made her want to squeeze her knees together.

She crossed her arms instead.

"Look," he said, pushing open his door. "The *truth* is that I didn't plan to drive into town tonight, and I've got my brother Deke's dog for the weekend, all right? I need to let him out or he's going to start gnawing on the nearest table leg. So while I'd love for you to come in and see my place, I've got no interest in coercing you into doing anything you're not comfortable with."

"Good," she said intractably. "Then you won't care if I wait here."

One big shoulder hitched in a careless shrug. "Suit yourself. Like I said, I won't be long."

Face set, she watched out of the corner of her eye as he climbed out, yanking his tie loose as he walked with the long loose stride that even now had the power to make her stomach hollow. Reaching an interior door, he switched on an overhead fixture so she wouldn't be in the dark when the automatic lights winked out and disappeared inside.

Well, good! For once he'd done exactly what she wanted. Telling herself it was about time, she gave a huff of satisfaction and crossed her legs, deciding a moment later that she could afford to indulge her curiosity by taking a look around.

She wasn't surprised to see the silver sports car parked in the next space over. Whenever she'd thought about Gabe in the past, she'd pictured him with just such a vehicle, living in a stylish penthouse atop one of the city's higher skyscrapers. Or occupying one of the newer mansions in some upscale neighborhood like Cherry Creek or Country Club.

Yet the car was the only visible symbol of the contained, sophisticated loner she'd thought she knew. While the rest of the garage, she realized, appeared to belong to some athletic suburban soccer dad.

There was a trio of bikes and a pair of kayaks hanging from the rafters, along with enough other sporting equipment from snow skis to hockey skates to scuba tanks that he could stock his own store. There was a lawn mower, what she thought might be a snowblower, shovels, lawn furniture, a set of barbells, a workbench and a tall red tool chest. Everything was efficiently organized and looked to be well maintained.

Not to mention being more Martha Stewart than James Bond. And yet another glaring example of him not being the man she'd thought he was.

But then, she'd never been the person she'd pretended to be, either.

That's right. You've gone from shallow but daring to hiding out in a parked car because you're afraid you might be feeling something real for a change.

The thought had her rearing back against the seat as if she'd been struck. She wanted in the worst way to deny it, but the longer she sat there, in the looming quiet, alone due to her self-imposed isolation, the more she could see it was true. And that being able to take care of herself financially wouldn't mean a thing if she kept following her old pattern of running away any time she felt the slightest connection to another person.

Taking a deep breath, she got out of the car. Then before she could lose her nerve, she walked over to the door and let herself into the house.

A quick look around showed she was in what appeared to be a combination mudroom and pantry, with high ceilings, a checkerboard floor and gleaming cherrywood cabinets.

Listening, she heard the low murmur of Gabe's voice. She followed the sound, walking into a spacious kitchen with stainless steel appliances, more of the same glossy cabinets, a vast expanse of black granite countertops and a big island with half a dozen large, padded bar stools lined up along one side like buttons on a shirt.

Continuing on, she entered the adjoining family room, which boasted a huge fireplace and a burgundy leather sectional anchored by a stunningly beautiful Oriental rug. Stopping briefly to listen, she gave a faint start as a shaggy canine shape suddenly bounded by on the other side of the sliding-glass doors. Then she followed her ears down a wainscoted hallway and was rewarded by the sight of Gabe in what was clearly his den.

As she'd already surmised, he was on the phone, standing with one hip planted against a mahogany desk the size of a small country. What she hadn't imagined was that he would've shed his jacket and tie, unbuttoned his collar and shoved up his shirtsleeves.

Her mouth foolishly went dry at the sight of his

exposed forearms, which were lightly dusted with black hair and corded with muscle.

"That's great, Jake." His eyebrows knit in a slight, surprised V as he caught sight of her in the wide doorway. "What?" He held up a finger to indicate he'd only be a minute. "Yeah, I'll be sure to tell Cooper. And yeah—" he chuckled "—you're right that he's not going to like it."

The soft sound of his laughter tickled her nerve endings like the lash of a velvet whip, raising goose bumps on her flesh.

It made her wonder what would happen when he finally put his hands on her. Because he would, she realized with sudden insight. Something fundamental had changed between them the day of their encounter at Annabelle's, and as she'd learned at the party tonight, there was no going back, no putting the genie back in the bottle.

Unless something unforseen happened—say a meteor streaked out of the sky and crashed down on one of them—it was only a matter of time before their attraction led to its logical conclusion.

So why wait? Why not put an end to this sexual limbo?

She had to admit there was an undeniable allure in the thought of taking charge, doing the unexpected, making Gabriel feel off balance for a change. Plus it was only sex, which in her experience was overrated and overhyped. They'd come together, do the horizontal tango and then—

What? For a moment she was perplexed to realize she didn't know. And then it occurred to her that was actually the whole point. Once they got the sex out of the way, then they'd see.

Her decision made, she lifted her hands and, one by one, began to pull the pins from her hair, dropping them deliberately onto the carpeted floor. When the last one was out, she combed her fingers through the curly mass, gave her head a gentle shake, and sent the liberated locks tumbling down.

Eight feet away, Gabe suddenly straightened.

She reached back, holding his gaze with her own as she unzipped her dress and slowly pushed it off her shoulders. Wiggling her hips sent it sliding down her body. Naked except for her lavender-colored push-up bra, matching thong and Jimmy Choos with their stiletto heels and peekaboo toes, she stepped clear of the pool of fabric at her feet, raised an eyebrow—and waited.

"Listen, Jake," Gabe said abruptly, "something's come up. I'll call you back tomorrow." Without taking his eyes off of her or waiting for his caller's response, he hung up.

The sound of him dropping the handset into its base seemed very loud in the sudden silence. Yet he didn't say a word, just took his own sweet time looking her over before finally leveling his gaze at her face. "What the hell, Mallory?" His voice was extremely quiet, his eyes intensely green.

She gave a slight shrug. "I thought about what you said."

"Regarding…?"

"Us. Having sex. And I decided yes. I'm up for it. The question is—" she gave him a look from beneath half-lowered lashes "—are you?"

Pushing away from the desk, he padded toward her. "You really need to ask?"

With a thrill of anticipation, she saw that despite his measured step, there was a dull flush beneath the olive-toned skin stretched over his killer cheekbones. She braced, expecting him to do what any other red-blooded male would—push her up against the nearest wall and pick up where they'd left off on that snowy sidewalk a week and a half ago.

Yet she should have known he wasn't prone to acting without thinking. Coming to a halt when a good foot still separated them, he reached out to cup her face, his palm cradling her jaw while his thumb came to rest against her chin. "First—" his shrewd gaze probed her own "—I think you better tell me what brought this on."

"Excuse me?"

Those expressive eyebrows rose. "Ten minutes ago you'd barely talk to me except to say you weren't setting foot in my house. An hour before that I had to practically twist your arm so you'd agree to let me drive you home. But now it seems you're hot to get it on with me. So the real question is—" he tapped the pad of his thumb against her bottom lip "—what's changed, Mallory?"

She gave him her coolest smile, "Didn't anyone ever tell you it's a girl's prerogative to change her mind?"

He just looked at her.

"Oh, all right," she said. "I got to thinking about it and realized this thing between us has been going on for a long time and I thought maybe we'd both feel better if we just went ahead and got it out of the way. Of course, that was back in the last century when I was still deluded enough to think that my stripping naked would be enough to turn you on—"

Thrusting both hands into her hair, he cut her off in midtirade by kissing her.

Except…*kiss* was too tame a word to describe what he was doing with those warm, skilled, sculpted lips. It was a claiming, Mallory thought hazily as his mouth slanted over hers. A possession. Or maybe an instant, overpowering addiction. Reaching up, she curled her fingers into his shirtfront to anchor him in place and parted her lips to accommodate his.

His response was immediate. His tongue breached her mouth, strafing her teeth and the inside of her cheeks, a hot, slick invasion that made her moan. Cupping her shoulders, he reeled her in even closer. His palms kneaded her flesh, while his fingertips skated up and down the outer ridges of her shoulder blades, making her arch like a cat being stroked. The heat from his solid, cotton-covered chest felt delicious against her breasts.

And then, to her shock, he lifted his head and eased back a fraction, dislodging her hands. "What's wrong?" she demanded, struggling to catch her breath.

He gave a slight, husky laugh and she felt her nipples tighten in reaction. "Nothing. Absolutely nothing. Only…why the hurry?" He took a full step back and it was all she could do not to pursue him. "Like you said, this has been a long time coming. We've got the whole night. I want it to be one to remember."

A faint sensation of alarm rippled through her. What she'd envisioned between them when she'd set this in motion had been something down and dirty, hard and fast, a quick union meant to scratch an itch, nothing more. While what he was proposing….

She dampened suddenly dry lips as he circled around behind her. "What…what are you doing?"

She heard a rustle of fabric as his clothes hit the floor, then nothing but the thump of her heart as he bent his head and grazed the ball of her shoulder with his lips.

"What do you think?" Maddeningly refraining from touching her anywhere else, he unhurriedly began to lay a trail of kisses until his mouth found the curve where her shoulder joined her neck.

"But I didn't expect—" She couldn't seem to stop her head from lolling back as he nipped at the tender spot, then soothed the tiny hurt with his tongue. "That is, I thought…" She'd thought they'd go up in flames so fast he'd never find out she wasn't nearly as skillful at this as he was. Except now…with his mouth…doing that…she couldn't seem to think why it should matter.

His hand found her hip. Big and shockingly warm, it slid across her stomach. "What did you think, Mal? That all I'd want is to throw you down and take you right here, right now? Trust me, we'll get to that." His thumb settled gently against the indentation of her navel, drew a lazy circle. "Just…not…yet."

Spreading his fingers, he pressed her back against the solid wall of his body. She bit her lip to suppress a moan as the crinkly hair on his thighs pressed against her bare bottom.

"You've got the most beautiful skin," he murmured into her hair, reaching to cup her lace-covered breast in his palm. "Soft. So damn soft. It used to make me crazy when we'd run into each other at some party and you'd be so close, yet so far out of reach. The whole time we'd be talking I'd think about what it would be like to lay you down, peel off your gown, run my hands all over you."

Heat, liquid and silky, bloomed deep between her thighs. She squirmed, then squirmed some more as he nuzzled the tender, silken seam where her neck met her ear.

"I…I wondered, too." Was that breathless, husky voice really hers? "About us. But I never imagined—"

She broke off as he slowly rubbed his fingertip over her lace-covered nipple and sensation rushed through her, pooling deliciously at her tight, aching center.

She shivered even as a part of her protested it wasn't enough. She wanted to feel his hands on her, experience the touch of those hard palms and slightly calloused fingertips on every inch of her skin.

Her bare, overheated, aching-for-his-touch skin.

"What?" He slid the damp heat of his mouth up to press a kiss to the corner of her lips. "What didn't you imagine?"

She took a long, shuddery breath. "That being with you would make me feel…like this."

Like so much else in her life, in the past her displays of sexual desire had been mostly a pretense, an act she'd put on because it was expected.

But not this time. Not with him. She wanted, she needed, she *ached*, and all with a fervor that was demolishing the very foundation of the walls she'd once depended on to protect herself.

She didn't care. What mattered was the heat from his body blazing against her own, the magic of his mouth at her throat, this unfamiliar craving…for Gabriel. Squeezing her eyes shut, she reached down and managed to release the fastener of her bra. Then she held her breath as he pushed the lacy cups out of his way, covering the soft mounds in his hands as her breasts sprang free.

She moaned at the sheer pleasure of his touch. Then moaned again as he began to shape her sensitive nipples with his thumbs and forefingers. Time dissolved as the stiff little points grew even harder and longer, her need for him stronger.

Desperation started to consume her. She rotated her hips in a mindless attempt to alleviate the ache deep at her core, and felt a thrill of anticipation as she registered the hot, heavy weight of his erection nudging against her. She heard his breath hitch, and she executed another little bump and grind, pouring gasoline on the fire with an instinct she never dreamed she possessed.

"Please," she entreated. "This is… Oh, Gabe, it isn't enough." Turning her head, she pressed hot kisses to the corner of his eye, the top of his cheekbone, the curve of his ear. "I want more. I want you."

"Dammit, Mallory." He no longer sounded the least bit amused. "You're not playing fair."

"Don't you get it?" To her chagrin, her voice trembled the slightest bit. "I'm not playing at all."

He swore. Yet even as his heartfelt profanity sliced through the air, he was whirling her around and sweeping her into his arms.

"What're you doing?" she exclaimed, twining her arms around his neck as he began carrying her down the hallway.

"I want to see you in my bed. God knows, I've pictured you there often enough." Slowing, he bent his head and slanted his mouth over hers in a kiss that was all teeth, tongue and carnal intent.

By the time he straightened, she was dizzy with desire. Burying her face in his throat, she held on tight as he bounded up the wide, curving staircase that punched upward to a second-story gallery.

Not the least out of breath, he crossed a small landing and strode into what was obviously the master suite. As he flipped on a lamp with a thrust of his elbow at the wall switch, she had a quick impression of high ceilings, a stone fireplace and a wide bed covered with a dark glossy spread.

Then he set her on her feet and her surroundings ceased to matter. Her attention was all on his starkly masculine face, with the obvious hunger stamped on his hard mouth and the heat glittering in his heavy-lidded eyes.

And oh, that body. He was all rangy lines and solid muscle, with wide, olive-bronze shoulders, powerfully curved arms and small, flat nipples set in the slope of rock-hard pectoral muscles. Then there was a ripple of washboard abs covered by more taut, golden skin and a shallow dimple of a navel dotting the slash of silky hair that disappeared like an inverted exclamation mark into his briefs.

Briefs that appeared to be strained to the limit by the heavy jut of his cotton-covered sex.

The room suddenly seemed far too hot. And to be lacking something essential. Like air.

"Mallory."

The sound of his voice jerked her gaze to his face. "What?" She took a deep, desperately needed breath.

His eyes, so hot only seconds earlier, were now hooded, his mouth grim. "If you're thinking of calling this off, do it now."

Shocked, she realized he meant it. That despite everything they'd already shared, and the indisputable proof that he was more than ready to finish what she'd started, he'd stop right now and let her walk away if that's what she wished.

Except there was nothing in the world she desired less. Not with this craving for him hazing her brain, this persistent ache deep inside that she was trusting him to alleviate. "Are you crazy?" Tossing back her hair, she drew herself up, trying hard to ignore the fact that she was clad in nothing but her panties and high heels. "I told you what I want. But if *you'd* rather pass, I'll just go gather up my dress and—"

The proud little lift of her chin demolished one more wall in the crumbling fortress of Gabe's control. "The hell you will," he gritted out, taking half a second to peel down his briefs before lifting her off her feet and tumbling her onto the mattress.

This wasn't how it was supposed to happen, he thought a little wildly as he followed her down to feast on the soft, yielding sweetness of her mouth. He shouldn't be so overwhelmed by this driving desire to claim her. Or be burning up with the fevered need to watch her face when he buried himself deep, deep inside her. Not when his plan had been to take it slow, to see to her satisfaction at least once, maybe twice, before even thinking about his own.

Only that wasn't going to happen. She was making him so hot and crazy that if he didn't find a way to reel it back in soon he was afraid he was going to disappoint them both.

Making space for himself between her thighs, he slid down to kiss her throat, the smooth line of her collarbone, the valley between her breasts. Shaping one lush globe in his hand, he paid homage to the soft undercurve, the plump top swell, holding off as long as he could before he finally zeroed in on her thrusting nipples.

"God, you're pretty. All over, but especially here. Your breasts are the perfect size for my hands. While these—" he lashed one stiff, erect tip with the end of his tongue while gently rolling the other between his fingertips "—are the perfect shape for my mouth."

"Gabriel!" Digging her hands into the bedspread, she held on as if her life depended on it as he finally settled his lips over her and sucked.

Lord, she was sweet. Sweet and chock-full of surprises, not at all the woman he'd always thought she was. The nymph, the siren, the worldly sophisticate—it was pretty clear it had all been an act. While this Mallory, his Mallory, had an unexpected vulnerability that satisfied a need in him he hadn't known he possessed.

By the time he raised his head, they were both gasping for air. Pushing up on one arm, he allowed himself a second to look at her, the finely modeled cheekbones, the delicate chin, those breasts, full and round, the rosy nipples wet from his mouth. Then he started to reach for her panties, only to freeze as her lashes fluttered up and her hand gripped his arm.

"Wait." Wetting her lips, she fought for breath. "Let me—I want…" Abandoning speech with a frustrated huff, she simply let go of his arm and let her fingers roam over his chest to explore the tight bead of his nipple, the corded sinew and muscle that ridged his torso. Then her seeking fingertips skated along his hip bone, dipped into his navel.

Brushed slowly against his iron-hard erection.

He jerked, gritting his teeth as that light, uncertain touch alone pushed him closer to the edge. "Mallory—"

Ignoring his strangled warning, she took a deep

breath and closed her hand around him, measuring him with the grip of her palm for the barest instant before her gaze flashed up to meet his. "Wow," she said breathlessly, before once more dampening her lips. "Now, Gabriel. Now, please."

The stark request propelled him right over the edge he'd been dancing on from the second he'd watched her hair come down. Rearing up on his knees, he slid the thong off her body, then wrestled a condom out of the nightstand, swearing at the tremor in his hands as he suited up.

The next second he was settling back into the notch of her thighs, smoothing a hand over her warm, wet center. Finding her slick and ready, he shifted his weight forward, fighting not to just plunge himself inside her as the tightness of her body slowly gave way to his first blunt probing.

His hands clenched against the mattress at the slick, hot squeezing sensation of her body gloving his. "Okay?" he gritted out.

"Oh, yes."

"Good." Pushing deeper and deeper, he lowered his head to kiss the underside of her jaw, the point of her chin, the sweetness of her lips.

Her hands came around him, stroking his sides, his back, flexing against the base of his spine. "Except…"

"What?"

Moaning softly, she shifted restlessly beneath him, her teeth strafing his bottom lip. "I need…I want…"

"What, sweetheart?"

"I want you." Digging her fingernails into his butt, she pushed against him, arching and rocking… "Deeper."

His shoulders bunching, he drove forward. Pulling back, he waited a beat and repeated that hammering stroke, only to freeze for a moment as she made a frantic sound and her hips slammed up.

Her whole body tightened. Then the silky tightness of her sex squeezed around him, gripping his length as she cried his name and to his shock his own climax came roaring up, tearing a harsh sound of disbelief from his throat as it slammed into him without warning.

Pumping his hips, he poured himself into her, his whole body clenching when she gave a second startled cry and came again.

Spent and unaccountably shaken, every muscle in his body went lax. He collapsed against her, driving her into the mattress, where they lay shivering together, fused from cheek to thigh.

When he could finally dredge up the strength, he carefully rolled them onto their sides, not yet ready to give up his place inside her. He let his mind drift for a while, forcing himself not to think but to simply enjoy his own unfamiliar lassitude, the faint scent of Mallory's shampoo, the sluggish return of his muscle control.

Eventually, he opened his eyes. Studying the striking face across from his own, he was struck by how much she'd revealed to him tonight. And how much he had left to learn.

"Gabriel?" she murmured, her voice still raspy with pleasure. "Are you awake?"

He smoothed an errant tendril of hair behind her ear with his finger, one of the few parts of his body that still seemed to be fully functional. "Sure."

She forced her lashes up, although it clearly took an effort. "Can you move? More than your finger?"

"Absolutely." If he wanted to. Which at the moment, he didn't.

"Do you think—would you mind—could you get these darned shoes off my feet? I can't believe I just made love with them on."

Then again… Pushing up on one elbow, he let his gaze take a leisurely stroll down her lithe, slender body to the only thing she still wore, her black-and-pink stiletto heels.

She had more dips and swells than a carnival ride, and like a teenager viewing that first swift drop off the highest point of a roller coaster, the longer he looked, the more his exhaustion faded, replaced by a jolt of pure anticipation.

The effect on his body was immediate and impossible to hide, and made Mallory's eyes suddenly go wide.

"If you insist," he murmured as he moved down to the foot of the bed, slid her shoes from her feet, then reverently placed them on the floor. "Although personally, sweetheart, I think we ought to get these babies bronzed." Wrapping his fingers around her ankles, he eased them over his shoulders.

Then pressing a kiss to the inside of her knee, he took the first step leading them toward the long, thrilling drop he had planned.

Seven

Mallory surfaced slowly.

Stretching languorously on whisper-soft sheets, she gave a sigh of pleasure at the firm resilience of the mattress beneath her and the perfect weight of the silk blanket enveloping her. Just for a moment, she thought she must be back in her own plush bed in the airy bedroom of the house where she'd grown up.

Until she stretched again and the muscles in her thighs protested. Waking more fully, she went stock-still as she registered the unfamiliar tenderness at her core and the events of last night filled her head.

And knew without a single doubt that she was in Gabriel's house, in Gabriel's room. In Gabriel's bed.

Her eyes snapped open. Taking one hurried look around she realized three things.

It was morning.

She was alone.

And she didn't regret one moment of what they'd done last night. Whatever you wanted to call it—and having sex seemed far too bloodless a term to describe the power, the passion, the tenderness she and Gabe had shared—it had opened her eyes to a world she'd never known existed.

Not once in her twenty-eight years had she suspected that she could feel such need, much less inspire it. And that with the right person nothing that brought them pleasure would feel wrong or embarrassing or awkward. Or that afterward she'd feel complete rather than diminished the way she always had before.

It clearly called for a complete overhaul of her naive assumption that one time with Gabe would be enough. Because now that she knew what was possible, she wanted…more.

Much more.

Yet as she stared up at the coffered ceiling overhead, she realized she wasn't sure how that would work, since she'd never had an actual, full-blown affair before.

Although, really… How hard could it be?

The thought brought a foolish little smile to her face. And even that was all right, she decided as she sat up. After all, it was beyond ridiculous to get embarrassed over a mental image when you'd cherished every last moment…and inch…of the reality.

Combing her hair back with her fingers, she tucked the sheet beneath her arms and leaned back against the headboard, looking around with interest.

In the dawn light limning the edges of the large shaded windows, she saw that the bedspread was a rich dark green, not black as she'd thought the night before. The rest of the room also reflected Gabe's taste, from a burnished walnut antique armoire dominating one wall to a large black on white painting above the fireplace, its stark, curving lines proving on closer examination to be the barest outline of a voluptuous nude.

An oversize chair was positioned to one side of the fireplace, a paperback book opened spine up on the table beside it. Her dress and underthings were draped across the matching ottoman, her shoes placed neatly beside it.

The dog, whose name it turned out was Moose, and whose acquaintance she'd made when Gabe had finally remembered to go down and let the animal in last night, was nowhere to be seen.

There was a black nylon carry-on bag parked by the door.

She was considering the implication of the latter when steps sounded on the stairs. Then Gabriel strode in, fully dressed, a cup of coffee in his hand.

His gaze immediately homed in on her. "Good. You're awake." Striding over, he set the cup on the nightstand beside her and sat, the mattress dipping under his weight.

Feeling just the slightest bit self-conscious in light

of the disparity in their attire, she automatically tilted up her chin. "You look nice."

His gaze skimmed her face, her bare throat, the shadow of cleavage showing above the sheet. His green eyes darkened. "So do you." Leaning forward, he anchored his fingers in her hair and claimed her mouth.

God, but the man could kiss, she thought, as his hard lips slanted softly over hers, inciting a riot of feelings. Forgetting to hold on to the sheet, forgetting about everything but him and the sensations he made her feel, she parted her lips and drank him in, a now-familiar tangle of desire starting to twist through her.

Then almost before it started, it was over and he was pulling away. Still cradling her face, he rubbed the pad of his thumb over her lips before finally dropping his hand. "The coffee's for you."

"Thanks." She made no move to take it, just pulled the sheet back up and waited. Even Moose the dog, who hadn't impressed her as being the smartest mutt on the block, would've figured out by now that something was up.

"Look, I hate like hell to do this, but a situation's come up and I have to go out of town."

Well, of course. That explained the bag. As well as the air of edgy energy that surrounded him and the leashed tension he was doing his best to hide. He wasn't on the verge of telling her "it's been nice, now don't let the door hit you in the fanny on your way out." He had business.

Suddenly able to breathe again, she loosened her grip on the sheet. "Where are you going?"

"Belgrade, to meet my brother Dominic. And I'm afraid I have to take off for the airport soon if I'm going to make my flight."

"Oh." She sat up a little straighter. "In that case, you'd better move so I can get dressed—"

He didn't budge. "There's no reason to rush. As a matter of fact—" reaching into his pant's pocket, he extracted a silver ring with a pair of keys on it, along with what looked to be a business card, dropping them next to the coffee mug "—you're more than welcome to stay."

"Excuse me?"

"Between the fridge and the freezer there's plenty to eat, the Jag's got a full tank of gas, and I'll leave my gas card for you in case you need a refill. The way it looks now, the earliest I'll be back will be the end of the week. So why not take advantage and make yourself at home?"

Why not indeed? It would be wonderful, Mallory thought, to spend more than one night in a real bed, to do her laundry without having to go to the laundromat, to have a car to drive instead of a bus to catch. To take an honest-to-God hot shower without running out of water and to sleep without being constantly awakened by people shouting or babies crying.

Except…then what? It was already difficult to transition each day from the affluent world at work to her gritty existence on Lattimer Street. And although there was nothing she'd like better than to move as soon as she could, she was currently deeper in the hole than she'd been when she'd been hired, thanks to the price of taxis and incidentals and because she'd had to invest in some clothes since too little in her wardrobe had been business appropriate.

For the foreseeable future she was going to have to stay where she was. So just how would it feel to live, even briefly, in such safe, comfortable, attractive surroundings, only to have to give them up at somebody else's whim?

Not too great, she imagined. And even if she could find a way to make peace with the situation, what about the truly alarming discovery that she hated the idea of Gabe leaving?

Here she sat, breathing in his scent, her lips still tingling from his kiss, with him so close that his every exhalation tickled against her cheek, and already she was missing him.

It wasn't supposed to be like this. She wasn't supposed to *feel* like this. Last night should have lowered the stakes between them, put her crazy yen for him in perspective, freed her to walk away.

Instead, she wanted to throw her arms around him, drag him back into bed, beg him to stay.

She settled the sheet more securely around her, took a shallow breath. "Thank you, Gabe." To her profound relief, her voice sounded remarkably even and steady. "But I can't."

"Why not?"

Somehow she managed to conjure up a careless

smile. "Honestly? There's a certain crowd at work who already think I shouldn't have been hired. I'm sure they'd really go to town if I showed up driving your car or they found out I was staying at your house. I think it's just better right now if I try to keep a low profile."

She braced, expecting an argument. But to her surprise, although he didn't look happy, after a second he inclined his head a fraction. "All right. Frankly, I think you're worrying about nothing, but it's your decision."

"Gosh." Her smile became genuine. "Gabriel Steele being reasonable. Do you think I could get that in writing?"

His eyes glinted, even as a corner of his mouth kicked up. "Careful, sweetheart. Don't push too hard."

"I wouldn't dream of it."

"Yeah, right." Once more, he leaned in and brushed his mouth over hers. Then he stood. "Don't worry about the dog. Right now he's outside, and if you'll let him in when you leave, Deke should be by around noon to get him. Also, be sure and take the keys, as well as the card, which has my security code written on it." He indicated the items on the nightstand with a thrust of his chin. "That way, if you change your mind, or something comes up, you'll be able to get in."

"All right. Is that it?"

"No." Pausing near the door, he hefted the bag and looked back at her. "I'll see you next week, so take good care of yourself in the meantime, all right?"

Ridiculously, a lump formed in her throat, since she couldn't remember the last time anyone had expressed even polite interest in her welfare. She swallowed, telling herself she was just overtired. "I will. You, too."

"Bet on it." And then he was gone.

"I see you have your nose to the grindstone as usual."

Seated at the desk in her spartan little office at Bedazzled headquarters, Mallory glanced up at the woman standing in her doorway. "Lilah. Hi."

"Do you have a minute to chat?"

She made a phtting sound. "Like you even need to ask? Of course I do." Setting aside her latest to-do list, she got up and came around to move the box of brochures that someone had dumped on her visitor's chair. "Come. Have a seat."

"Thanks. I know it's ridiculous—" the princess-pretty blonde lowered herself down with an appreciative sigh "—since all I've done today is shop for draperies for the baby's room, but getting off my feet for a while sounds heavenly."

Of all the things that had happened to Mallory lately, her burgeoning friendship with Lilah Steele had to be one of the most unexpected. They'd crossed paths occasionally over the years, of course, but had always traveled in different circles and had very different objectives.

Lilah had been raised by her strict, demanding grandmother to have exacting standards and high expectations. Mallory, obviously, had not.

Yet when she'd approached the other woman after their initial talk in Gabe's car ten days ago, about the idea of holding the fashion show at a private home, Lilah had been enthusiastic. Even better, she'd suggested they try to secure Cedar Hill, her grandmother's palatial estate, for the event. The property was one of Denver's largest and most exclusive, and since it had never before been opened to the public, its use would likely garner added interest and publicity.

With insight on Abigail Anson Sommers from Lilah, Mallory had put together a presentation, called on the autocratic old lady and enlisted her cooperation. And ever since, the two younger women had been busy working out details and finding that for all their differences, they just seemed to click.

Now, she looked at her new friend with sympathy and not a little concern. "Still not sleeping well?"

"No. The heartburn is better, but for the past few days Junior here—" she touched a proprietary hand to her pregnant belly "—seems to have decided it's fun to dig his feet into my bladder at bedtime, so I spend most of the night running to the bathroom. But enough about me." A concerned frown knit the blonde's smooth brow. "Did the police have any luck finding whoever was trying to get into your apartment the other night?"

"No. And honestly, I shouldn't even have mentioned it. Most likely it was just kids. Or maybe Mr. Androsky from down the hall. He tends to get trashed the days his pension check shows up and he may have simply confused my place for his." She waved a hand. "Whatever it was, it's over. And except for a few scary moments for me and some pry marks on my door—

which believe me, was hardly a thing of beauty before—no harm was done."

Lilah didn't look convinced, but to Mallory's relief she let it go. "Any word yet from Mrs. Buckingham?"

"Yes! I can't believe I didn't already mention it. She called first thing this morning. Once she got past her amazement that I wasn't in rehab somewhere and that I'd actually managed to hoodwink someone into giving me a real job, she said they'd be happy to help." Since not even Cedar Hill had a place to park several hundred cars, Mallory had contacted the principal at their old high school, Taylor Union, which was only a scant mile away from the mansion, to ask if they could use the school's parking lot. "Not only that, but in exchange for us acknowledging TU on the program, she offered to donate the use of their buses to shuttle people back and forth."

"That's great," Lilah said enthusiastically.

"It's better than great," Mallory countered, flashing a smile. "It's one more thing I can check off my list."

"Well, you can add another. I spoke to Gran yesterday and she suggested we go ahead and hold the after party at Cedar Hill, too."

Mallory sat up straighter. "Really?" Traditionally, there was always a private party to thank the volunteer models after the fashion show, and not having to shift to another site would mean one less thing for her to worry about. "Lilah, that's fabulous! Thank you."

"I didn't do anything."

"Oh, yes, you did. Without you, I doubt your grandmother would have agreed to any of this."

"I'm not so sure about that. She's very impressed with you—and believe me, that's no small feat. But then, even Nikki Volpe and her crowd, who aren't inclined to cut you any slack, acknowledge that you've been working like a dog to get things back on track."

"It really hasn't been that bad. The bulk of the arrangements for the ball itself were well in place when I took over. Mostly it's been a lot of little things that have needed attention."

"Except for the fashion show."

"Except for the fashion show," Mallory agreed, "and with your help even that's coming together. I talked to a supplier in Littleton this morning who can provide us with the runway, chairs and buffet tables. I've ordered the chocolates and champagne, confirmed with Dillon & Diegos regarding the stylists and with Marchant's about the clothes. And I'm scheduled to meet with the man from Scaffoldi's about the tents out at your grandmother's on Friday."

"Good grief," Lilah said with a most unladylike groan. "It's wearing me out just hearing about it. Do you ever sleep?"

Mallory's eyes glinted with good-natured self-mockery. "Darling, please," she scolded in her best uptown voice. "I spent the better part of twenty-eight years on one long vacation. I'm sure I could stay up for a year and not even put a dent in my reserves."

A dimple flashed in Lilah's cheek. "I take that to mean you're as sleep-deprived as I am. Although I know my situation will greatly improve once Dom gets home."

As Lilah had previously explained, Dominic had gone overseas to check on several operations so he wouldn't have to worry about them when it was time for their baby to be born. "He has a talent for relaxing me."

"I just bet he does," Mallory said, amused by the contrast between her friend's demure expression and the anticipatory gleam in her big blue eyes. "Any word on when that will be?" she asked, reaching for her to-do list.

"Yes, actually. He called this morning and he should be home by Sunday."

"That's great."

"Yes, it is." There was a brief silence during which Lilah considered her knowingly. "It's all right to ask, you know. About Gabe."

She picked up her pen, staunchly ignoring the way her pulse leaped at the mere mention of that name. "What about him?"

"Apparently there was some sort of security breach at the Makedonska Museum that required his expertise, which is why he went to Belgrade. But since they've about got things wrapped up, he should be coming home this weekend, too."

"Well, good for him." She made a quick notation to ask the tent man if he supplied his own electrician, and tried to tell herself that the sudden cartwheeling of her stomach was just a delayed reaction to drinking too much coffee.

After all, Gabriel's longer-than-expected absence had proved to be a good thing, allowing her to focus solely on her job. She'd devoted every waking hour of the past ten days to putting Bedazzled's business back in order, and as Lilah had mentioned, it was starting to pay off.

And even if the thought of seeing him again did make her feel a little nervous and unsettled, well, she supposed that was only to be expected. The single night they'd spent together had shown her a whole different side of him. And of herself.

"I'm sure he's more than ready to get back," Lilah observed. "Although I, for one, am going to miss seeing what new clever thing he can come up with to give you. And I'm not the only one. Your little surprises have been the talk of the office."

Her hand went still. Her first "little surprise," a beautiful but functional briefcase, had been delivered the day after he'd left, with a small, unsigned note that she'd known was from him since it had read, "Bronzed those shoes yet?"

In the time since, she'd received a bottle of her favorite scented hand lotion, a new bus pass, an exquisite lithophane night-light, a Starbucks gift card, a bouquet of lilacs in a lovely little china bowl and a small foam cooler packed with a dozen precooked entrees from one of Denver's best restaurants.

Although none of the items had been terribly expensive, it was obvious some real thought had gone into the selections, and that meant more to her than anything else. Never before had a man cared enough about her to actually spend time—did she dare to say the word?—*wooing* her. It made her feel special, cherished, as if she actually mattered.

It was also absolutely terrifying, since now every time she thought of him she felt a little more of her defenses slipping away.

Setting down the pen, she looked at Lilah. She hadn't said a word to anyone about the gift giver's identity, which meant there was no way the other woman could know it was Gabe for sure. Unless, of course, Gabe had confided in Dom.

Yet even if he hadn't, even if Lilah's comment was pure speculation, she wasn't going to lie about it. Their growing friendship was much too important to jeopardize with a lie. Plus it would be a relief to have it out in the open, to perhaps even confide some of her confusion about what she was feeling to another woman.

She set down the pen, pushed her list away. "How long have you known they were from him?" She wouldn't swear by it, but she thought her friend's slim shoulders relaxed a fraction.

"I was pretty sure right from the start," Lilah admitted.

"Oh. I guess that means he sends gifts to women on a regular basis." And the idea didn't fill her with disappointment. It *didn't*.

"No. Truthfully, I don't think I've ever known him to pay another woman this sort of attention. Usually it's just the opposite. Women are constantly throwing themselves at him."

"Then how—"

Lilah gave a slight shrug and smiled. "I've seen the two of you together. And I've seen the way he looks at you when he doesn't think anyone else is watching. Plus until your flowers came in it, that pretty little bowl used to decorate a shelf in his office."

"Oh." It was silly, but the idea that he'd actually given her one of his belongings was mildly alarming, for reasons she wasn't ready to think about. "Does everyone know?"

"I don't see how. I certainly haven't said a word."

She blew out a breath. "Good."

"But why the secrecy, if I might ask?"

"Of course you can. I wasn't trying to be secretive. Just …private. This is all so new—the job, our…relationship, me actually caring about more than the forecast for spring skiing in the Alps or whether I should wait for Mr. Kenneth to make up with his boyfriend before I let him near my hair with his scissors. For once in my life, I didn't want everyone talking about my business."

Lilah nodded. "Makes sense."

"Also… I don't know. At first, everything seemed so straightforward. My need to feel strong and independent versus Gabe seeing me as some loose end leftover from the mess with my dad that he needed to tie up. But now…"

She trailed off, only to have Lilah unexpectedly finish her sentence. "But now you think there's more to his feelings than that."

"Yes. I do." Just hearing herself say the words made her feel panicky and elated all at once.

"I'm sure you're right. And I'll tell you why."

Tipping her head to one side, she said, "Just how much do you know about Gabe's background?"

Mallory thought about it. "Pretty much what everyone does, I guess. That he comes from a military family, that he's the oldest of a bunch of brothers, that his business is a huge success and everyone seems to respect him."

"That's all true, as far as it goes. But what you need to know if you're going to have a chance of understanding him is that when he was fourteen he lost his mother in a car accident. Jake, the baby of the family, wasn't quite two, with the other seven boys ranging in age between them. As Dom tells it, their dad, an army mechanic who was the big, strong silent type, just lost it. Oh, he provided for the family financially—what he didn't drink away at the base bar. But other than that, the boys were on their own.

"I think they all would've wound up in foster care if not for Gabriel. They were all pretty traumatized, but he stepped up, made sure they had clean clothes and enough to eat, oversaw homework and bedtimes, arranged for day care and doctor's appointments, pretty much took on the role of parent. Eli once told me that it was Gabe, not their father, who got up in the night to comfort him and the others when they had bad dreams or cried for their mother.

"Through it all, he did well in school, always had at least a part-time job. Eventually, he went to the local college on an ROTC scholarship, although he was still essentially raising the younger boys. Then their dad unexpectedly remarried, and he was finally able to throw himself into the military career he'd always wanted.

"Dom says he was burning his way up the ranks, doing special operations work overseas, when their father's second marriage broke up and Steele Senior suddenly announced he was retiring to the Philippines. Gabe felt he didn't have a choice but to resign his commission and come home so he could provide a stable, financially secure home for the youngest boys, Josh, Eli, Jake and Jordan."

Absentmindedly Lilah pressed a hand to the small of her back and shifted in her chair. "Not too surprisingly, his brothers are convinced he walks on water even though they're the first to point out that he can be relentless when he thinks something should be done that hasn't been.

"I guess what I'm trying to say is that he's not someone who takes things lightly, Mallory. When he cares, he cares deeply and when he commits to something, he sees it through. But having said that, as far as I know, he's never opened himself up to anyone but family. Certainly not a woman. So just…be careful with your heart, okay?"

Busy trying to sort through everything she'd just heard, it took Mallory a moment before Lilah's last statement sank in. When it did, she momentarily forgot her tangled feelings regarding Gabriel, surprised that Lilah would be concerned for her.

"I… Thanks," she said awkwardly. She fell silent, and

then, because she was afraid she was making more of the other woman's caution than she should, she reverted to humor. "Although I don't think you need to worry," she said lightly. "Just ask Nikki, and she'll be glad to tell you that we Morgans don't have hearts to hurt."

"Right," Lilah replied. "Like I'm going to be influenced by a woman who told me just two days ago about her plan to end world hunger by getting rich people everywhere to save their leftovers? Please."

Mallory gave a snort of disbelief. "You're not serious."

"Oh yes, I am. And the really sad part is, even though she has all the sensitivity of a rock, just thinking about food is enough to make me hungry these days. So what do you think?" Climbing to her feet, the blonde slid her purse onto her shoulder and looked hopefully at Mallory. "Do you have time for lunch?"

"Considering its noon, and I've been here since six? Yes. Besides, I can always eat."

As for Gabe... As she followed Lilah out the door, she promised herself that unsettling or not, she would think about him later.

Eight

After seventeen grueling hours of travel, Gabe had every intention of going home, taking a long shower and getting a good night's sleep in his own bed. What's more, after nearly two weeks of his brother Dominic's constant company, he planned to do all those things alone.

So how he wound up standing rumpled and jet-lagged in the deserted hallway outside Mallory's Be-dazzled office Friday evening was beyond him.

Unless it had something to do with the fierce anti-cipation that raced through his veins at the sight of her. Not yet aware of his presence, she sat engrossed in something on her computer. Despite the lateness of the hour she looked fresh and professional in a pale yellow wrap dress that brought out the sunny streaks in the curling mass of her hair.

Damned if he didn't want to stride in, scoop her up, lay her down and—

"Are you going to say hello?" she inquired, eyes still riveted to the lighted screen. "Or are you just going to stand there and stare at me?"

He felt a stab of surprise. Then he felt profoundly pleased—and maybe a little relieved—that she also felt this powerful connection. "I haven't made up my mind." He took the first step through the doorway. "It's a helluva pretty view."

"You're such a sweet-talker." Despite the lightness of her voice, her hands resting on the keyboard had begun to tremble. The next instant she was on her feet, starting around the desk as if to meet him halfway, only to stop, draw herself up, seemingly rein herself in. "I— How was your trip?"

"Long." Ever since his brother Jake had gone away to college, he'd considered being able to just pick up and go anywhere in the world at the drop of a hat one of the real perks of his job.

He never tired of seeing different locales, of immersing himself in other cultures, of pitting himself against whatever tried to come after a Steele Security client. The instant he'd go wheels up out of Denver, his focus would zero in on the task at hand, and there it would stay until the problem had been satisfactorily dealt with.

Until Belgrade. Where, no matter how hard he'd tried—and he'd given it one hell of a herculean effort—he'd been unable to banish Mallory from his mind.

She started to twine her fingers together, then caught herself. "When did you get back?"

He ordered himself to be patient, to give her a second to get used to his sudden presence, even though it was taking more willpower than it should have for him to hang back. "About an hour ago. We got lucky and were able to catch a flight a few days ahead of schedule."

"You haven't been home yet?"

"No. There was something I needed to get first."

Her eyes sparked with an emotion he couldn't identify. "What's that?"

"What do you think?" Abruptly, he'd had enough. Forbearance was all very nice, but... Erasing the distance between them, he pulled her into his embrace, something taut inside him relaxing as she made a sound midway between relief and pleasure and locked her arms around his waist.

He wasn't sure how long they stood there holding each other, his face buried in her hair, her cheek pressed to his throat. A little uneasily, it occurred to him that what he'd thought he wanted was sex, yet this simple embrace was fulfilling an equally compelling need.

"So how are you?" he said when he finally lifted his head.

She gave him one last squeeze, then leaned back and smiled up at him. "Great. Absolutely great."

"You better be careful, Mal, or I'm going to think you missed me."

"Well, maybe I did. A little."

The admission pleased him. Perhaps too much.

"So." She reached up, toyed with the open collar of his dark gray shirt. "How did you know I'd be here instead of at my apartment?"

He shrugged. "When I couldn't get you on your cell, I called Stan."

"Who's Stan?"

"He's the night security guy for this building. Both he and Rich, the day guy, moonlight for me when I need an extra pair of eyes or ears. I asked him to check the building log and he confirmed you were still here."

"And let you in."

He nodded. "He knows I can be trusted."

"How deluded of him."

His mouth twitched. "Does that mean there's no way I can convince you to come home with me?" That hadn't been part of his plan, either. When he'd realized he intended to see her tonight, he'd been sure he'd find that he'd exaggerated his desire to be close to her.

Clearly that wasn't the case.

"I wouldn't say that." She gave him a look that he felt in the pit of his stomach. "Although actions do speak louder than words…"

"Amen to that." He bent his head, felt her lashes tickle against his face as he skimmed his lips over her temple and along her jawline. He kissed the sleek softness of her throat, lingered there until he felt her melt against him, found her mouth. Their lips met and clung, and he let himself sink into her, driven by the grinding need for the taste and scent and feel of her that had been building in him almost from the minute he'd walked away from her thirteen days earlier.

By the time he eased back to rest his forehead against hers, her hands weren't the only ones that were shaking. Less than thrilled with the discovery, he put a quick stop to it, assuring himself it was simply an outgrowth of being tired. "How'd I do?"

"How 'bout I tell you when I get my mind back?"

The words and her breathy delivery went a long way toward restoring his equanimity. "I take it that's a yes?" He rubbed a circle on the small of her back. "You'll come to my place?"

"I'd heard that you were quick."

"Smart-mouth. Let's get your stuff and go then."

Stepping quickly around her desk, she shut down her computer and picked up her purse. "I'll need to stop by my place and pack a few things."

"No problem." Hustling her out the door, he clicked off the overhead lights.

Minutes later they were in his SUV and on their way. "Nice night," he observed, savoring the dry balmy air against his face.

"How was the weather in Belgrade?"

"Okay. Humid compared to here. How's your job going?"

"Well, I don't think you'll find my picture in the dictionary next to indispensable quite yet, but I'm working on it."

"Maybe working too hard, if tonight's an example."

She gave a throaty chuckle. "Hearing that phrase applied to me has to be a first. It's also sort of ironic considering the source, who—correct me if I'm wrong—just came off at least a hundred-hour work-week."

"Yeah, well—"

"Don't you dare say that's different," she warned lightly. "The only thing different is that you've been working for years and I've been doing it about ten minutes. Besides, I found out just this morning that there's an office pool on how long it's going to be before I throw in the towel, and I sort of lost my head and bet a hundred dollars on never. So now I can't afford to do anything but see this through."

"Like there was ever any question of that," he said with a snort.

She was momentarily silent, then reached over and squeezed his thigh. "Thanks," she said softly. "That's got to be one of the nicest things anyone's ever said to me."

"It's the truth."

"Yes, well, it means a lot, coming from you. Which reminds me." She twisted toward him on the seat as they slowed for a red light. "I also need to thank you for the wonderful presents. I can't…you really shouldn't have, but honestly, I love every single one."

He glanced over at her and saw to his gratification the unguarded pleasure on her face. Truth to tell, the first item, the briefcase, he'd bought purely on impulse while cooling his heels at the airport. The instant he'd seen it, run a hand over the buttery leather and taken a moment to appreciate its clever but elegant design, he'd known she had to have it.

Then, when he'd realized how much he enjoyed picturing her surprise when she received it, he'd been hooked on the idea of doing more, driven by a need to make her feel special—maybe even a little cherished—that he didn't entirely understand.

Still, seeing the quiet glow on her face, it occurred to him that a subtle change seemed to have taken place in their relationship. That she might actually be starting to trust him just a little.

The realization brought satisfaction…and a razor-sharp prick of concern regarding the future.

"That's odd," Mallory said suddenly.

Shooting a glance her way, he frowned at the perplexed expression on her face as they approached the ramshackle old building she called home. "What's odd?" he asked as he drove past the structure, pulling in at the only available spot at the curb a few doors down.

"My apartment's dark."

"Shouldn't it be?"

"No. I always turn on the small lamp by the sofa when I leave. In case I'm late like this. I guess I must've forgotten to switch it on this morning. Either that or—" her keys in hand, she gave a slight, dismissive shrug and reached for her door handle "—the bulb burned out."

"You're probably right," Gabe said at the same time that he caught her by the arm, tugged her around, plucked away the keys. "But on the off chance you're not, you're going to stay right here."

"While you do what?"

"Go check things out." He retrieved the Maglite from the glove compartment and snapped it onto his belt. "In the meantime—" he raised a hand to forestall the protest he could see forming on her lips "—I want you to be sure to lock the doors behind me when I leave. And promise me that you will not, under any circumstance, set foot from this car." He leveled a look at her that had once set toughened soldiers quaking in their combat boots.

"Or what?" she shot back, completely unfazed.

As was often the case with her, he wasn't sure whether to swear or laugh. "Or I'll be worrying about you instead of paying attention to a potentially dangerous situation."

"Dear God." Her gaze locked on his face, she worried her bottom lip for a second, then stopped and squared her shoulders. "All right. I promise. As long as you swear you'll be careful. And understand accept that if you're not back in five minutes, I'm calling 9-1-1."

"I'm always careful." He leaned forward and gave her a fast, hard kiss on the mouth. "Plus I'm trained for this, remember? And chances are good I'll be back in less than a minute with nothing to report."

"Famous last words," she murmured as he climbed out.

He waited a second, gave a quick nod of approval as

he heard the door locks engage. Then he blanked his mind of everything but his current objective and headed inside.

Whoever had broken into her apartment was long gone by the time Gabe walked in to find her door hanging by a single hinge.

That, however, was where the good news ended, Mallory reflected, as he ushered her into his house hours later.

Apparently angered that she'd had nothing worth stealing, the intruder or intruders had thoroughly trashed her place. Her sofa and bedding had been slashed, the sparse contents of her kitchen cabinets dumped onto the floor, her lamps smashed and the Goodwill tables she'd been so proud of reduced to kindling.

Far more upsetting, someone had taken the time to paw through her underthings, lay them out around the room.

While everyone from Gabe to the police to the apartment manager agreed the destruction looked to be the work of teenagers, Mallory feared she'd been violated by someone who knew exactly what he was doing. That made her feel sick—and wonder if she'd ever find the courage to live in the apartment again.

She was doing her best to hide the tumult churning inside her, however. It didn't seem fair to do otherwise, to reward Gabe's kindness and his steadfast support with tears or a hysterical outburst.

Yet it appeared she wasn't doing as good a job hiding her feelings as she thought when he switched on the lights in his bedroom and frowned, taking a good, hard look at her face. "You okay?"

She dredged up a smile. "I'm fine. Although I'm betting you can't say the same. I think this comes under the heading of be careful what you wish for."

Drawing her deeper into the room, he set down the bag she'd hurriedly packed by the ottoman. "How's that?"

"Isn't it obvious? You ask me to spend the night, and now you're stuck with me."

"Is that what you think?"

She shrugged. "Honestly, Gabe, you don't need to worry. I'm not sure when I'll be ready to go back to my place. But until I am, I have a little money set aside, enough to rent a room somewhere. First thing in the morning I'll start looking—"

"Screw that."

"What?" She couldn't have heard that right.

"Maybe I want to be stuck," he said flatly. "God knows, I'm tired of worrying about you all the time."

Her spine stiffened. "I thought we settled that. I'm not your responsibility."

"No, you're not. But that doesn't mean I don't care what happens to you, dammit."

If for an instant he looked a little taken aback at the forcefulness of his admission, Mallory barely noticed. She was too busy trying to breathe as his words kicked a major support out from under her defenses.

"I admit it made me feel a little crazy to find out that someone's been sniffing around your door," he informed her, pacing over to the window. "And when

I think about what could've happened if you'd been home when the bastards broke in, it scares the hell out of me. But it's just because I want you to be safe, Mal. If that's a crime, you may as well convict me now, because it's not going to change."

He'd actually been frightened? For her? The one person on earth she thought of as totally fearless? Her throat went tight. "Gabriel—"

"As far as finding somewhere to stay," he steamrollered on, "if paying your own way means that much to you, then fine—rent a room from me. I've got three that are empty. Although I wish like hell you'd just agree to share the one we're standing in."

"All right." She swallowed. "I will. I do."

"What?"

"If you want to be my landlord, at least temporarily, okay." It would only be until she figured out where she went from here, she promised herself. "But do you think…could we discuss it later?" To her mortification, reaction was finally beginning to set in and her voice was starting to shake. "Right now, would you m-mind terribly—could you just hold me? Please?"

He was across the room and scooping her up before the last word was completely out of her mouth. With a sigh of relief, she looped her arms around his strong, warm neck and let him carry her over to the bed, where he sat and scooted back against the headboard with her across his lap.

"I'm sorry. I don't mean to be such a baby." Except that she did. It was undeniably sweet to be able to lean on someone else—on him—if just for a moment. Burying her face in his shoulder, she closed her eyes, soaking up the heat that seemed to roll off him and radiate right down to her bones, displacing the chill that up until then she'd thought might never go away.

"I keep thinking about what might have happened, too," she admitted. "And the thought of somebody touching my personal things totally creeps me out. And then, for you to say you care…" Her breath shuddered out. "Nobody's ever cared before…."

"Shh." Rubbing his hand over her back, he began to rock her in the universal motion of comfort she'd experienced rarely in her life. "Easy, baby. You've been through a lot tonight, but you're okay now. I didn't mean to upset you."

"Oh, you didn't," she protested. "Not the way you mean." Listening to the steady beat of his heart beneath her ear, feeling the strength of the hard, lean body supporting her own, it dawned on her that she felt safe for the first time in months—maybe years.

For a second the irony of it stole her breath. That the one man on earth she'd always considered a threat to her peace of mind was now the one person she trusted…

It was the most unexpected gift of all. And it made her want to give back something equally important. Yet the only thing of value she had—even it was questionable—was a small measure of truth about herself.

She drew in a breath, forced herself to relax her hold on him enough that she could lean back, face him when she spoke.

"I wasn't exactly up-front with you in the beginning, about being broke," she said quietly. "I *was* irresponsible, and I did recklessly spend too much money, but… My father didn't just steal from all those investors, Gabe. He cleaned out my trust fund, too."

He stiffened. "Jesus, Mal. Why the hell didn't you tell me?"

"Because it was nobody's business but my own. And I—" She hesitated, finding the next words even harder to say than she'd imagined. "I was ashamed that he would do that to me. I mean, I always knew I was low on his priority list. Somewhere above him having a faultless manicure but below whoever he was currently sleeping with. As a kid, I did everything I could to get his attention, pulling stunts that always got everyone who participated but me grounded for life, while my dad—he barely noticed."

She sighed, slid her fingers into the open V at the top of his shirt, needing that contact with his warm smooth skin even as she realized the words were starting to come a little easier.

"I think that's when I finally accepted it was no use. And decided that if he wasn't going to care, neither was I—about him, about me, about anything. I was just going to have fun. So when he disappeared, it was a really rude surprise to discover how much it hurt. And then to find out he'd stolen my trust money…"

"That selfish sonofabitch." Just for a second, before he could mask it, he looked utterly menacing. Then to her complete surprise, he gathered her close once again.

Despite the gentleness of his embrace, she could feel the tension thrumming through him. "If I'd had the slightest clue—" He broke off, but the grimness of his voice said it all.

"It wouldn't have made any difference. Because it wasn't just his fault. Up until he took off, I was just phoning my life in, not paying attention. And then, when I realized what he'd done, what I'd allowed him to do by being so careless with my own affairs, I felt so incredibly stupid. I'm ashamed to admit it, but I wasn't sure what to do, so for a while I didn't do anything and that just made everything worse."

He gently stroked his hand over her hair. "You were in shock."

"Maybe." She blew out a breath. "Mostly I was just clueless. It took getting evicted from the house, then having the hotel where I'd gone to stay throw me out, for me to realize that if I wanted to survive, I was going to have to take care of myself. And because I wanted to do it right, start off with a clean slate, I promptly sold off the only thing of real value I had left, my grandmother's jewelry, and paid off all my debts, thinking it was the honorable thing to do. Of course, in hindsight I can see that not leaving myself a cushion—on the off chance that I couldn't find a job that paid enough to live on—was a mistake, too.

"I guess what matters—" she tipped back her head, looked at him "—is that I don't ever want to feel that way again, Gabe. As if I'm not smart enough or competent enough to run my own life."

Inexplicably, something dark and unsettled flashed through his gloriously green eyes. "Mallory, you're none of those things."

"Maybe not now, but I was. Which is why I can't tell you how much your backing off, not pressing me all the time to do things your way, means to me."

"Mallory—"

"No. Don't." She pressed a finger to his mouth. "You don't have to say anything. Just…I need you, Gabriel. Make love with me."

She felt him jerk at her words. Moved—and amazed—that she could affect him so, she shifted in his arms, brushing her lips over the silky strip of skin behind his ear, the outer edge of his eye and down along the elegant line of his cheekbone until she finally reached his mouth.

His hard, beautiful, indisputably male mouth.

Sliding her hands into his cool, slippery hair, she tipped her head and softly, softly molded her lips to his.

The kiss was exquisite. A sweet meeting of need, an exchange of comfort, an acknowledgment of barriers tumbling down. Nestled together, time slowed as they savored each other, exploring the bow of an upper lip, touching tongue to tongue, feasting on a plump bottom curve, teeth gently shaping moist, tender flesh.

It was like mainlining champagne, and with every sip, every nip, every caress of tongues Mallory felt her distress over the break-in, her uncertainty about the future, her sorrow over her father, fading away.

The only thing that mattered was Gabriel. His taste

on her lips, his scent filling her head, his elegant hands trailing fire over her skin.

Shoes hit the floor, clothing was peeled off, underthings stripped away and discarded. Murmuring his name as they knelt, facing each other in the middle of the big bed, Mallory was bombarded by sensations as they continued to kiss.

There was the slippery coolness of the comforter against her knees and the tops of her feet. The satiny tickle of her hair trailing over her back and shoulders. And Gabe, all warm, powerful muscle and lean angles, his hands cradling the small of her back, his chest abrading her tender nipples as they swayed together, mouths still fused.

The were like two perfectly matched puzzle pieces, she thought hazily.

Moved by a need larger than herself, she opened her eyes, driven to consider Gabriel's strong, compelling face, to admire the slash of his eyebrows and to-die-for cheekbones, his straight nose and tough but sensitive mouth. And as she looked, she felt something fundamental inside her change.

As if sensing her scrutiny, Gabe raised his dense black eyelashes to lock his glittering gaze on her own. "Are you all right?"

"I'm great."

A faint smile curved his mouth. Lowering his head, he kissed the underside of her jaw, the tops of her shoulders, the notch of her collarbone.

"Before, I didn't know—" her voice wobbled as his

head dipped lower and he closed his mouth over one straining nipple "—I could feel this way. That it was possible to want…the way I want you."

For a bare instant, he went still. And then, as if he'd been holding it in, he said fiercely, "Good. Because you're mine, Mal. *Mine*." He raked his teeth over her, a low proprietary growl issuing from his throat. Then he sealed his lips around and sucked. Hard.

The breath exploded from her lungs and she arched, only the support of his hands keeping her upright as she shuddered from the pleasure of his touch—and from his unexpected words, which fulfilled some primitive, unexpected need to be claimed she hadn't known she possessed.

But she did need—she needed him. That became crystal clear as he lowered her onto her back and knelt between her parted thighs. Sliding his hands beneath her bottom, he bent down and trailed his lips over her midriff, pausing to dip his tongue into her navel.

He nuzzled the satiny skin of her abdomen and she felt a shivering excitement. It was matched by growing anticipation as his mouth began to trail lower and lower. "Gabe—"

Her mind seemed to blank and her entire focus to zero in on his slightest movement as he slid the pad of his fingertip along the aching cleft of her sex, and into the silky heat inside. "You're beautiful. So soft, so ready… So wet. You make me crazy, Mal…"

Settling his mouth against her there, he kissed her, deep and intimately, the flick of his tongue startling a cry from her and sending her heels digging into the mattress.

Caught between the upward thrust of the arm braced beneath her, the slow advance and retreat of his broad, marauding finger, the steadily increasing suction of his mouth, Mallory gave herself over to his power. Pleasure built, slow and steady, at first dancing along every sensitized nerve ending, then slowly coalescing into the single, throbbing point between her legs. Robbed of speech, forgetting to breath, she strained against him, wanting, wanting....

Him. Just him.

Forever him.

The realization, along with the rapid, repeated stab of his tongue, sent her spinning and she came apart like a house of cards in a high wind. "Oh. Oh. *Oh*. Gabriel!"

The last syllable of his name was still hanging in the air as he came rocketing up and caught her close. His hands biting into her hips, he thrust himself inside her, big, hard and hot, his sudden, unexpected possession detonating another, even stronger ripple of pleasure. She wrapped her arms around him, meeting him thrust for heavy thrust while that second orgasm began to roll through her. "Don't stop, don't stop, don't, don't, don't—"

His mouth found hers, caressing, demanding, giving. Feeling as if she were riding the crest of an unstoppable wave, Mallory held on tight as he drove her higher and higher, until suddenly something inside her gave way. Caught by a profound punch of pleasure, she cried out, then cried out again as Gabe's big body began to quake and she heard him call out her name as he came.

Breath sawing harshly in and out of oxygen-starved lungs, they sank bonelessly into the mattress, holding tight to each other. It was a good while later when they finally managed to wrestle back the covers and slide between the sheets. Bunching a pillow under his head, Gabe settled her against him, leaning down to press a kiss to her temple as she nestled close, her cheek against his chest.

"Mal?" Yawning, he smoothed a hand over her shoulder.

"Hmm?"

"I'm sorry about the circumstances, but I'm glad you're here."

There seemed no way to respond to that with anything less than honesty. "Me, too."

"As for the rest of it, don't worry. We'll figure it out."

We. She told herself his automatic assumption that he'd be part of some future discussion should have alarmed her. Yet as she felt him settle a little farther into the bed, heard his breathing deepen as twenty-four hours without sleep and his trip across numerous time zones finally caught up with him, she decided that just for tonight, she could let it go.

There'd be plenty of time tomorrow to reestablish some boundaries. Right now, however, there was no place she'd rather be than lying here with Gabe in the dark, safe in the warm circle of his sheltering arms.

Because oh, dear Lord. Somewhere along the line she'd foolishly gone and fallen in love with him.

Nine

"Correct me if I'm wrong," Mallory said, making no attempt to hide her glee as the basketball Gabe had just launched at the hoop in his driveway hit the rim, teetered for an instant, then bounced back to the ground without going in, "but I believe you just added an *E* to H-O-R-S-E. Which means I win." She smiled triumphantly. "Again."

Propping his hands on his hips, Gabe shook his head and did his best to look disgruntled. It was damn hard to pull off, however, while she was standing there looking so pleased with herself.

With her face glowing, her hair drawn up in a ponytail and her slim, leggy figure displayed by a pale pink velour jogging suit almost as soft to the touch as her skin, she looked quintessentially female—soft, silky, seemingly too delicate to lift more than a pom-pom. Yet she'd just taken him two times out of three at the old match-me-if-you-can hoops game, a feat he'd never hear the end of if his brothers got wind of it.

And he didn't give a damn.

He'd never spent this kind of concentrated time with a woman before. Hell, prior to Mallory, he'd never even invited one to stay overnight at his house. After growing up in a big family, his time spent in the military, and then the past few years riding herd on his rowdy younger brothers, he'd become fiercely protective of his privacy.

Yet with Mallory it was different. Granted, she'd been there hardly more than a week. And it wasn't as if she was exactly intrusive. She'd been careful to maintain her boundaries, paying him up front for room and board, continuing to ride the bus, spending long hours at work, asking for nothing from him she couldn't repay—both to his admiration and his annoyance.

But for all of that, she still managed to bring to his life a softness, a feminine perspective and even the occasional, much-needed touch of levity that he hadn't known he was missing. She also continually surprised him, whether it was with a perceptive comment about an item in the news, a previously unsuspected devotion to M&M's—not for their chocolate content but because they shared her initials—or his current discovery that she might look like Society Princess Barbie but had a jump shot like LeBron James.

"I believe this means you're on deck to cook tonight," she said, effortlessly bouncing the ball from one slender hand to the other.

"Considering I already put dinner in the oven before we came out here, I think I'll survive," he said drily.

"For which I'm eternally grateful." Taking one quick spin, she launched the ball right through the net—again—before turning gracefully toward him. "For your continuing survival, of course." She grinned. "But also that you're in charge of the food. If we had to depend on me, we'd starve."

"No need to worry about that." He caught the ball on the rebound. "I like to cook."

"I know. And there's just something so wrong about that." She leaned contentedly against him as he looped an arm around her shoulders. "No one so brazenly male—" she pressed a kiss to his jaw as they walked back toward the house "—should be so adept in the kitchen."

He lobbed the ball toward its allotted bin in the garage, then followed her into the house. "It's not like I had a lot of choice. Growing up, it was either learn to cook or starve."

She widened her eyes in mock horror. "No takeout?"

"Not a big option with a limited budget and a lot of mouths to feed."

"No, I guess not." She was silent a moment, then said soberly, "Lilah told me you lost your mother in your teens. It must've been hard."

"No worse than yours taking off," he said easily. Seeing the faint flicker of surprise in her eyes, he found himself reaching for her. Pushing a curl that had come loose behind her ear, he let his fingers linger a moment on her soft cheek. "You've got to know that's common knowledge, Mal. It's one of the first things I ever heard about you."

"Oh, I do. It's not that. It's just... KiKi Morgan Manthauser's idea of good parenting was giving the nanny a raise. But given the way you turned out—" heading into the kitchen, she pushed back her sleeves to wash her hands, her nose crinkling appreciatively at the smell of roasting chicken "—your mom was clearly in a whole different league."

"Yeah, that's probably true. God knows, we were her whole focus. And she was good at being a parent— smart, strict, organized, but fun, with a knack for saying what you needed to hear, even though you might not think so at the time. She had a gentle, sensitive side, but she could be tough as a drill sergeant, too, the way you have to be to run a household that size. For the first fourteen years of my life, she was pretty much the sun we all revolved around."

Taking Mallory's place at the sink, he scrubbed his hands, then took the towel she handed him and dried off. "But it's been twenty years, Mal. It was tough, for a lot of different reasons, but I don't think it was as bad for me as it was for Taggart, who was closest to her, and lost without her, or even Dom, who was just old enough to decide he couldn't be hurt if he didn't let himself care about anybody again. The fact that he found Lilah, and that Taggart has Gen, is nothing short of miraculous."

"But what about you? Don't tell me that losing your mom didn't have an effect on you, too."

"Sure it did. But I was so busy looking after the younger kids, there wasn't a lot of time to dwell on it. I couldn't go my own way like Dom, or act out the way Taggart did and risk getting sent off to some tough-love military school. I had responsibilities."

"That you chose to take on," she pointed out. Having finished setting two places at the island counter, she poured them both something to drink, then seated herself as he carried their plates over and joined her.

"Yeah, but it's part of my nature." He'd come to grips with who he was a long time ago. "And it gave me the incentive to do something with my life, so I can't complain about that."

"What about your dad?"

"What about him?"

"Didn't it ever bother you that he let you take so much on your shoulders at such a young age?"

He shrugged, dismissing the old man's behavior the way he had since the day he'd turned sixteen. Flush with the success of getting his driver's license, it had been a definite downer that the first thing he'd had to do was use it to retrieve the elder Steele from a brawl at an off-base bar. But it hadn't been until later that night, as his father had gone from belligerent to maudlin to prostrate with his never-ending grief, that

Gabe had decided he'd seen enough, that for him to survive he was simply going to have to get on with the business of life.

"You do what you can," he said now. "He made his choices. I made mine. Besides, I prefer to think I'm in charge of my own destiny."

She mulled it over for a moment. "I guess, given my own less-than-sterling antecedents, I'd like to think that, too. Heaven knows, I'll never have children of my own if I don't think I can do better than my parents did. Of course, that's setting the bar really, really low." A rueful smile tipped the corners of her mouth. "Or maybe, in their case, not setting it at all."

"You'll do fine." And she would, he thought, as he glanced sideways at her sitting there with her chin propped in her hand. Out of the blue, he had a sudden vision of her, that striking face alight as she fussed over some sturdy little dark-haired boy.

Jesus. Where did that come from?

Telling himself firmly it was simply a reaction to all this talk of the past, he deliberately steered the conversation to a lighter subject. "Where'd you learn to play ball like that, anyway?"

Looking faintly relieved herself, she answered easily. "I spent every summer of my misspent youth going to camp. It was my dad's solution to not knowing what to do with me. I'm also an excellent shot with a bow and arrow and play a killer game of softball."

"Pretty impressive for the current queen of the social scene."

"Please." She flicked her fingers dismissively. "One successful fashion show hardly qualifies me as that."

It had been more than that, and they both knew it. Even without the enthusiastic write-up in that morning's paper, the verdict from participants and attendees of yesterday's exceedingly successful event had been overwhelmingly positive.

The setting, the tents, the food, the clothes and her choice of a popular radio personality to emcee the event had all gotten raves. Even Abigail Sommers, whom he'd known for years and who handed out praise as if she were being forced at gunpoint to part with a precious family jewel, had paid Mallory a number of heartfelt compliments for how impressively the show itself, and the party afterward, had gone.

"Just cross your fingers that the ball next weekend goes as smoothly," she said. "And that I'll still be able to get into my dress after the way you've been feeding me."

As far as he was concerned, she could wear what she had on and still be the most beautiful woman there. But he was always willing to do what he could to help. "If you're really worried, even though you shouldn't be, we could always burn off some calories with a little postdinner exercise."

"But the dishes—"

"Will wait." He leaned sideways, gently nipped her ear, then slid his mouth south to the crook of her neck and nuzzled her there. "I, on the other hand, am not so sure I can."

It was all that needed to be said. Sliding off the bar

stool, she came up on tiptoe and kissed him once on the mouth, then took his hand and set a course for the bedroom.

Shifting restlessly onto his side in bed later that night, Gabe spared a glance for the clock on the nightstand. The digital readout read two-forty-five.

His mouth tightened impatiently It wasn't often that he suffered from sleeplessness. He'd long ago perfected the art of switching his mind off, diving straight into dreamland and waking refreshed and ready to go five or six hours later.

So why was he lying here, spinning his wheels in the dark, tension churning in his gut?

Well, duh. The answer to that happened to be curled bonelessly beside him, her breath tickling his back, one slender arm draped trustingly around his waist.

He couldn't count the number of times in the past week he'd had lethal thoughts about Cal Morgan and what the bastard had done to Mallory. Or found himself once more hearing Mallory's distraught voice in his head saying, "I felt so stupid. I don't ever want to feel as if I'm not competent to run my own life again."

The thought of her being hurt and subsequently doubting her own worth twisted him up inside, made him want to shield and protect her, as well as assure her that from now on she had someone on her side she could depend on. Someone she could trust.

Except wasn't *trust* precisely the problem? Wasn't it the bogeyman in the room that had recently taken to stalking him, popping out at crucial moments to stab at his peace of mind?

All right. So maybe his conscience was bothering him just a little bit about certain steps he'd taken at the start of their relationship to provide Mallory with some help getting on her feet. It had seemed like the right thing to do at the time. And even now, given how well things were going for her, he couldn't honestly say he regretted it.

But he wasn't an idiot. He knew she wasn't likely to view what he'd done the same way. At least initially, until she had time to think about it, to get things in perspective and realize he'd had no choice but to take the actions he had for her own good, she was probably going to be angry.

Just the thought added to the tension twisting through him. Not that he doubted for an instant that they'd get past it, since he had no intention of accepting anything less. He might not be so far gone that he had thoughts of happily ever after—he'd learned the fallacy of that as a youngster—but he was damned if he was ready to give her up, either.

The night of the break-in he'd shocked the hell out of himself when he'd heard himself staking a claim, informing her in no uncertain terms that she was *his*. Yet the minute he'd said it, he'd known it was true. She belonged with him, at least for the foreseeable future, he thought, shifting onto his back and pulling her securely into his arms.

What's more, sometime over the past few weeks her

happiness had really begun to matter to him. More than he would've thought possible just weeks ago. And that meant he'd do whatever it took to look out for her.

Which was precisely why he wasn't going to say anything now, he thought, covering her hand with his own and pressing it to his heart. There was less than a week to go until the ball, and he was damned if he was going to risk ruining her big night just so he could get a few extra hours of sleep.

Afterward, however, they were definitely going to have to talk.

So this is what genuine accomplishment felt like, Mallory reflected, fielding yet another sincere congratulations from a passing partygoer as the Bedazzled Ball glittered its way past midnight.

It was having someone she didn't even know tell her they were having a great time.

It was looking up to see elegantly clad men and women dressed in a veritable wildflower garden of colors sitting at small, intimate tables on the balcony overhead, chatting and enjoying the spectacle of the dancing below.

It was gazing out at that very same dance floor to see a hundred plus couples dip and sway to a band she'd handpicked.

It was breathing in the sweet night air wafting through dozens of French doors thrown open to a terrace she'd transformed into a fairyland of twinkling lights and fragrant flowers.

It was having just been informed—by Nikki Volpe

of all people—that the preliminary tallies showed this year's event had raised the most money in the charity's entire history.

And it was knowing that while she'd had a hand in it all, it wouldn't feel nearly so sweet if she didn't have someone with whom to share it, she decided, as she accepted her first glass of champagne that evening from Gabe's outstretched hand.

"Thank you." Indulging herself, she took a moment to simply admire him in his faultlessly cut Armani tux. "For the drink. And for being such a good sport tonight. As busy as I've been, I noticed you took time to dance with all the elderly ladies on the board. That was really sweet of you."

He shrugged. "It was fun. Plus a number of them are long-standing Steele clients, so it was nice to have a chance to visit with them."

He wasn't fooling her for a moment. He could brush off what he'd done as self-serving, but beneath that tough guy facade, the man had a compassionate streak a mile wide.

And it just so happened that at this perfect moment in time, he was hers. Wondering if there was such a thing as being too happy, she took a sip of bubbly and gave a small, breathless laugh. "Umm. That tickles."

His eyes lighting with appreciation for her good humor, he touched his hand to her back, which was dramatically bared by the high-necked emerald gown she'd chosen for its perfect fit—and because it was the same green as his eyes. "Enjoy. You deserve a moment to savor your success." Leaning closer, he added softly for no one's ears but her own, "Just keep in mind I have plans for a private celebration when we get home."

Arching an eyebrow, she reached out and ran her fingertip over his lapel. "Do tell."

His mouth quirked. "All I'm prepared to say is that it involves a better brand of champagne and a certain pair of high heels."

Anticipation sparkled through her like the wine in her glass. "Oh, my."

"No matter what he's promising, I can do better," a different male voice promised confidently from just behind her.

"Not on your best day, little brother." With deceptive ease, Gabe took a step that effortlessly put him between Mallory and his brother Cooper.

Bemused, Mallory turned to smile at the other man, and found he'd arrived just a few steps ahead of Lilah and Dominic. The three brothers somehow wound up standing shoulder to shoulder, a sight that made her feel slightly light-headed.

Lilah came to her rescue. With a wry look on her lovely face, the blonde moved to Mallory's side, linked their arms and drew her slightly away from the men. "Breathe," she advised, her voice ripe with amusement. "I know it can be a little overwhelming the first time you find yourself face-to-face with all that unbridled testosterone, but it doesn't do to let on. As it is, none of them suffers from a lack of confidence."

Lilah was a hundred percent right. Like some recruiting poster for the tall, dark and devastating club, each man had a physical presence that came from being in top-notch shape and an ease of manner that stemmed from knowing they could handle anything that was thrown at them.

Individually, they were a sight to make any woman's pulse flutter. Together, it was a wonder they weren't hip deep in bodies from the female occupants of the room swooning at their feet.

"Just wait until the Fourth of July," Lilah advised, "when the whole family gets together to celebrate. It's always too hot for words." She fanned her face with one delicate hand. "And I'm not referring to the weather."

Unable to help herself, Mallory chuckled, thinking again that things just couldn't get any better. The ball was a success, it was beyond terrific to have a friend with such an unexpected sense of humor and the man she loved and respected desired her in return.

While it was true the two of them had yet to talk about a future, and she wasn't taking anything for granted, for the first time ever she was starting to feel as though she was making a real place for herself.

"You about ready to call it a night, sweetheart?" Stepping close to his wife, Dominic's entire demeanor turned protectively tender as he briefly touched one big hand to Lilah's cheek.

"Yes, I certainly am," she replied, with a little sigh of contentment as he reached around to knead the small of her back with one big palm. "I just need to go grab my wrap."

"I'll get it," Mallory said promptly. "As one of my last official duties of the night, I really should go make sure everything's going all right in the cloakroom."

Clearly enjoying her husband's attentions, Lilah didn't demur, just fished her ticket out of her evening purse and handed it over. "Thanks. You're a doll. We'll head in that direction and meet you."

"Okay. I'll be back in a minute," she said with a polite smile meant to include the other two men. Before she could take more than a single step away, however, Gabe tugged her close and kissed her boldly on the mouth.

"Don't be long," he said, watching with satisfaction as she blinked up at him a little dazedly before hurrying away.

Glancing around, he found he was the center of a number of pairs of interested eyes. Yet it was only the reactions of the three people closest to him that he gave a damn about.

Lilah's expression reflected warm approval. She'd clearly taken to Mallory and it was obvious the two of them were becoming genuine friends.

Dom's reaction, though more guarded, also seemed to be positive, as well as a little smug, no great surprise since he'd had a hell of a good time in Belgrade needling Gabe by murmuring, "the bigger they are, the harder they fall" under his breath at the most inappropriate times.

Only Cooper appeared to have some reservations. Not that anyone who didn't know him like a brother would notice—the smile he sent Gabe was totally pleasant. But Gabe saw the shadow of concern in his eyes just the same.

He wasn't in the mood to worry about it tonight, however. So it was just as well that Dom slapped the younger man on the shoulder and said, "Come on, kid. Do me a favor and hunt down a valet to bring the car around, will you? That will give me a sporting chance to get my lovely bride to the door without every woman in sight trotting up to share her labor and delivery story." He gave a slight shudder. "Trust me. Some of the stuff is scarier than trying to evade a sniper while picking your way blindfolded through a minefield."

Family, Gabe thought minutes later, as he watched the members of his get swallowed up by the crowd. As crazy as they sometimes made him, he couldn't imagine his life without them. For exactly that reason it had been good for them to see him with Mallory, he reflected, to let them see for themselves that she was currently an important part of his life.

"There you are, dear." Separating themselves from an elderly trio of friends, sisters Eleanor and Annalise DeMarco, longtime Steele clients, permanent Bedazzled board members, and both spry and sharp as tacks—although they'd long passed their eightieth birthdays—approached. "Alone at last, you handsome young devil."

Smiling, Gabe held up a hand in surrender. "I'm not sure I can handle another dance, Anna, if that's what you came for," he said to the older, more effusive of the two, who was resplendent tonight in diamonds and pale blue silk that closely resembled the shade of her hair. "You wore me out the first time around."

"Oh, you!" she said, her faded brown eyes twinkling. "That was nothing. If I were forty years younger—"

"Hmph," Eleanor, tall and angular and wearing mauve and rubies, interjected tartly. "More like fifty."

"I swear I'd put you through your paces somewhere other than the dance floor," her sister said, giving Gabe a naughty wink.

"She always was a trollop," Eleanor said with sniff a of disapproval, throwing a long-suffering gaze his way.

Amused as he always was by their bickering, Gabe let them go on for a few more minutes before he finally intervened. "Ladies, you know I'm always glad to see you, but as it happens I was just on my way to find Mallory."

"Who is precisely the reason we came to talk to you," Eleanor said, abruptly perking up.

"Yes, she most certainly is," Annalise agreed with an actual nod of approval at her sister.

"You know, of course, that we were a little dubious when we first agreed to take her on. There was all that unpleasantness with her father—"

"Odious man," Anna remarked.

"—and despite the time she'd spent as a Bedazzled volunteer over the years, she did have a rather flighty reputation."

"Clearly exaggerated, we can see now."

"But whatever her difficulties in the past, she's come nicely up to the mark now and we just wanted to let you know how truly grateful we are that you brought her to our attention," Eleanor said firmly. "Even without your extremely generous pledge, this year's event has been the most successful ever—"

"No doubt in part due to the wonderful fashion event your young lady put together."

"—and we couldn't be more pleased with her performance. Now, don't worry—"

"No, no, we wouldn't want you to do that," Anna said.

"Sister and I will continue to honor your request for anonymity. But we thought you'd like to know that we board members have been talking amongst ourselves tonight and have decided to ask her to stay on for next year. We really can't thank you enough for twisting our arms and insisting we give her a try."

He couldn't contain a smile as he imagined Mallory's elation when she learned the good news. "I just gave things a nudge in the right direction. The credit is all Mallory's."

"Apparently not," said a cool, achingly familiar voice.

His heart dropped to his shoes and he slowly turned, almost afraid of what he would find.

For good reason as it turned out.

Because Mallory stood not a foot away, staring at him as if he were a stranger, a shattered look in her eyes.

Ten

"Dammit, don't look at me that way," Gabe said fiercely.

Swallowing hard, Mallory said nothing. No matter what, she assured herself as he pulled her with an inescapable grip into the first deserted meeting room they came across outside the hotel ballroom, she was not going to break down.

Not when she'd managed to keep a firm grasp on her composure while Anna and Eleanor DeMarco had fussed over her, smiling and patting her shoulder as they'd reiterated what she'd already heard them tell Gabe.

How the ball was a smashing success. How exceedingly pleased everyone on the board was with what she'd managed to achieve in such a short time. And how, in light of her impressive performance, the board had agreed that the coordinator's job was hers for the upcoming year if she wanted it.

It had been her moment of triumph, the fulfillment of what only six weeks earlier had seemed like an unattainable dream.

So she'd smiled and nodded, said *thank you very much* and *yes, please*, acting thrilled in a truly Oscar worthy performance.

And all the while her mind had been riveted on what the sisters so very discreetly had *not* seen fit to say.

That she owed her success to Gabriel who had promised a large amount of money to the charity in order to secure her present position for her.

The knife that seemed to be jammed in her heart twisted a little harder at the reminder.

Somehow she'd gotten through the exchange with the sisters without losing her aplomb. Just as she'd managed not to succumb to the tremors that had threatened to overtake her when Gabe had encircled her wrist with his hard fingers before she could bolt.

She hadn't let loose with the furious denial that had crowded her throat when he'd declared, face grim, "We need to talk." Much less dug in her heels and shrilly refused to budge when he'd hustled her out of the room like some fugitive he was determined not to let escape.

No. Her effort to be viewed as someone other than the despicable Cal Morgan's useless daughter was far too new, and her quest to be taken seriously still too important to her, to jeopardize either by making a scene.

But there was nobody watching now.

"Just how should I look at you, Gabriel? Why don't you tell me?" Feeling his touch like a brand to her soul, she tugged at her wrist, profoundly relieved when he let her go. "Should I simper with gratitude because you bought me my job?"

Stepping back out of reach, she saw a nerve jump in his jaw, and the small seed of hope that she may have gotten it wrong withered inside her.

"Or wait, maybe I'm supposed to gaze at you with admiration for the way you duped me into actually believing you respected me."

"I *do* respect you," he said forcefully.

"Oh, please!" Turning away, she fought to hide the pain that was starting to radiate through her like cracks spidering across a shattered windowpane. "Don't insult us both! I told you I could take care of myself. And you went behind my back anyway! You manipulated me, dammit!"

"*No.*" Catching her by the shoulder, he swung her around. "I merely provided you with an opportunity— and look how well you did with it!"

She knocked his hand away, filled with increasing sadness and frustration as he refused to see reason. "But don't you see? It was an opportunity I couldn't secure on my own!"

"So? What does that matter when you weigh it against everything else? I mean, honestly, are you going to stand there and tell me that if you'd known I was involved, you'd have passed up the job to flip burgers someplace?"

"That's not the point!"

"The hell it isn't." Untying his bow tie with a jerk, he heedlessly yanked the top few studs free on his shirt, his face growing more and more shuttered. "All I did was get your foot in the door, Mal. You did the rest."

"Okay, Gabriel. Let's say you're right. If, as you just so arrogantly pointed out, I couldn't afford to turn down the position, then why bother to lie about it? I'll tell you why. Because you knew all along that going behind my back was wrong!"

"Jesus!" He raked a hand impatiently through his dark hair. "Do you think, just for a minute, you could try to be rational here? The truth of the matter is I tried being up-front with you, but you wouldn't have it. So what was I supposed to do? Turn my back, walk away, leave you to starve in that ratty little garret where you were already three months late on the damn rent?"

"How on earth do you know I was… Oh, my God." She raised a suddenly shaking hand to her chest as she stared at him in horror. "Oh, my God. I should've known it was too good to be true. There never was a cousin Ivan, was there? It was you. It was you all along."

His sudden stillness spoke volumes and then he exploded into motion. "You're right!" Pacing away, he whirled to look her square in the face. "I arranged for you to get that money. Just like I arranged for you to get the job. But no matter what you want to believe, it was never about me trying to control you. What I will agree, is that I should've told you—and I should've done it long before now."

"So why didn't you!"

"Because, again, I was trying to look out for your best interests. Once I got to know you and we started to feel this…connection…I knew what I'd done wasn't going to be easy for you to accept. So I decided to wait, rather than risk ruining tonight for you."

In that instant, with her world crumbling around her, she lost the desperate grip she had on her temper. "Would you listen to yourself? *You* knew, *you* decided. *You* thought it would be best to spare me the hardship of the truth." Sick with betrayal, she finally lashed out. "Gosh, Gabe—how very Cal Morgan of you!"

His face went white.

And just like that, her anger vanished, washed away by a profound grief for what she'd believed they had— and what she'd just lost. Yet she still had a spark of pride and she'd rather die than admit to him that her heart was breaking.

"Whatever connection we did or didn't have, it's over. I don't want to see you. I don't want to hear from you. What I *do* want is for you to leave me alone. Do you hear me, Gabriel? Please. Just leave me the hell alone."

Then no longer caring what anyone else might think, she turned and wrenched open the door, picked up the full skirt of her gown and fled down the corridor. She sped across the lobby, dashed out under the portico and along the curving sidewalk, her only thought to put as much distance between them as she could manage.

She was halfway down the street when it dawned on her she didn't have her purse.

Not that it mattered, she realized a little hysterically, slowing as she fought to catch her breath. What good would it do her? The ten dollars she'd tucked inside it would barely begin to cover the cost of a cab ride to Gabe's. And even if she used it for the bus, between transfers and the reduced nighttime schedule it would take her well over an hour to get out to his place.

Where Gabriel would no doubt be waiting for her. And even if somehow by the grace of God he wasn't, what then? Did she pack a bag, call a cab, go to a hotel where with his resources he'd have no trouble tracking her down if he chose?

And why should she believe Mr. Master-of-every-one-else's-universe wouldn't do precisely that? She'd have to be crazy to think he'd leave her alone simply because she'd asked.

But where else could she go? What other choices did she have?

God help her, she didn't know—she couldn't think. The only thing that seemed clear was that she couldn't stay here, she thought, stumbling a little as she resumed her pell-mell pace and the first tears began to track down her face.

By the time a gleaming white limo with darkly tinted windows swept past her moments later, she was a mess.

She'd cried her mascara into rivulets down her cheeks, her hair was coming down and her feet, which she'd bared rather than risk breaking her neck in her high heels, were bruised and filthy.

God. Could this night get any worse?

Up ahead, the limo abruptly veered toward the curb, stopped, then slowly reversed. Her heart began to pound and she picked up her skirts to run—until a rear window glided down and she recognized the occupant.

When the door promptly swung open seconds later and the figure beckoned her with an autocratic crook of a hand, she only hesitated a second. Then with a sob of relief she crossed the sidewalk and climbed in.

Seconds later, the vehicle rolled away and disappeared into the inky Denver night.

Eleven

Gabe knew instinctively from the insistent peal of the doorbell that whoever was pushing the ringer wasn't Mallory.

Yet apparently his heart wasn't as certain as his head or he wouldn't feel such a crushing mix of disappointment and despair when he strode down his front hall, yanked open the door and found Cooper standing there.

For a second it was almost more than he could bear.

Then he got a grip, reminding himself that he'd brought this on himself. And that he'd get through it since the only other alternative was giving up—and that was no option at all. Still, with the exception of his unfulfilled longing for one special woman, he was no more in the mood for company now than he had been for the past six days.

Erasing all expression from his face, he considered his brother. "What're you doing here?"

"I came by to give you a report on the Landow search."

"Have we found him yet?"

"No."

"Okay." He inclined his head a fraction. "Thanks for the update." Giving the door a firm shove, he turned away.

"Aw, hell." In a move Cooper never could've pulled off if Gabe had been anywhere near the top of his game, the younger man shot his foot into the rapidly dwindling gap, slapped his hand against the glossy wood panel and shoved, blowing past him into the house. "That wasn't exactly the truth," he said, prudently backing out of reach a few feet down the hallway. "The real reason I'm here is that everyone's worried about you."

For maybe half a second, Gabe considered teaching his brother a lesson about the consequences of shoving in where you weren't wanted. In the next instant, the irony of the thought struck him, and his mouth twisted. Jesus. After the way he'd screwed things up with Mallory—

Reining in his emotions, he closed the door. "Everybody being...?"

For the first time Coop looked faintly apologetic. "Well, all of us guys...but mainly Lilah and Gen."

"And what? You drew the short straw?"

"Something like that."

It figured. The last time one of his brothers' wives

had gotten worried, he'd been the one in Cooper's place—and wound up taking a roundhouse to the face from Taggart for his trouble.

"Goddammit," he said but without any heat, padding past Cooper as he headed down the hall. "You've got five minutes to say or do whatever you have to so you can go back and convince the girls I'm fine and they need to just leave this alone."

"Yeah, well..." Trailing behind, Cooper followed him into the family room. His sharp gaze skimmed the pillow and blanket piled on the floor, the dishes sitting across the way in the sink and the newspapers littering the bar, before coming back to Gabe's face. "I don't know," he said dubiously. "You're looking a little rough around the edges here, bro."

He ran a hand over his unshaven cheek, glanced down at his denim-clad legs, then shrugged. "So I'm taking a few days off. Big deal. I'm allowed."

"Well, sure, but..." Walking into the kitchen, Cooper poured himself a cup of hours-old coffee, took a sip, then grimaced. "You want to talk about it?" he said quietly, dumping the contents of the mug into the sink.

When Gabe just looked at him, Cooper sighed. "Look, Deke says when he ran into you at Jilly's Java Sunday morning you were still in your tux and looking pretty grim. And Dom says Mallory sent word to Lilah that same afternoon that she was going to be unreachable for a while but would be looking for a new place to live. Which Lilah admits she passed on to you.

Then you don't come into work… Come on, Gabe. A two-year-old with one of those big fat crayons could complete this picture."

Gabe felt a muscle jump in his cheek. Most of the time he genuinely liked his family. Then there were moments like this when they made him feel as hemmed in as a tiger stuffed into a cat carrier.

Still, there didn't seem to be any way out of the conversation but to be honest. "Okay. So we had a fight. We'll work it out." Or so he hoped with every inch of his being.

"Is there anything I can do?"

"Except give me some space? No." Hell, there was nothing *he* could do—despite the fact that sitting on his hands was taking an ever-increasing toll with each day, each hour, each minute that passed.

But that didn't change the hard truth—that whatever happened next was up to Mallory.

Of course, that wasn't how he'd felt Saturday night, he reflected.

He still wasn't sure how long he'd stood in that meeting room, cut to the bone that she would ever compare him to her father. At the same time his gut had screamed at him to go after her, chase her down, *make* her listen to reason.

Eventually, his sanity—or so he'd considered it at the time—had prevailed. Deciding they both needed some space to cool off, he'd made his way to the hotel bar where he'd nursed a scotch and asked himself why he was surprised by what had just happened. Hadn't he predicted she'd overreact exactly the way she had? Wasn't that precisely why he'd held off telling her in the first place?

Hell, yes. But she was an intelligent woman, and once she calmed down and realized she was being unreasonable, he'd been confident they'd get past that particular bump in the road.

That line of thinking had sustained him all the way home. And though he'd felt a distinct uneasiness when he'd crossed the threshold and realized there was nobody there but him, he'd shrugged it off, as well, figuring one of her coworkers had seen her distress at the hotel and taken her in for the night.

By dawn, when he'd gone out to get coffee and run into Deke, he'd been starting to feel less sanguine. And as the morning had progressed without any word from her, he'd found himself wandering restlessly through his too-quiet house, seeing little traces of her everywhere—in the trio of lacy panties folded next to his socks in the laundry room, the book she'd left on the nightstand next to the bed, the bouquet of daisies on the kitchen table.

And he'd started to wonder: What if she'd actually meant it when she said she never wanted to see him again?

But that simply wasn't acceptable. He was a man who made things happen and he wasn't ready for their relationship to end. Hell, they were just getting started.

Still, like a fatal crack in a faulty foundation, with that first doubt he'd felt something inside him shift.

Then while he'd still been attempting to cobble things back together, Lilah had called to tell him Mallory was safe and that he shouldn't worry.

Then she'd quietly added she was sorry and hung up.

And standing there in his kitchen clutching his silent phone, he'd realized that was it. There hadn't been a word about Mallory returning. Not a hint where she was. No message for him at all.

Still like a sharp stick in the eye, he'd gotten the point. *We're through and I'm not coming back.*

Desolation had slammed into him, nearly taking him out at the knees. Sliding onto a bar stool, he'd dimly realized that despite what he'd told Mallory a couple of weeks ago, the only other time he'd felt this sort of pain had been nearly two decades earlier. That was the day he'd finally accepted that while the father he'd worshipped was still breathing and walking around, inside his dad was as dead as the woman they'd buried nearly two years before.

Yet that couldn't be right, Gabe had thought, the crack in the bedrock of what he believed about himself widening into a crevasse. Because he'd loved his father with all a firstborn son's fervor, while his feelings for Mallory…

Sweet Jesus. The truth had blown through him like a howitzer blast, practically knocking him off the stool.

Because the truth was he'd been pretty much a goner the first time he'd seen her at that very first party all those years ago.

Reeling, all he'd been able to think was that he had to find her. That no matter what it took, he had to track her down and tell her how he felt. That she had a right to know his heart before she made any decisions about their future.

He'd climbed to his feet, scooped up his keys—only to falter as the last thing she'd said to him had suddenly sounded in his head as clearly as if she'd actually been in the room.

I don't want to see you. I don't want to hear from you. What I want is for you to leave me alone.

And that's when it had dawned on him that if he was ever to have a hope of regaining her trust, he had to back off. That he had to give her space and trust her to make her own decision about their future.

So that's what he was doing, even though the waiting was killing him.

"Listen," he said, plucking the cup out of Cooper's hand and herding him out of the kitchen and back down the hall. "I'll be fine. When have you ever known me not to be? I just need some time to myself for a change. Tell everyone I'm taking a little vacation. God knows I'm overdue."

"Well, yeah, that's true." Despite his agreement and the fact that he was allowing Gabe to ease him out the door, Cooper's gaze was still troubled. "Just—take care of yourself, all right?"

"You got it," Gabe replied. Standing at the door, he watched for a moment as his brother got into his red SUV, pulled out of the drive and sped off down the street, passing a white limo coming the other way.

Then he turned around and went back inside. To wait.

* * *

Mallory glanced out the limousine window for the hundredth time.

"Good grief, my dear, quit looking so nervous," Abigail Anson Sommers said tartly. "As I've already told you, there's no need to rush into this. You're welcome to stay at Cedar Hill as long as you'd like."

"I know. And I appreciate your offer more than I can say," she said, turning back to the elegant old lady. "But I need to do this. I need to try, at least."

Because Abigail's offer notwithstanding, she really *didn't* have another choice, she thought as the limo slowed for the final turn into Gabriel's driveway and her already jittery stomach bounced up into her throat.

Not if she was going to have a hope of getting on with her life.

For nearly a week now she'd waited for Gabriel, expecting him to marshal all his impressive resources, do whatever it took to track her down so he could tell her, in his big, bold, take-charge kind of way, that he didn't intend to let her walk away.

Only he hadn't shown up.

Not the first couple of days, when she'd been so angry and hurt that she'd easily used up a lifetime allotment of curses and tears.

Not during the next two days, either, when her emotions had finally settled enough for her to get some perspective on what had happened between them, forcing her to face some hard truths. Not only about Gabe but about herself, as well.

And heaven knew, there'd been no sign of him in the past forty-eight hours, as she'd grown more and more restless and impatient while wondering what on earth was keeping him.

The woman she'd been three months ago would have concluded his absence meant he didn't care. But the woman she was now—who through recent trials and accomplishments was stronger, steadier, possessed of some genuine, hard-won confidence and a growing sense of self-worth—refused to believe it.

And that was the Mallory who'd awakened this morning to a startling thought. What if Gabriel had actually taken her angry, overwrought, parting shots to heart? What if all this time he'd stayed away because that's what she'd told him she wanted?

At first she'd blown it off, telling herself not to be ridiculous. People said things they didn't mean in the heat of an argument all the time. As savvy as he was— and as secure in his masculinity—certainly after the past few weeks he had to know she cared about him.

Except… She'd never actually told him. Not straight-out. And the more she'd thought about it, the clearer it had become that as much as she missed him, and despite the sharp little thorn of insecurity his failure to appear had lodged near her heart, she'd *needed* this time.

She'd needed it to examine how she felt. Needed it to decide just what it was that she wanted.

"Well if you feel so strongly, then obviously you must see this through," Abigail said briskly, reaching over to give Mallory's hand a quick squeeze as the limo purred to a stop. "Just one further piece of advice, child. Don't try. *Do*."

Oh my. Was it her imagination or had Lilah's elegant, autocratic, octogenarian grandmother just channeled Yoda?

Unbidden, a spurt of laughter squeezed past the lump in Mallory's throat and impulsively she leaned over to press a kiss to Abigail's paper-thin cheek.

"Thank you, Mrs. Sommers. For everything. I don't know what I would have done without you. If you hadn't rescued me off the street and taken me home with you…" She paused to steady her voice. "I'll never be able to repay you."

"Oh bosh!" Abigail said brusquely.

As the chauffeur opened the door, she shooed Mallory away. But not before Mallory saw the hint of moisture sheening the older woman's eyes.

"Good heavens, Clarence," Abigail went on imperiously, addressing her grizzled employee, "this younger generation is appallingly sentimental, don't you agree?"

"Yes, madam," he said solemnly, giving Mallory a wink before handing her out of the car and escorting her to the front door. "You'll do fine, miss," he said, tipping his cap.

Then the limo backed out of the drive, and impulsively trying the knob, she found to her surprise that the door was unlocked.

So after one more deep, steadying breath, she walked inside.

She found Gabe standing at the tall windows at the back of the house. He was gazing moodily out at his big backyard, looking quite unlike his usual elegant self, dressed as he was in a faded black T-shirt and ancient jeans, with his hair mussed, his feet bare and what looked to be several days' worth of black stubble shadowing his face.

As if only then registering her footsteps, he started to turn. "Dammit, Coop, what could you possibly—" The words died on his lips. "Mallory. You're here."

"Yes. Yes I am."

For an instant his eyes squeezed shut and then he took a swift step toward her and her heart lifted—only to plummet again as he jerked to a stop and his expression closed up.

All right, she thought, trying to control her hammering pulse. For a moment she'd hoped this was going to be easy, that they would simply fall into each other's arms and kiss and talk and everything would instantly be all right again…

Except she'd learned real life didn't quite work that way. Sometimes, no matter how frightened or unsure or how big the risk, you just had to lay your heart on the line and hope for the best.

She breathed in, breathed out. Cleared her throat and plunged in. "There are some things I need to say."

Thrusting his hands in his front pockets, he inclined his head. "Okay."

Eyeing the rigid set of his shoulders, she began slowly, "We both said some pretty hard things the other night, and I'm not going to apologize for most of them. But I do regret one thing. You are everything my father isn't. You're strong and dependable and honorable and a man to be counted on—and if I made you think for a minute that I didn't believe that with ever fiber of my being, I'm sorrier than I can say."

Taking a breath, she again tried to gauge his reaction, her stomach tightening even more as he simply stood there, not giving away a clue as to what he was thinking. "Don't get me wrong. I still don't agree with the way you did things." Her heart gave a little lurch as the line of his mouth grew even more forbidding. "But I know you truly thought you were looking out for me. Your methods may have been high-handed, but your intentions were pure. And that means a lot."

She swallowed. "I guess what I'm trying to say—" she dredged up a slight, tentative smile, still praying fruitlessly for a glimmer of response in return "—is that I love you, Gabe. I know I've made my own share of mistakes, but if you'd be interested in giving us another chance—"

Before she even finished what she had to say, he was across the room. Hauling her into his arms, he demolished every last inch of space between them.

The joy—the relief—was so intense that for a while it was all she could do to absorb it. Eventually, however, she realized the thumping she felt was the furious beat of his heart and the last of the coiled tension that had been strangling her the past hours abruptly unwound.

Oh, no, not indifferent, she thought, holding him

fiercely as he rocked her against him, his face buried in her hair.

Not indifferent by a long shot.

"God but you gave me a scare," he said finally. Loosening his hold on her, he brought up his hands to cradle her face as he rested his forehead against hers. "Walking in here, looking so damn serious and beautiful. I thought—"

His throat worked, and the sight of him—big, strong, and normally so articulate—struggling to find his voice made her own throat ache.

"I thought you'd come to say goodbye. Before I ever got the chance to tell you how sorry I am for hurting you. Or admit what a fool I've been. The truth is, there's a lot I need to tell you—some of it about the past and my feelings for my dad that I'm only starting to see myself. But for now that can wait."

He leaned back just a little more, exposing all the naked emotion on that compelling face. His eyes, green and clear, met hers directly and this time he wasn't holding anything back. "What won't wait is this—I love you, Mallory. Looking back, I was pretty much a goner from the first time we met, only I was too stubborn to see it then." His strong, sensuous mouth quirked a bare fraction. "I was convinced I didn't want that kind of complication in my life, and I think I would've gone right on believing it if I hadn't walked into Annabelle's that day.

"But seeing you there, all alone, knowing you were in trouble… As much as I wanted to, I just couldn't walk away—not and live with myself. And you know what?"

She shook her head, pretty sure she was staring up at him with her heart in her eyes—and knowing she'd never find anyone else who would cherish her more.

"It was the best decision I ever made. And if you'll give me the chance, I swear I'll spend the rest of forever making sure you feel the same way."

His lips found hers then. And standing there, with the sunshine pouring in through the window around them, Mallory knew that with Gabriel Steele she'd always be safe.

* * * * *

2 FREE

BOOKS AND A SURPRISE GIFT!

We would like to take this opportunity to thank you for reading this Mills & Boon® book by offering you the chance to take TWO more specially selected titles from the Desire™ series absolutely FREE! We're also making this offer to introduce you to the benefits of the Mills & Boon® Reader Service™—

- ★ **FREE home delivery**
- ★ **FREE gifts and competitions**
- ★ **FREE monthly Newsletter**
- ★ **Exclusive Reader Service offers**
- ★ **Books available before they're in the shops**

Accepting these FREE books and gift places you under no obligation to buy, you may cancel at any time, even after receiving your free shipment. Simply complete your details below and return the entire page to the address below. You don't even need a stamp!

YES! Please send me 2 free Desire volumes and a surprise gift. I understand that unless you hear from me, I will receive 3 superb new titles every month for just £4.99 each, postage and packing free. I am under no obligation to purchase any books and may cancel my subscription at any time. The free books and gift will be mine to keep in any case.

D8ZED

Ms/Mrs/Miss/Mr ....Initials ....

BLOCK CAPITALS PLEASE

Surname ....

Address ....

....

....Postcode ....

Send this whole page to:
UK: FREEPOST CN81, Croydon, CR9 3WZ